Transference Dreamwalkers:
Volume Two

By Brooke Terry

© Copyright 2024 Brooke Terry
All rights reserved.

No portion of this book may be reproduced in whole or in part, by any means whatsoever, except for passages excerpted for the purposes of review, without the prior written permission of the publisher.

For information, or to order additional copies, please contact:

Beacon Publishing Group
P.O. Box 41573 Charleston, S.C. 29423
800.817.8480| beaconpublishinggroup.com

Publisher's catalog available by request.

ISBN-13: 978-1-961504-08-0

ISBN-10: 1-961504-08-0

Published in 2024. New York, NY 10001.

First Edition. Printed in the USA.

Transference Dreamwalkers:
Volume Two

*For all those who have had a dream come true
and decided to keep dreaming.*

Darby's Cabin
Calvenia
Bolivar
Clearview Lake
Dunbar
Hurley
Fox River
Pond of Sali's Tears
The Iris
Karlow
Deniz
Glass Sea
Tortia
Baratana
Otto's Pass
Vito's Point
Dream Hollow Mountains
Arvenia
Forest of Visions

Arvenia
Calvenia
Dunbar
Clearview Pond
Hurley
Karlow
Fox River
Deniz
Glass Sea
Baratana
Tortia
Otto's Pass
Vito's Point
Dream Hollow Mountains
Terra
Avendale
Spruce Mountains
Mirror Lake
Wusylla
Soleia
Moreland
Balsam River
Merimak River
The Notch
Inverness
Westfall
Treacherous Seas

PROLOGUE
500 Years Ago, The Court of Avendale

King Deryn slouched as he waited for the last of the commoners to enter his throne room. It had been a long day, and his back was throbbing from sitting so long without moving. Try as he may, he could find no cushion to keep him from aching after a long day spent sitting on this rock. When his father was king, he had designed the throne and had it carved from stone with intricate designs and gems inlaid at the top and on the sides. It looked magnificent, but comfort was obviously not taken into consideration when it was created. Deryn raised his hand and spoke to the guards along the entrance. "Send them in."

As the doors opened, Deryn shifted his weight in an attempt to find a comfortable position. When he looked up, he was pleased to see that only one man had entered. *Thank the gods. He is the last for today*, he thought to himself, not bothering to hide his disdain. He was a king. He shouldn't be wasting his time listening to lowly common peoples' complaints. He had more important things to worry about.

Deryn continued to examine the massive rubies on his fingers as the man approached the dais the throne sat upon. He began speaking, and Deryn struggled to spare half of his attention for the man. When Deryn finally looked at him, he was struck by his size. He stood well over six feet, was a burly man and was dressed in heavily-worn traveling clothes. Because of his tattered appearance, Deryn was even less inclined to listen, but something the man said shook Deryn from his thoughts.

"…heard rumors of an imminent war with Calvenia." The man finished. He stood still and confident as he stared at the king, waiting for a response. His boldness made Deryn's blood boil.

Deryn narrowed his eyes at the stranger. "Who are you?" he growled.

"That is of no importance, your majesty. What is important is that I have something you desperately need." The man replied softly. Deryn was not amused.

"That is enough." He said to his guards. "Get him out of my sight." He flicked his hand casually at the guards to indicate that the man had run out of time. The guards moved quickly to take away the stranger, but the man stood his ground, not indicating any distress. He simply said, "My great king, aren't you tired of waiting in the shadows while lesser men's victories outweigh your own?" Now a smirk played across the man's face, and Deryn grew even more tired of his insolence, especially when remembering his latest defeat while trying to reclaim lost territories to the west.

"OUT, I SAID!" King Deryn roared, throwing himself off his chair and gesturing heavily at the doors. The guards grabbed the man by the arms, but he pulled himself free and ran closer to the dais.

Bewildered, King Deryn watched as the man pulled a chain from under his traveling cloak to reveal an unimpressive, white crystal. The two men stared silently at one another, until the stranger finally spoke. "This little crystal could change the future of Arvenia and forever record your name in its history as the greatest ruler that has ever sat upon the Arvenian throne."

King Deryn raised his hand to the guards, telling them to stop their attempts to remove the man from the court. King Deryn seated himself once again on that uncomfortable throne he despised and said quietly, "I'm listening."

A wicked grin broke across the man's face, and his deep brown eyes glittered with malice. "Do you know what a dreamwalker is?"

CHAPTER ONE
Ansley

Ansley had always wondered what it may feel like to be a wielder of air. Flying and floating in her dreams above rolling hills, like those in her beloved Terra. She could see herself swooping down to let her fingers touch the tips of her favorite wildflowers and then soaring back into the clouds. It had always been her wish to experience it someday, but at this moment, as Ansley's world spun and twirled around her, she decided she would rather that her feet never leave the ground.

Ansley sat on her grandmother's couch with her hands covering her face. Whenever she opened her eyes, she felt the world move beneath her again. *This is all too much...* she thought in despair. A hand rested gently on her shoulder, grounding her, and a soft, cool nightly wind blew in through the door that was still open. Ansley hastened a peek through her fingers at the man sitting beside her, thinking she had indeed succumbed to those sleepless nights of the past week and imagined herself a solution to all of her problems. But, no, he was still there. He was tall, even though he was seated, and his wavy locks fell naturally into a wind-blown look. Ansley sighed and covered her face once more, closing her eyes as tightly as she could.

"Ansley, it's okay. Just try to breathe." Rhyn whispered, as he soothingly rubbed her shoulder.

Ansley shrugged away his hand and stood quickly. Rhyn's eyes were wide as though she were an animal he was trying not to frighten away. "How do I know you aren't Magnus?" Ansley growled, as she narrowed her eyes at this stranger. It was a fair question to ask. Over the past few weeks, Ansley had experienced so much deception and loss that trust seemed a luxury she could not afford. Her parents and brothers had been murdered at the hands of cult members who had been linked to Orco, the god of death. After an assumed success at finding the cult leaders and dispensing justice, Ansley had been devastated to learn, merely hours ago, that the true culprit was the handsome boy she had met in her dreams. Her heart had broken with the lies she had ingested, and she simply could not handle any more. Now she found herself face-to-face with a double of the man who had betrayed her trust. "Overwhelmed" did not seem a strong enough word to describe her feelings.

Rhyn merely sat still and shook his head silently. "You know I don't look anything like Magnus, but you still want me to prove who I am to you, Ansley? What could I even begin to tell you that would earn your trust? I'm afraid that is an impossible request. Look, I know you have had a horrible month, and you are within your rights to think the worst of me; however, the truth is simply this: I am Rhyn of the Brooks. My family protects our dreamers and claims the River as our star guide. I inherited when I was eleven, and I am a wielder of air. I have no tribe except my brother, Rhys, who is currently the hostage of a psychopath. And I need your help if I hope to ever see him again." Rhyn finished, his blue eyes glistening with unshed tears of shame.

Ansley moved toward the door and shut it just as a fresh breeze blew in, soothing her nerves. Then, she walked back to where Rhyn sat on the couch. "You know him, don't you?" Ansley whispered, almost afraid to hear the answer.

Rhyn sighed and looked away from her for a moment before replying. "No, I do not. I was hoping it was someone wanting money from my family, but I fear that this Magnus is much more dangerous than that." Rhyn paused for a moment before adding, "My brother disappeared weeks ago, and we have been searching for him since then. I was starting to worry that he may be dead, caught by a stray wolf or bear while he was out in the night finishing his chores. Then, after searching my dreams every night for some sign of him and trying to pull him back to me with our tether, I finally found him. And what I saw…well, it was not pleasant."

Ansley realized she had been holding her breath while listening to Rhyn. She let the breath out slowly, terrified of what he may say next. What had Magnus done to Rhys?

Rhyn sighed. "He was chained and soaked in his own blood. When I came to him, he could barely open his eyes because he was so weak. He begged me to help him and come to find you. Last night was the first time I knew anything of this Magnus. I was with Rhys only for a moment before I lost the tether again. As soon as I could ready my horse, I came to find you."

Ansley shook her head silently. She glanced over Rhyn's shoulder to the dark hallway leading to the bedrooms in the small home. Her grandmother, Damon, and Kenna were silent. She wished for a moment that they would wake up and join her with Rhyn. Why did she have to deal with all of this alone?

"Ansley, I can help you, but I need you to trust me. We have a small shot at this. I will not leave my brother in the hands of a torturer and murderer." Rhyn grabbed Ansley's hand and squeezed it gently between his strong, warm hands. "Please…"

Ansley sighed. "Alright. I will try to help you, but that doesn't mean I have to trust you. If you are who you say you are, then you must know something about me, or was all that about Rhys and me being connected a lie too?" Ansley asked.

"That wasn't a lie. That's why Magnus took him. Rhys told me that Magnus thought he needed Rhys to get to you."

"*Me*? Why am I important to anyone?" Ansley whispered, her forehead wrinkling with confusion.

"I don't know, Ansley, but I do know that he has taken my brother in hopes of gaining your trust and luring you in. He is cruel and determined to find you at any cost. He will not stop until he achieves whatever purpose he has set his mind to. But he will regret choosing to use my brother to achieve his goals." Rhyn said, his words laced with hate.

Ansley nodded silently and waited awkwardly as the room grew silent. She tried to understand what Rhyn was telling her, but she could not make sense of Magnus seeking her trust. He had chosen and used Rhys to get to her, and it had worked. But how had it worked? Was she that naïve that a handsome face could persuade her to forgo her better judgement? Rhyn gently placed his hand on top of hers, drawing Ansley out of her inner struggle for answers.

"Ansley, it is the middle of the night, and I know your grandmother and the others are asleep. I will not ask you to leave them, and I would prefer if you ask them to help us too. We need back-up. We cannot succeed without the help and guidance of experienced dreamwalkers." Rhyn stood from the couch and moved back toward the door. "I will come back to you tomorrow, once you have had time to rest and speak with them. Then, we should begin planning our next move."

Rhyn reached out and grabbed the door handle, pushing it silently outward. Ansley's thoughts raced, but she remained silent, unable to speak. Rhyn turned back to look at her one more time before saying, "I am sorry to have to come to you this way. I hope you know that I would never have come to you if I had any other hope in rescuing Rhys." He stared at Ansley for another moment before adding, "Until we meet again." Then he saluted her as a fellow dreamwalker, by putting his forefinger to his brow, before disappearing into the night.

Ansley stepped toward the open door still dumbstruck. She stared out into the darkness and watched Rhyn until he faded into the night. The stars twinkled silently, and the stillness of the night seemed to push down upon her. She took another deep breath to steady herself, but it was no use.

Ansley thought over the previous events of this night. Before Rhyn had arrived, Ansley had been summoned to the dream realm by Rosalie, a wraith that had appeared to her in the desert when she had faced her trials in her inheritance ceremony. Although Ansley had assumed Rosalie was a benevolent guide of the inheritance ceremonies all young ones face before gaining their skills, she had been wrong. Rosalie had sought out Ansley because they were connected, and she knew she must warn her. During her dream tonight, Rosalie had cautioned Ansley and urged her to find a way to save Rhys and defeat Magnus. From her vision, Ansley had learned that Magnus was Rosalie's son, so she had begged for Rosalie's help in defeating him. Rosalie had explained to Ansley that she could not because she was a wraith and was trapped in the dream realm. Ansley swallowed nervously as she remembered the dubious mission Rosalie had set her on.

The whole interaction had left her head spinning. And now, between her dream with Rosalie and realizing Rhys had a twin brother that was determined to rescue him, there was no hope of her getting any rest tonight. Ansley turned back toward the house, closed the door, and stepped back into the warm room. *What had just happened?*

*****

Damon lay awake in the dark, staring into the shadows laying over him like a heavy blanket. The darkness was so thick that he could tell no difference between when his eyes were open or closed. Damon sighed deeply, trying to stay awake. If he were to close his eyes, he knew that the nightmares would come.

He shifted onto his side trying to find a more comfortable position that didn't disturb the wounds he had accumulated from the encounter with Dane. Only hours before, Damon and Kenna had been pulled by Dane, a member of Kenna's own tribe, into a dream where he trapped them and intended to steal their skills. Before this had happened, Damon had been scrying for Dane's location, not knowing that he was duplicitous. Scrying had weakened Damon, and according to the elders' assessment, it had taken a few decades from his lifespan. And on top of that extreme fatigue, Dane had punched Damon many times while holding him prisoner with Kenna. Right now, Damon was a mess, and he felt like it too. *If only Lya could see me now*, Damon thought to himself sadly. *I would be in for another thrashing.*

Damon closed his eyes to allow himself to rest for a few moments. He wouldn't fall asleep. He was not even tired. He would just close his eyes for a few moments and try to think of his lovely wife, Lya…

*

Damon opened his eyes to find himself sitting on a grassy hill overlooking the farmlands stretching for hundreds of miles before him. Cattle and horses moved silently along, finding small patches of grass to satisfy their hunger. The silence was heavy but peaceful.

Damon covered his face with his hands in frustration. He was not even tired! How could he have fallen asleep so quickly?

A sound to his right startled him, so Damon looked in that direction to find his older brother, Rory, riding his dapple-gray mare up the hill. Rory smiled and waved at Damon in greeting. Damon tried to hide the horror he felt in seeing him and lifted his hand slowly to greet his brother.

"Damon! What are you doing up here when there are still more cows to milk and stalls to clean?" Rory laughed and said, "I know you've always preferred an easy life, but until you come of age, you are mine to boss around, boy!" Rory swung his leg over his mare and landed gracefully on his feet. Rory was probably around nineteen years old in this dream. His golden-brown hair was wavy like his brother's, but that was where the resemblance ended. Where Damon was gloomy, Rory had always been light-hearted and quick to laughter. Rory had spent his childhood playing while Damon had spent his brooding.

Rory grabbed his horse's bridle and gently moved the mare closer to where Damon sat. Rory's smile faded, and his sharp green eyes narrowed with uncertainty upon seeing the look on Damon's face. "Damon, what ails you? Are you unwell?"

Damon reached up and stroked his bare chin, admiring the smooth, stubble-free feeling of his youth. Damon stood slowly and put his hand upon Rory's shoulder. "Nothing, Rory. Just thinking of what will need to be done here when harvest arrives."

Rory's eyes softened, and a smile pulled at the corners of his lips once more. "You know better than to dwell on the future, brother. Come! Mother has started dinner. We need to get the horses in for the night before the sun sets." Rory turned away from his brother and led the mare back down the hill toward his last awaiting chore for the evening. Damon began to slowly follow Rory down. He watched Rory and noticed the way he carried himself so…jovially. His brother had been such a happy soul. Damon was ashamed to admit that Rory's easy-going spirit had always annoyed him. Why had he hated his brother so much?

A sigh escaped Damon's lips, and he reluctantly followed Rory to the home he hadn't seen outside of his dreams in decades. He wondered silently if it was even still there, nestled in the hills like a sleeping bear. The thought followed him as he rolled up his sleeves to ready himself to help with the milking.

*

Damon drew in a deep breath and sat up in his bed. *Gods!* Damon thought as he rubbed his face with his hands. The dreams had tormented him every night for almost seventy-five years now, and once he was in them, there was no pulling himself back to reality. A curse from the gods he supposed.

Damon flinched as a floorboard squeaked to his left. He instantly grabbed the naked blade that he kept under his pillow each night and thrust it forward in the dark.

"Ahh…damn it, Damon!" The person hissed. "It's me!" The shape lit a candle quickly, illuminating Ansley's face.

Damon lowered his weapon which was inches from Ansley's nose. At least he hadn't lost his aim in all these years of exile. "Ansley, what in the gods' names are you doing sneaking in here in the middle of the night? I could have skewered you." Damon grunted as he moved his blade back under his pillow within easy reach.

Ansley raised a finger to her lips before whispering, "Damon, I need help, and as much as I hate to admit it, you are my best option. I need you to listen, and I need you to not tell my grandmother." Ansley's face was lined with shadows from the candle she held before her, and Damon could sense her unease.

Damon rolled his eyes before laying back down with his hands folded behind his head. "I'd prefer my nightmares to listening to a teenager's sordid secrets."

Ansley paused and bit her lip. "What about the secrets of the one truly responsible for killing my parents and causing all the trouble in Terra?"

Damon's brow furrowed in confusion, unsure what she could possibly mean. They had already destroyed the supposed group that was responsible for attacking dreamwalkers across Terra, including Ansley's own family. Following the attack on Ansley's family, the elders of Terra and her grandmother, Bianca, were spurned into searching for answers and justice for Ansley's lost family members.

Damon had come to Terra to help, and he had offered to scry for the location of these criminals in hopes of bringing an end to this bloody affair as soon as possible. His scrying had proved unhelpful when Dane had lured the others into a trap. Ansley had arrived to help Damon and Kenna escape. Kenna had demonstrated immense strength, revealed to the others that she was elite, and locked the dream, trapping those criminals inside before destroying the warehouse. After Kenna, Ansley, and Damon had successfully escaped, they had assumed the threat was over, and they had returned to Bianca's home to recover and tend to their wounds. But one look at Ansley told Damon she was not bluffing. It seemed that they had not been as successful as they had assumed.

CHAPTER TWO
Magnus

Rain pelted the large glass window and ran down in rivulets. Magnus sat in the silent chamber impatiently waiting. He began to drum his fingers softly on the wooden table in front of him. The steady drumming of the rain beat in time with his fingers, and he let the rhythm soothe his frustration. *He should be here by now*, he thought angrily, as heat filled his face.

Magnus had never been a patient man, and fortunately, that was something that was never expected of him. Especially here. But today, the king of Arvenia was testing his limits. Magnus sighed heavily as his thoughts centered on Ansley. He fiddled with the silver ring on his left hand as he often did while trying to solve a problem.

It had been only three days since he had last seen her, since Kenna and Ansley had returned from the dream in which Kenna had destroyed a handful of his followers. Before that, Magnus had been close to achieving his goal. He had plotted incessantly to gain Ansley's trust and determine if she was the dreamwalker of the Black line he had been searching for. But unfortunately, his efforts had been for naught, and his tedious planning had been foiled because one of his followers, Dane, had not been strong enough to capture Ansley.

But Magnus also wondered if maybe there were other factors at play that would have broken that bond he had worked so hard to establish. Magnus had not noticed a change in Ansley after she returned from dreamwalking, but he realized later that night that she was avoiding him in her dreams and almost completely blocking his attempts to dreamwalk with her. He could only guess who he should blame for this change in her. There was only one person who could have given Ansley insight into who Magnus was, and now he would have to form a new plan to try to bring the girl to him and ensure his political maneuvers did not fail.

Dane had been given one assignment, and he could not even succeed at that. Fools. They were *all* fools. These followers of his. Magnus's followers claimed to follow Orco when he was their true master. Typicals always looked for a god to cling to. Well, Magnus would make himself just that. A god of the waking realm. Then, these pitiful typicals and dreamwalkers would worship him like the powerful god he deserved to be. He twisted the thin silver ring, admiring the texture of the worn, old metal.

He recentered his thoughts on Ansley once more. He was not sure how Ansley had managed to summon Rosalie, but he knew it had happened. Ansley had not allowed him to enter her dreams since that night, and when he reached out to her, he felt only emptiness where there had once been an earth-shattering joy. But, no matter. He was still linked with Ansley, and that had been his most crucial objective in meeting her in person. He achieved this easily enough when he had her take the "blood oath".

His thoughts lingered on that odd day that she had arrived at the storehouse. It was as if she could sense Rhys was there. She had been moments away from discovering him, but thankfully, she trusted Magnus enough to believe his tale. *If only her naivety could have lasted a few more days…*

Magnus's thoughts were interrupted by a loud creaking from the massive door opening. Magnus looked in that direction, scowling at the man who entered.

King Orlan, who was the descendent of those men who had conquered this land and made it their own, was dumpy and sweaty. He was a poor excuse for a man, let alone a king. His people were fortunate they rarely, if ever, laid eyes on him. If the Arvenian people ever learned what type of king Orlan truly was, Magnus believed they would stage a revolt and replace him with someone more suited to ruling.

Orlan stood a measly five foot four, almost unheard of in his line of royals. His face was pale and round, like that of a child who had eaten too many sweets. Orlan's hair, which had once been blonde and long enough to reach his shoulders, had begun to fall out. The courtiers finally talked his majesty into shaving his head to improve his look. The king had been even less attractive without his hair. Magnus never knew that someone could have such a lumpy head. Thankfully, his marriage to Queen Aileen (formerly a princess of Tortia) had been arranged, and the poor woman had only met Orlan upon their wedding day. In contrast, Queen Aileen was a tall, thin, and striking woman whose pale green eyes had no equal among those at court. That pathetic lump of a king had been a little too lucky, but his children had been luckier. They took solely after their mother's looks.

Orlan ascended to the throne at seventeen, when his father, King Finley, died in a skirmish within his own castle walls. Calvenia had sent assassins, and while they were not successful in killing the king themselves, they wounded him greatly. Finley died within the week from an infection. All great healers knew that a wound to the gut would almost always end in death, so the prognosis for King Finley had not been good, though he had been treated by the best.

Finley was all that his son was not. Tall, strong, and

commanding, Finley led the country of Arvenia for over thirty-five years. He was the type of king that Magnus actually enjoyed working with. Magnus turned his silver ring once more, in memory of the one who had gifted it to him. Orlan was a poor substitute. He could not even be in Magnus's presence without stumbling over his words in fear. *So be it*, thought Magnus. *Better fear than insolence.*

Orlan took a few steps towards the table where Magnus sat. "Sssir. Magnus, ssssir. Do forgive me." Orlan mumbled as he bowed his lower half forward in reverence to his guest. "A king's work is never done it seems." He smiled with this statement, but seeing the look on Magnus's face, his smile turned into more of a grimace.

Magnus cleared his throat impatiently. "Yes…Well, shall we begin? Care for tea, or perhaps something stronger, my lord?" Orlan asked with a flourish of his hand.

Magnus simply shook his head. Orlan seated himself in his dark chamber. The two men looked across the table at one another for several silent minutes before Magnus laced his fingers together and began speaking. "Your Grace, you did not send the soldiers to fortify the borders like I recommended last quarter."

Orlan swallowed and nodded several times. "Yes…you are correct. Well, you see, there are not enough soldiers to send safely to the Spruce Mountains like you suggested." Orlan finished without meeting Magnus's eyes. Magnus glowered at Orlan who subsequently raised his hands in the air, "I know, Lord Magnus. I am sorry this displeases you; however-"

"Displeases me, Orlan? It is you who should be displeased. This is, after all, your country I am helping defend, is it not?" Magnus's voice was barely more than a whisper, but the words sunk into Orlan like poison. He shuddered with his eyes closed before attempting a response.

"Yes, my lord." Orlan began nodding his head vigorously, but his eyes betrayed his unease with the idea of recruiting more soldiers from his parishes. His country had been on the brink of war for years, if not generations. Arvenia and Calvenia had always been competitive, but once Arvenia had assisted in the overthrow of the Calvenian monarchy, the Calvenians had grown even more cold-hearted towards their southern neighbors. Magnus did not judge them. He knew their hate was warranted, especially for a useless lump such as Orlan.

"You must force the men to enlist, Orlan." Magnus added. "These borders along the mountains are vulnerable. Although the mountains are treacherous, they can be scaled in several places. Calvenia will use any advantage to get into your country, and if they cross the Balsam River, you are practically invaded. Avendale will not stand against invaders, your grace."

Orlan stared blankly at his hands on the table. A long silence drew out before the men. "How did we bring ourselves here, Lord Magnus?"

"*We*? Orlan, you are mistaken. In this situation, you alone are to blame. It was your council that sent messages that the Calvenian spies intercepted regarding the dreamwalkers' crystals you have here in Avendale. What were you trying to accomplish with sharing that information in a message? You know Calvenia looks for any reason possible to attack Arvenia, and tensions have always been high between our countries regarding how dreamwalkers are handled. Now you have landed yourself in a potential war that will only result in your destruction if you keep refusing to take action!" Magnus slammed his fist onto the table, making Orlan and the unlit candelabra on the table shake.

"I understand, and I thank you once more for your counsel, Lord Magnus. You were a great friend to my father, and he would be grateful to know that you are such a help to me in this time of need." Orlan rose from the table, his purple velvet robe falling to the ground behind him. It was meant to make him look kingly, but Magnus felt it only made the man appear a child, wrapped in a favorite blanket. "It seems I have some matters to attend to. Please stay and make yourself comfortable here until you are ready to travel. The weather may delay you, but you are always welcome in my hall. Your quarters will be readied."

Magnus inclined his head to the king as Orlan exited his council room. Magnus sighed and rubbed his temples to relieve his growing headache. *Friend of his father indeed. And his grandfather, great-grandfather, and beyond. When will I end this taxing relationship with the royals? Maybe I should allow the Calvenians to do it for me.*

Magnus pushed back from the table and stood. A heavy bolt of lightning struck in the courtyard below the window. Its brilliance illuminated the dark chamber, and Magnus felt that he had also been struck by it, with inspiration. Orlan had his matters to attend to, but Magnus's were much more pressing. The king would have to handle his own problems from now on.

CHAPTER THREE
Kenna

The sun set with a dazzling display of purples, oranges, and navy smears across the horizon as Kenna rested her head on Edric's bare chest. The two had been apart for what seemed like ages but was really only a few weeks. Kenna could not remember the last time they had been parted for this long. Edric traveled as a sailor, but the seas were dangerous in the harvest season. The seasons had begun to change again last month, and the winter would soon be upon them. Because this was Edric's dream, he could form any season here. If it were left up to her, Kenna would choose an unending summer, but this was Edric's dream and he chose autumn, the time when the leaves change and the cool winds begin to blow.

Kenna looked up at her husband and stroked his cheek lovingly. They had met here to celebrate the end of her quest and her success in finding the attackers responsible for killing so many dreamwalkers. Kenna had originally been the only one from her tribe who saw merit in chasing down the ones responsible, but her tribe came to understand the true disparity of the situation when Laurel, her tribe member was attacked. Thankfully, Laurel was not harmed, but she had yet to return to dreamwalking. Jameson, the tribe's leader had placed guards around her home to ensure her safety. Edric had volunteered to remain in Willow to help Jameson look after Laurel and Sophie, the tribe's shifter. With those responsible for attacking Laurel dead, Kenna was thankful that Laurel could finally rest easy once more.

Edric smiled down at Kenna, and his light green eyes sparkled, reflecting the setting sun. "My love, when will you come back to me?" Edric whispered.

Kenna grinned back at him. "Are you sure you would not prefer to live apart? It seems that our love life has more fire when the distance between us is greater." She grinned at Edric before leaning in to kiss his soft lips. Edric's rough beard tickled her chin. He had let it grow while she had been away, and Kenna thought that it suited him.

Edric kissed Kenna's hair before sighing deeply. "I would prefer for us not to part again for some time, my darling." Edric's eyes scanned the darkening horizon. Stars began to glitter above them as they lay draped in a blanket on the soft grasses. He was quiet for some time and had begun whistling a familiar tune. Kenna puzzled over this tune for a moment, but she was unable to name it. Edric often enjoyed singing, but whenever he was in a complacent mood, he would whistle that certain tune. Kenna wondered what significance it held for her husband and all at once had the odd feeling that she knew nothing of the man holding her. It raised chills down her bare arms despite the warmth provided by the fur blanket they snuggled under. Kenna looked back at Edric, and the feeling faded. What was she thinking? This was her Edric, not some stranger.

"I miss the sea," Kenna sighed and leaned back into Edric's warm arms. He held her tightly, making her believe he could protect her from anything that might come along. "How is Willow? How is my store?" Kenna pressed Edric.

Edric chuckled softly. "I was wondering when you would ask. Willow is quiet. No travelers have been in since the seas have turned. We are entering our cold season now, so work will be slow for me for some time. I'll finally have time to work on those new tables, chairs, and shelves you asked me to build." Edric added. *"The store is well stocked for now, but with no sailors bringing in wares or their business, it will not be long before it is time to close for the season."*

Kenna nodded in agreement. She had been away longer than she had planned.

"Do you plan to return to teaching until next spring? You seemed to enjoy it last winter." Edric asked softly.

Kenna frowned. He was digging. She had known for some time that Edric was ready for a child. She had enjoyed teaching, but she knew what returning to it this winter would entail: her remaining there, indefinitely, if Edric had his wish. "We will see. I suppose I have a week of traveling to make up my mind."

Edric nodded silently, and then changed the subject. "I am glad that you accomplished what you meant to do, but Kenna," Edric paused meaningfully, "don't you think it was too easy?" Concern knotted his brow.

"Yes, of course I do, but Dane was the only one involved that we could readily identify as a member of Orco's Cult and a facilitator of the attacks. I am afraid that we must believe that we destroyed them until we are proven otherwise." Kenna sighed. "But I do fear that when I leave Terra, events may take place that bring me back here."

Edric clenched his jaw. "It is not safe for you to be there with Damon."

"I don't know, Edric. I think I can trust Damon now. He has proven himself to be loyal thus far."

Edric scoffed. Kenna glared at him, and he shook his head in frustration. "I am trying to honor my mother by giving him a chance. He was very important to her, and I cannot help but wonder why." The gods knew he was difficult. Kenna looked out at the sky as the imitation stars glittered soothingly and reassuringly. She had recently shared with Edric her family's history with Damon. He was not pleased to learn more about the man she had spent the last several days with. "The bigger issue I face is what to do with my new discovery."

"But you have always known you did not inherit. Did you not know that you were...what is it called? Elite?" Edric asked. Kenna had just learned that she was what dreamwalkers called elite. This meant that she never "inherited" (was granted her skill by another dreamwalker). Kenna was simply born with her skill, and this inherent skill was stronger than the skills of other dreamwalkers who were not elite. Edric was a typical, another word for a mortal without skills, so this new discovery about his wife had not changed much in his opinion of her. But Kenna knew that this revelation was more significant than Edric thought. Kenna mused on this for a moment before answering Edric's question.

"I knew I was different, but I did not know that it meant that I was stronger than others dreamwalkers. I will admit that I always wondered why I felt unaccepted by others. Maybe it is because they knew deep down that I had something they did not."

"So, what can we do about that?" Edric questioned, trying to determine if Kenna had a plan or was just musing over this new information about herself.

"We find someone to train me. I think that-", Kenna was suddenly cut off by a loud rustling in the bushes behind where they lay. This drew her attention to the fact that Edric and she were both naked and barely covered by a thin blanket. She drew the blanket up to her chin as Edric

scrambled to his feet. "Who is there?" he boomed. Kenna rolled her eyes as she reached for her dress. Men! Modesty was certainly a womanly trait...

A head emerged from the foliage near the tree that stood behind them. A throat cleared, and Kenna locked eyes with Damon. His face flushed bright red, and he turned immediately and walked back into the bushes. "Oh! Kenna, when you are free, can I speak with you? Ansley has shared some new information with me that we need to discuss. Just—whenever you are ready. No need to rush things!" Damon yelled as he continued to walk away from the couple.

Kenna gestured in Damon's direction. "I guess I..."

Edric nodded and kissed her before grabbing for his clothes. "He better have a good reason for coming after you tonight," he growled. Kenna smiled naughtily and wrapped her arms around her grumpy husband.

"You can have dibs on every night until we are old and wrinkly, my love." She followed this promise with a deep kiss, savoring the manly taste of his lips. There was something in him that she would drink in if she could, but she could never place her finger on what exactly it was.

"Hmph!" Edric responded and turned away from Kenna.

*

Suddenly, Kenna was back in the soft bed in Bianca's small home. She could hear the cows and horses that were in the stable from outside, eager to receive their breakfast. Kenna rubbed her face with both fists before pushing her aching body out of the bed. The soreness lingered in her arms and back from the chains Dane had used to restrain her in the dream the night before. Kenna rolled her shoulders trying to ease the tension. She had hoped to spend a relaxing night forgetting all that had happened here in Terra, but now, even that small hope was extinguished. *Damon may be trustworthy, but he will never cease to madden me*, she thought angrily as she pulled on a fur cloak she had borrowed from Ansley and padded softly into the living room to find out what news had pulled her from such a good dream.

CHAPTER FOUR
Damon

Damon sat huddled at the table in the kitchen trying to ignore the aches in his bones brought on by the cool morning weather. It had been almost four hours now since Ansley had woken him. Damon shook his head thinking about what Ansley had shared with him. *How could she expect me to help her? The idiot has landed herself in an impossible situation, and without the elders' help, we could all be in more danger than we ever thought possible.*

Damon shivered and pulled his heavy, fur-lined cloak around his neck to keep the cold air out. He picked up his small metal flask and unscrewed the top as he shook his head. Damon lifted the familiar brew to his lips and took a gulp. It burned as it ran down his throat, but it drove away the cold from his limbs. He was thankful he had brought his whiskey with him on this trip. *I will likely need every drop to get me through this mess*, he thought angrily.

Damon tapped his fingers on the table, silently trying to decide what could be done about Ansley's situation. Even with Kenna's help, they may still be no match for this *Magnus*. The name sounded familiar to Damon, but he was unsure why. He had spent years in libraries, learning the history of his people, so there were a number of possibilities about where he had seen or heard the name. Damon took another sip of whiskey and wiped his mouth with his flannel shirt sleeve.

The sun was starting to rise outside the small, glass-paned window. Damon had sent Ansley to bed before reaching out to Kenna. His face burned with the memory of what he had interrupted. First, Ansley's dilemma, and now Damon had disrespected Kenna too. What was he thinking? He should have never dreamwalked to her like that. Even with a tethered dreamwalker, it was strongly frowned upon to disturb another dreamwalker's dreams. Damon took another sip of his whiskey, hoping to scorch away his shame. Damon glanced back at the window, his eyes looking in the direction of his home, and wondered where Lya was on this fateful morning. Was she still laying in their bed, snuggled up with her large feather pillow, or had she ventured out to tend to her treasured horses? Mila had better be watching over her mother. He had told the girl to do so, but his trust in his overeager and adventurous daughter was not as strong as it once had been. His sweet wife was aging, and the years had been hard on her. Thinking of Kenna and her husband made Damon wish that he could go home to his family.

But now, that may not happen for some time. Damon took one last sip of whiskey before tightening the lid on the flask and hiding it in one of his inner pockets. He heard soft footsteps moving toward him from down the hall. Kenna appeared in the kitchen, her eyes bright and full of irritation.

"Good morning. I'm sorry, I never thought that I would..." Damon began.

"Save it, Damon. What do you want?" Kenna hissed. Her breath was visible in the frigid air of the morning. The fire had burned out during the night. The sun was barely starting to peek over the horizon, and Bianca still slept quietly.

"Come, we won't have much time before Bianca rises." Damon rose silently from his chair and motioned to the door of the cabin.

Kenna followed him out of the cabin and to the edge of the woods. The sun finally rose, and rays of light filled the sky. Damon lifted his hand to shield his eyes from the brilliance of the light as he continued walking. He was thankful that the sun was rising. Hopefully, it would fight off the cold of the night. He led Kenna to a small clearing in the trees that he had used for Ansley's training. *This should be far enough from unwanted ears.*

He turned quickly, and Kenna, not seeing him stop, ran right into Damon's chest. They moved apart quickly and awkwardly, trying to avoid touching one another at any cost. One look back at her reminded him how she favored her mother, his daughter's namesake. Damon had always loved Vida's name because it had inspired such joy in his heart. *Probably more now than before.* Damon smiled to himself as he thought of his own daughter.

"Let's speak here. It should give us the privacy we need." Damon grunted and sat under one of the nearby trees. The warmth of the morning sun was slowly chasing the bite of cold from the air. Damon guessed that in less than an hour the temperature would start to creep up. The new season would not officially begin until the Winter Solstice had passed, but that was still over a month away.

Kenna sighed. "Damon, please. What is this all about? Why do we need privacy?"

"Ansley spoke with me during the night. The girl is in trouble. Do you remember her friend, Rhys, that we met a few days ago?" Damon asked quietly.

"Of course. He seemed nice enough. Isn't he of the Brooks family?" Kenna asked, leaning against a tree opposite Damon.

Damon cleared his throat. "It appears that he is not who he pretended to be. Kenna, Ansley says he is not a dreamwalker. She had a dreamvision that showed her the truth about Rhys."

Kenna's face was leached of color. "So, who is he? What does he want with Ansley?"

"I don't know, but I have a bad feeling about the whole situation. Ansley believes that he was involved in those attacks on the dreamwalkers. She thinks that is why my scrying found his storeroom." Damon responded thoughtfully.

Kenna nodded slowly, taking it all in. "Damon, do you think this series of attacks was bigger than what we thought?"

"I do think so, yes. I know you believe that you killed the leaders of Orco's cult, but it's likely that those we found were not the ones in charge. Dane may not have been the one responsible for the attacks. He was probably just a pawn."

Kenna shook her head. "How could it fail, Damon? I have locked dreams before, and it has never failed me. It is one of the first tricks I learned when I joined Jameson. He insisted that we all learn how to lock dreams and destroy them…in our own way." Kenna rubbed her face with her hands.

"Locking dreams is standard enough, but everything connected to this cult seems…off. Now, with Ansley discovering this about Rhys, I fear that we have just scratched the surface of what is really happening with everything. Now, we are faced with another uncertainty of this…*alliance* Ansley has with Rhys, and I am concerned of the implications. Kenna, have you ever heard the name Magnus Black?" Damon waited for his words to take effect.

Kenna shook her head in confusion, her brow furrowed. "No, I haven't. Is this someone I should know? You know the Blacks are from Terra. I have only ever lived on the east coast of Arvenia, so I am not familiar with the family lines here. Does Ansley not know him? He shares her family name."

Damon sighed. "No, she has never heard of him, which worries me. I've heard the name somewhere before but cannot remember where. Ansley insists that this *Magnus* is who Rhys truly is. She said he asked her to make a blood oath with him." Damon's eyes lifted to Kenna's, which had widened at his remark.

Kenna's face reflected the fear that Damon had been unable to shake from the moment Ansley had shared this with him. "Damon, what is a *blood oath*?" She whispered, her voice barely registering over the calm sounds of the morning. Damon shook his head thinking of his apprentice. *What had Ansley gotten herself into? How could she blindly trust someone that she had just met? Why had she asked for this stranger's help instead of Damon's?*

Kenna continued to gaze at Damon in fear as Damon's thoughts drifted to his own past. His brother, Rory, had always trusted others blindly too, and look where that had gotten him. Rory's face swam in his memories before he could will it not to. Damon's voice caught in his throat, and he found himself unable to speak for a moment.

Kenna misinterpreted his emotion, and she moved closer to where he sat in the shadows. "I do not know what is happening, Damon, but I swore to see this finished. I will help you however I can." She reached out her hand to his, and he shook it gently, accepting her offer.

Damon swallowed and responded at last, "We will likely need all the help we can find. But I believe it is in our best interest to leave Bianca out of this. She will want to help, but she is weak. We will be unable to protect her at the same time without endangering ourselves."

Kenna replied, "Yes. She is a strong-willed woman, but her role in this has ended. She has been at risk since she passed on her skill. Have you discussed this with Ansley?"

"Yes. She reluctantly agreed. She wishes to keep her grandmother safe too."

"Good. So, what is our plan?" Kenna asked. Damon frowned, understanding that Kenna had accepted that she would not return to Willow for some time.

CHAPTER FIVE
Kenna

Kenna paced in front of the large tree. Their tree. She knew he would be here soon, but she felt like she had been waiting for too long. Maybe it was the conversation she had with Damon that was weighing on her so heavily and making the moments pass so slowly. Kenna could not believe what they were facing. Just when she thought they were safe once more, she was faced with this. Edric would not be happy.

Damon's words drifted back into her mind. Magnus Black... who was this mysterious villain? Why had he targeted Ansley? She was just a girl! A thought flashed through her mind of her own youth, and Kenna sighed. Young girls are always the most trusting and vulnerable, aren't they?

Kenna stopped pacing and leaned against the tree trunk. She crossed her arms over her chest and tried to comfort herself and divert her thoughts from memories of her own naivety. The clouds passed over the sun, and a chilly wind whispered through the trees. Suddenly, a rain drop fell on her cheek. Kenna glanced upwards to the glimpses of the sky she could see through the thick branches and leaves above her. "What....?" The sky had suddenly turned as dark as her mood, and the rain started pouring in earnest now. Kenna huddled under the tree for cover, but it was no use. She was thoroughly soaked.

Thankfully, now she spotted a familiar figure walking toward her. His stride was so etched into her mind that sometimes when Kenna closed her eyes, she could still see his movements. She smiled and walked out from under the tree and into the rain to greet her husband.

"A bit rainy, huh?" Edric asked with a frown. Kenna nodded, and he pulled her in for a kiss.

"What took you so long?" Kenna asked over the downpour. She snuggled into Edric's arms as they walked together to their usual spot on the wooden bench under the tree. This was their favorite place to see one another in dreams. Probably because it was where they had one of their first dates in Willow.

"I don't know. I have been asleep for a few hours already, but I guess I wasn't dreaming yet." Edric pulled Kenna in closer and wrapped his strong arms around her, squeezing her worries away.

Suddenly, the sky lightened up, and the rain stopped abruptly. Kenna opened her eyes to find the clouds disappearing and sunlight beaming down on both of them. She frowned in confusion.

"Did you...?" Edric asked, pointing up to the sky.

Kenna swallowed uneasily. "I don't know. I'm a wielder of earth. Not water."

Edric shrugged and smiled at his wife as he said, "So, when can I expect you home?"

Kenna cleared her throat. "Well, there have been some unforeseen complications."

"Complications?" Edric asked quietly. "Complications that will keep you away longer, you mean?"

Kenna nodded. "I am sorry, Edric. I want to come home, but it seems that we have not rid ourselves of the danger like we thought. Even you yourself thought it was too easy. Damon suggested we travel to try to find some answers that will help us form a better plan. Some new information has come to light, and I think it has unsettled all of us. I cannot leave until I feel that our people are safe."

Edric looked at Kenna from the corner of his eye but nodded. He turned to look out over the now-peaceful lake and crossed his arms. "So, Dane was not the one in charge of all of this after all. I assumed he was more muscle than brains. Where are you going?"

"There are many more records kept of the dreamwalkers' history in Calvenia. Damon says while he has lived there, he learned of some sources and can take us to them. The country has been closed to Arvenians for some time now, making it harder for us to get in, but Calvenia may hold the answers we seek."

"Why would they have records in Calvenia?" Edric asked, suspiciously.

"That is where the first dreamwalkers were created. Or so the legend says. I know it is far from here and will likely keep me away for some time, so I thought I would ask you to come with me. You have never taken me to your homelands, and I have heard so much of it from you! I know you miss the rolling hills and wild horses you loved so! It would be a nice trip for both of us, and we could spend time exploring your family's history too…"

"No." Edric said. His voice was so soft that Kenna had almost missed it. The anger there surprised her.

"No? Why, Edric? Don't you want to go home and see your family once more?" Kenna asked. Her confusion grew quickly, and the strong lines of Edric's face gave her no comfort.

"No. Please do not ask me again."

Kenna looked at her husband and again felt that the person before her was someone she did not know as well as she had thought. He had never reacted this way to *traveling with her before. Edric, being a sailor, was always so full of joy and adventure.*

"Do you mind if I go then? Alone?" Kenna added, trying to get something more from Edric on why he had refused what she considered a good opportunity to spend some time together.

"If you wish to, I will not stand in your way. Just do not ask me to go with you. I won't do it." Edric said, still focusing his gaze on where the lake met the bright sky.

Kenna touched Edric on the arm, but he did not respond to her. She leaned in, kissed her husband on the cheek, and whispered into his ear, "I hope to see you soon, my love."

*

Then, Kenna woke up. She sat straight up in the bed, her heart so full of hurt and concern for Edric that she almost felt nauseous. What was he hiding from her?

CHAPTER SIX
Ansley

"I'm sorry, how did you say you are related to Rhys?" Bianca asked in earnest, frowning at Rhyn over her steaming cup of black coffee.

Rhyn did not hesitate. "His brother, ma'am. Younger brother actually." Ansley was glad they had discussed their story beforehand. She knew her grandmother was very intuitive, so if the plan was going to work, they needed to convince Bianca that their trip to Calvenia was for leisure instead of being part of a larger plan.

"Hmm…you do look like Rhys. So, why is he not with you today?" Bianca asked as she sipped her steaming brew.

"He had work to do with our storehouses, so he asked me to come look in on everyone after all the excitement this week. Are you well?" Rhyn asked. Rhyn had a good story, and Ansley was impressed with his interactions with her grandmother. She herself was having trouble suspecting him of telling any lies, and she knew the real plan. He was good at this, but she was not sure if it made her feel better or worse about this stranger sitting beside her.

"Ahh. Yes, we seem to all be healing nicely. Thankfully, Ansley only had a few cuts and bruises. I think Damon got the worst of it." Bianca responded amiably.

From the corner of the kitchen, Damon snorted and then took a sip from his flask. Ansley looked more closely at him and noted the grey hair that he had not had a week ago. Her grandmother was right, but it was not over yet. Who knew who would "get the worst of it" next time.

"That's very good news! I am pleased to meet you, Mrs. Black. I am sorry to meet you on such negative terms, but our family is always thankful to meet fellow dreamwalkers." Rhyn said with a smile.

Bianca smiled in return. "Yes, there are far too few of us these days. A long and bloody history we have had! I am hopeful that in the future the dreamwalkers will grow closer with Arvenia's typicals so we may find an alliance with them. I fear that too many of them fear us because they do not understand what we are. Ignorance can be our worst enemy."

Rhyn nodded silently, and his face looked grave. "Yes. My family has lost much to protect our secrets, but we are happy enough with our lives. The Brooks have lived for many decades south of Avendale, and it is a peaceful area. We are lucky that we have found a trade to support ourselves easily enough."

"What does your family do?" Bianca asked. Ansley nervously looked back and forth between her grandmother and Rhyn and was surprised to see trust blooming there already.

"We mine and shape metals. Our storehouses are filled with grains and various farming equipment. My great-grandfather was a blacksmith and taught his son the trade. As you can imagine, such a noble trade was then passed on to his-"

"Son?" Bianca interjected, following the conversation with genuine interest.

"Daughter." Rhyn replied. A smile formed at the corner of his lips as he added, "My own mother."

Bianca raised her eyebrows. "Well! Good for her! I am always telling Ansley that we women depend more on men than we should. We have two hands and a brain. Why shouldn't we use them?"

Bianca and Rhyn laughed at her joke, and the conversation ended in a peaceful thoughtfulness. Ansley looked expectantly at Damon, whose turn it was to continue the story.

Damon cleared his throat. "Since we are wrapping up this...*adventure* we have had, I suppose I should mention that I aim to return to Calvenia at the end of the week. I have served my purpose here and mean to return home."

Bianca looked surprised. "Home? Why, Damon, I am sure the elders would let you stay here. After all you have done to help us in this difficult situation, is Terra not still your home?"

"Not anymore." Damon said. His face twisted into a frown, and he turned to look out the window.

"Very well then. I must say that I am glad that you have come here. There are so many reasons I am in debt to you, especially for training Ansley. I have no experience with seers, so I knew any information I gave her would be unhelpful."

Damon turned back to Bianca and glanced at Ansley as he said, "Yes. About that. I am pleased with the progress Ansley is making, but I cannot willingly release her from my instruction. I believe she needs more mentoring, so I was hoping to bring her with me to Calvenia for a few months."

Ansley swallowed in response and glanced at her grandmother. A look of shock crossed Bianca's face, but then a calm settled on it as she seemed to push down her hesitations. "Ansley? What do you think about it?"

Ansley's mouth dropped open. Her grandmother was letting her decide? She swallowed again and formed her words carefully. "I have spoken about it with Damon already, and I agree with him. I want to learn more about this *transference* that the elders mentioned. Damon says there is a large collection of historical documents about dreamwalkers in Calvenia. If I can find answers somewhere about this new skill I have, it will likely be there."

"Yes. There is much she can learn in Dunbar." Damon added. Dunbar was the capital of Calvenia, and Damon had explained that it was roughly two hours from his home, if you were traveling by cart. This made Dunbar the ideal place for the group to search. Damon was hopeful that one of the halls of records in the capital would hold answers that could help them defeat Magnus.

Bianca nodded, taking it all in. "If you think it will benefit you, I can hardly ask you not to go. After all, Damon is likely one of the most experienced seers of our age. But I do ask that you write to keep me updated on your progress and plans to return home."

"Are you okay with this, Nana?" Ansley asked quietly.

Bianca's eyes glistened with unshed tears. "Ansley, my dear. I have known from the moment I held you in my arms on the day you were born that I could not keep you forever. After all, how can you catch a shooting star?"

*****

Rhyn sat on the bed in Ansley's room as she began packing her things. He watched her silently, not wanting to disturb her thoughts, or so Ansley believed. *He is good in that way,* she realized. In the whirlwind of the last twenty-four hours, Rhyn had given her space to think and feel. It was something Ansley had needed, so she was thankful she did not have to ask him for it.

Ansley sighed. "Well, that went better than I had hoped." She looked up from her traveling bag that now held several pairs of linen and woolen shirts folded neatly in a stack.

Rhyn looked at Ansley waiting for her to continue. When she did not, he asked, "Were you surprised with her reaction?"

"Surprised? Of course, I was! You may not know this since you just met her…and me…but my grandmother has always made decisions for me. She and my father trained me prior to my inheritance ceremony, and sometimes, I wished so hard that I could shut her voice out of my head." Ansley placed her hands on either side of her face and closed her eyes. "To be able to make my own choice is new and a bit terrifying."

Rhyn nodded. "I know it seems like a leap of faith, but Damon seems steady. He will protect you, Ansley."

"That is not what I am afraid of, Rhyn. I am afraid of us going somewhere and getting involved in something that will permanently take me away from my grandmother. She will know nothing of the circumstances that led to my death, and I know she deserves better than that. This was my first opportunity to choose for myself, and I chose to lie to her!" Ansley sat on her bed with her back to Rhyn. Unexpectedly, she felt her face grow warm with her emotions and clenched her fists in frustration. "I am thankful I can choose for myself, but did I make the right choice?"

Rhyn placed his hand on Ansley's shoulder. "Ansley, you really have no choice here about telling her. Damon insisted, and Kenna agreed that it was best. They have been walking much longer than either of us, and Ansley, we need their help. Your grandmother is too blinded by her love for you. She would only be a liability on this mission."

Ansley nodded silently and focused on taking a few deep breaths. Slowly, her breaths started to come more easily. She noticed that she had made indentations with her nails on the inside of her hands from clenching her fists so tightly. As she looked at the small half-moons, she whispered, "Yes, but what would my father think?"

Rhyn sighed. "I did not know him either, though Rhys told me he saw him a lot with you in your dreams. I would like to think that any parent, in this situation, would approve of the caution you are taking with your grandmother. He may not have agreed with lying, but your father was also a son who loved his mother. I'm sure that he would not have wanted either of you to be in danger."

"Maybe you are right." Ansley replied, looking over her *shoulder* at Rhyn. The calm in his expression soothed her anxious heart. "But if my father were here, I would not have gotten into this situation."

"But you did. Do not be harsh with yourself, Ansley. We have seen that Magnus is an expert in deception. You have made the mistake in trusting him, and now, it is simply time to correct it. Consider yourself lucky that you have friends who are willing to help you on this dangerous path."

Ansley glanced into Rhyn's eyes, the same eyes that she had fallen into weeks earlier under false pretenses. She thought she could see a fire in Rhys's eyes back then, but in Rhyn's eyes, she saw only hope. Ansley was thankful for that. Fire burns, and she thought that by now, she had tasted enough of fire.

CHAPTER SEVEN
One week later…
Damon

The wind was cool and whipped Damon's traveling cloak furiously around his legs. Damon looked to the north, towards Calvenia and what awaited them there. The weather was not favorable for their travel, and he expected it to rain once they were out on the water.

Damon had a terrible time finding someone willing to take them across Otto's Pass. He had approached many captains along the dock, but all had refused him. Damon was offering gold, so it was not the fare but the dangers awaiting them on the foreign shore that deterred the captains. It had been many years since he first had set foot in Calvenia, but tensions between the two countries were not as high then as they were now.

Damon pulled the small bag of gold from his pocket for their captain. He had hired a young man to take them across. The poor fool had agreed heartily to it when Damon had approached him in a pub near the docks. He could not resist the bag of gold lying on the bar in front of him. By the look of the boy, he sorely needed it too.

Damon felt a drop of cool rain fall on his hand, and he glanced up at the sky. *He better hurry if we are to make it over before the storm.* Damon had traveled this route only twice before. Once on his way out of his homelands, and once on his way back to answer Alden Black's summons about a month ago. He was glad that his time in Terra was over. Although he had not told the others about his family,

Damon was eager to return home. He missed his wife and daughter desperately.

Damon turned and looked behind him. Ansley and Kenna were huddled together for warmth and protection from the cold winds. It seemed that Caeli, the god of the winds, was not looking favorably upon their journey. Damon sent up a silent prayer to appease the god, and he swore that the winds roared more loudly in his ears afterwards. He held up his hands and mumbled, "Hey, can't blame a man for trying."

Damon turned back to his companions and spotted Rhyn walking toward him. Rhyn pulled his cloak tightly around his arms as he moved toward Damon. Rain drops began to fall sporadically, and the temperature seemed to plummet even more.

"A message just arrived from the captain. He worries that the seas are too rough for travel." Rhyn yelled over the roaring winds as he held the hood of his cloak to prevent it from blowing off his head.

"Damn boy! Send the messenger back," Damon replied, glancing at the boy standing beside Ansley expectantly. Damon realized that the boy ahead was likely as old as the one set to sail them across the Pass. "None of the other captains would even attempt crossing because of the issues Arvenia is facing with Calvenia right now. We need to leave today! Time is our best weapon, and we have wasted too much of it already. Besides, the closer we get to winter, the more dangerous the currents that plague Otto's Pass. Tell the messenger we will not take no for an answer. We sail today!" Damon roared in reply.

Rhyn just nodded and turned to send the messenger back to their would-be captain, who was very likely the boy's brother. Damon sighed. Ondo, the god of waters, must hate him just as much as Caeli. He supposed it was his lot in life now for the poor choices of his past.

Damon stood on the edge of the dock, glancing out to the treacherous seas. *If Rory were alive now, where would he be? Would he be a captain? Or perhaps a fisherman?* Damon mused. But in his heart, Damon knew his brother would never have lived as long as he had. Whatever his skill may have been, Rory would not have been cursed by the gods to walk the earth in penitence. Rory would have lived a life full of joy and love. Damon could almost picture his older brother chasing after children and grandchildren. Damon imagined Rory lifting them onto his shoulders, as they laughed, like he used to do with Damon when he was small enough.

A hand on Damon's shoulder pulled him back from his daydream, and he was surprised to see that it belonged to the captain himself. *Barely old enough to have hair on his chin!* Damon hoped that the boy's skills on the water were as good as he had claimed. He removed the bag of gold from his inner cloak and placed it into the boy's open hand. The boy swallowed as he pocketed the gold quickly and motioned for the others to join them at the dock.

He led the group to a small boat tied at the end. It looked big enough for around twenty-five passengers, but it also looked old. Damon assumed that this boat had probably seen as many winters as he had and many more than their captain. He rolled his eyes as he stepped into it first. He hoped this would not be the last mistake he made. His life may be cursed by the gods, but he didn't plan for it to end anytime soon.

The others followed him in and settled on the benches the captain had instructed them to use. They were a small group and with the storm, it was important to shift their weight evenly throughout the boat. Once they had all settled in, the captain raised the sail and prepared to move out into the cold, dark depths. The wooden planks of the boat creaked as the boy walked around, checking that everything was ready to set sail, and Damon shuddered. *I hope his feet don't break through this old piece of wood.*

The boy handled the boat deftly and maneuvered them into Otto's Pass with skilled hands. He raised and turned the sail to catch the angry winds, and the boat began moving quickly. Damon let the salty winds whip his face. He closed his eyes and pictured his home and family. In his imagination, Mila was running towards him with a smile full of mischief. In his mind's eye, she was always a toddler, but she had just turned seventeen while he was away. Damon had never missed her birthday before, and he knew that she would coax something out of him to pay back that debt.

He looked over at Kenna where she sat on the far side of Ansley and sent a prayer to Matrisa, the goddess of family and hearth, that his wife would not murder him on sight. He chuckled deep in his throat at the thought of Lya's face when he introduced Kenna to her. Ansley turned to him, "What are you laughing about?"

Damon just shook his head and replied, "The irony that the gods fill my days with." How was he ever going to explain his reasons for bringing his ex-lover's daughter home with him?

CHAPTER EIGHT
Magnus

The mountain tops were covered in snow and ice, and the crisp wind that whirled through the trees promised more snow by nightfall. Magnus drew in a deep breath of mountain air and savored it. *I could stay up here for an eternity and not need anything but this air, this view, and this wine*, he thought as he took a small sip from his glass.

He stood on the balcony and rested his free hand on the polished wooden railing. The sky was beginning to darken. He guessed that the sun had set only an hour ago behind Alyanna's Thumb. Magnus had watched the sun set for many hundreds of years behind that spectacular mountain, but it never ceased to amaze him.

Alyanna's Thumb was one of the most well-known mountain peaks in northwest Arvenia. The mountain base rose into a twisted shape, and the ridges along the sides resembled fingers. The top-most stone of the mountain jutted up above the surrounding trees almost forty feet into the sky. It strangely resembled a hand giving a gesture that was used to convey either "congratulations" or a "job well done". Magnus found the idea preposterous and childlike, but he could not deny that the mountain did resemble a closed fist. The mountain's namesake, Alyanna, was one of the first princesses of Arvenia. Her history was a strange one, but it did not interest Magnus.

Like his feelings towards his mother, his feelings towards most women were of dismissal and annoyance. Magnus preferred the company of men in all aspects of his life, though he had shared a bed with women in his past. His distaste for the betrayal he had experienced by the most influential woman in his past was projected onto all his future associations with women. It was a flaw of his, and he could freely admit that. Magnus took a sip of his fine wine as he thought on how strange childhood must be that it can leave such a lasting impression on a person. *Hundreds of years have passed, and still my scars from that woman haunt me.*

Magnus continued to gaze out upon Arvenia's mountainous skyline and Avendale's lights to the south of his castle. His thoughts wandered as he glanced toward where he believed Terra was and longed for an answer to his troubles. *Why had it always been so difficult to achieve his goals?* He thought angrily. Magnus had thought of another way to draw Ansley to him, but the tool he had discovered was not working the way he wanted it to. Rage blinded him momentarily, and he saw the sky turn red, matching his mood. Magnus hurled his unfinished wine over the railing and roared in disgust.

"Am I interrupting something, sire?" An uneasy voice spoke from the doorway behind Magnus.

Dane stepped out onto the balcony with Magnus and folded his arms behind his back, waiting silently for Magnus's answer.

Magnus did not turn. Instead, he spoke out to all of Arvenia. "Don't stand there and pretend you don't know what ails me," he murmured in a low growl, "My plans again have hit a snag. What are we to do to ensure this new approach is more successful?"

Dane moved slightly closer to Magnus's right elbow. He had healed some in the last few days, but Dane continued to favor his left leg, and he dragged his foot along on that side, making a quiet scraping noise on the balcony. "My lord, perhaps you do not need the girl. Maybe your plan would be better suited in using another dreamwalker?" Dane inquired, trying to offer advice and instead falling into the trap Magnus had set for him.

Magnus clenched his jaw in silence and swallowed this critique from his inferior. *How dare he speak to me so*...Magus took a deep breath before answering, "You fool! You are as useless to me as the others! Do you think that you are wiser than I? Do you think that I have not considered *all* the options? *Perhaps* my plan would have been more successful if you had succeeded in the one task I set for you?" Magnus suggested softly, his words laced with venom. With this he turned and faced Dane. Dane, upon seeing Magnus's eyes alight with anger, bowed his head in submission and took two steps back from him. "You're right, master. Please forgive me?" Dane said quietly.

"Leave me." Magnus replied dejectedly.

Dane did not turn from him though. Instead, he raised his head and bit his lip before adding, "Sire, they have not made moves to follow us here. They are where you left them in Terra."

Magnus's eyes widened and then narrowed. "How do you know this?" He inquired, suspiciously.

Dane shrugged and said, "Well, I-umm, I dreamwalked last night. I still have access to Kenna's dreams."

Magnus frowned at Dane in annoyance. *Maybe he is not as useless as I originally thought.*

"And," Dane added hopefully, "From what I overheard, it seems that Ansley only shared her information with a few of them. Neither Bianca nor the elders of Terra have been told. I believe it is just Kenna, Damon, and Ansley who know that you were disguising yourself as Rhys."

"Ahhh." Magnus said as a malicious grin pulled at the

corners of his lips. "It seems that naivety may be our biggest ally. She will regret that decision, and we will see to that."

"But...why is she so important to you? This girl?" Dane inquired of Magnus. Magnus sighed but did not answer immediately. Instead, he played with the thin, worn silver ring on his left hand as was his custom when he was deep in thought. He finally answered, "We have a history, she and I. She does not know it, and neither does her grandmother, but we are tied together in ways that cannot be broken. She is the one thing that keeps me from attaining my rightful place on the throne in both this world and the dream realm. If I cannot harness her skills, then we will never succeed."

"Master, should we not fear Damon? Or Kenna for that matter?" Dane asked with a frown.

"You will learn, Dane, that power can be bottled. We need not fear either of them. We have enough skills to last us for years against any that may challenge me. I merely seek power beyond what I have. True power. And I want all of it. Ansley's skills are crucial to me attaining the power I seek."

Dane's confusion was clear, but Magnus did not care enough to offer him an explanation. It was best to keep his followers from being too well-informed of his plans. That was how he maintained his control over them for so long after all.

"Where is our guest?" Magnus asked Dane. "I need to pay him a visit tonight."

"He is chained in the dungeons, master. He seems unwell. Should we not have him…?"

Magnus had turned to glare at Dane, who suddenly swallowed his last few words. "I will let you know when he needs assistance. Until then, see to it that he is alive.

That entails food, water, and sleep." Magnus said with a laugh. "He may be dreamwalker scum, but like the rest of you, he serves a purpose here."

Dane nodded, lowering his eyes from Magnus's face. "You are dismissed." Magnus said and waved his hand at Dane. Dane backed into the open doorway, blocking the candlelight that flickered inside Magnus's extravagantly decorated bedchamber. He had been the master of this castle since he was in his mid-thirties. Magnus had it decorated to fit a king, and if he was being honest, it put all of King Orlan's furnishings to shame. But, in truth, Magnus was the voice behind Orlan. He may as well live like it.

Magnus turned back to face the now jet-black sky. He could no longer see Alyanna's Thumb or the tree tops, but he could still see the distant lights of Avendale. He would take whatever steps were necessary to ensure that he ensnared Ansley this time. *I suppose I know what I need to do to make my tool more effective...*Magnus thought dryly, wishing he had not thrown his wine away so carelessly before.

CHAPTER NINE
Ansley

Ansley lifted her face and closed her eyes as the wind blew a salty mist over her from the south. She looked around at the group surrounding her: an exiled seer who was over ninety years old, a dreamwalker from the east coast of Arvenia who was elite, and a stranger who claimed he was the twin of the boy that Ansley had thought she was falling in love with. She let out a deep sigh and suddenly found herself feeling more alone than she had in a long time, probably since her parents' funeral. The loneliness ate away at her heart, but the strangest part was her ability to hide it away behind a smile.

Ansley glanced to her left where Rhyn sat. His hair was disheveled by the strong winds raging as the boat tried to move northeast towards the capital of Calvenia. The captain told them shortly after they left the harbor that it would take them around six hours to arrive at the dock of Deniz. Once they arrived at the Denizian port, they would find passage up the Iris to the capital. Ansley could not even remember what it was called. Another long sigh escaped her as she brushed her damp hair out of her eyes and tied it into a quick braid.

Her thoughts lingered on her grandmother's face, full of hope for Ansley when she had lied to her. *If she really knew why I left, she would be furious with me!* She tried to shift her thoughts away from the dread she felt, but the only other feeling she had was loneliness. Ansley couldn't remember the last time she had chosen not to trust her family with something so important. She yearned to run into her mother's arms and beg her for her help, but that was no longer an option. It was time for her to grow up, she supposed. With this thought, Ansley rested her chin on her hand and sighed once more.

"If you keep at it, you may get us there faster than the wind itself," Rhyn murmured behind a smile.

"What?" Ansley asked, softly.

"You just keep sighing so much that it sounds like you are trying to compete with the wind." Another smile tugged at Rhyn's lips. Then he added, "What's on your mind?"

"I don't want to talk about it." Ansley replied. She could not keep the hopelessness from her voice.

Rhyn frowned and looked around at the others, who looked busy with their own thoughts as they each stared out at the rolling waters leading to the horizon. Kenna sat at one end of the boat, and Damon sat by the captain, asking questions about the storm and currents. Ansley covered her face with her hands to hide the few rogue tears that were falling, but she could sense Rhyn moving closer to her. He placed his hand on her shoulder, and that gesture was all it took to break the dam holding back Ansley's emotions. She let the tears fall through her fingers as Rhyn squeezed her shoulder in silence.

"I know it was hard to be dishonest with your grandmother after all you have been through lately."

Ansley nodded and sniffled as she wiped her nose with her sleeve. Rhyn noticed this and handed her a small kerchief. She took it and glanced at his face, which was lined with concern and empathy. *Who was this man?* Ansley wondered.

She used the kerchief and kept it in her hand in the event her emotions betrayed her again. She cleared her throat before saying, "Yea. She's really all I have left. I just fear that I have broken the trust she places in me while also leaving her unprotected and alone."

Rhyn nodded. "That is understandable. So, why did you do it, Ansley?"

Ansley whipped her head up to glance at Rhyn. "What?" She asked in surprise.

"Why did you lie to her?" Rhyn asked again, waiting for an answer.

Ansley's blood began to pump loudly in her ears echoing the anxiety the question had provoked in her. "I didn't have a choice, did I? Magnus may be a typical, but he somehow has skills. He could have destroyed her!" She whispered in fear. "What would you have done? What would anyone have done?" She asked him sadly.

Rhyn nodded in agreement. "Exactly."

Ansley frowned in confusion, unable to understand Rhyn's point.

Sensing her confusion, Rhyn added, "If you knew that you had no other choice than to lie to her, then do not keep torturing yourself with it. I'm sure your grandmother will understand. Besides, she may have lied to you over the years too when it was the best way to protect you."

Ansley pursed her lips but could not argue. Maybe Rhyn was right after all. Father used to say, 'Courage is not never feeling fear. Courage is choosing to keep going in spite of the fear.' Ansley was surprised by Rhyn's support in this decision, but she had to admit that he had been surprising on all accounts. She wondered how he could be so compassionate with her when they had just met.

Rhyn patted Ansley's shoulder in a friendly way and turned away from her to reach into his travel bag. When he turned back, Ansley saw that he held a small flask. "Oh, no thank you. I…. I don't drink that stuff," Ansley sputtered.

Rhyn smiled and pushed it into Ansley's hand. "Give it a try. You may be surprised at the courage it gives you."

Watching him closely again, Ansley carefully unscrewed the lid of the flask and touched it to her lips hesitantly. Rhyn did not watch her reaction. Instead, he moved back down the bench in the boat to even out their weight again. Ansley took a small sip, and her mouth erupted with a variety of flavors. Berries, specifically blackberries and maybe strawberry, and a touch of peach. It was not sweet, but it was not tart either. The flavors were delightful and brought to mind thoughts of early summer. Ansley looked at Rhyn in surprise. He did not catch her glance quickly, but when he did, a rolling laugh echoed out over the strong winds.

"You like it?"

Ansley nodded. "I have never had anything like it. What is this?" She asked eagerly as she took another small sip.

"My family has a small vineyard. I may be biased, but I consider our wines to be the best in Arvenia."

"So, you made this?" Ansley asked, and then she took another sip.

"Yes." Rhyn smiled at Ansley, and she suddenly felt a warmth travel up her spine. She was unsure if it was the wine or the smile, but what did it matter? She liked them both.

Ansley lifted the flask once more to her lips, but before she could take a sip, Rhyn reached out for it, "Easy there, Starlight. This may not be whiskey, but it can knock you out just as quickly." Ansley smiled back at Rhyn in defiance before taking one longer sip of the flavorful wine. Then she replaced the cap and handed it back to him. Rhyn shook his head and simply said, "See for yourself then." Ansley swore that she heard him chuckle again, but she had turned her attention back to trying to warm her freezing hands. She tried to blow a little of the warmth from the drink into them, but the heat had disappeared almost as fast as her loneliness.

*****

Ansley's hands turned white from gripping the bench so tightly. She swayed uneasily with the boat as it moved through the waves. What had been a choppy sea when they had set out from the dock had become a whirlpool. Ansley gripped the bench to try to remain in a seated position, but now even her head seemed to swim. Watching the waves move in front of their boat made her stomach turn flips.

Without thinking it through, Ansley dunked her head down between her knees and tried to catch her breath. She felt Rhyn move close to her once more and heard him chuckle. *Gods! How can he be so calm when the boat moves so!* She opened her eyes and noticed that he had placed a small bucket under her head and in between her feet. Ansley pushed herself up to look at him, and he merely pointed to the bucket. "I told you about the wine. Bad choice to try it out when we are on the sea."

Ansley tried to focus her eyes on Rhyn but only grew dizzier. "Where did you.." she started to ask him but stopped as her stomach heaved. She felt the burning of the wine again and wondered why it had not moved down out of her throat yet. Wait…no…now it was coming back up….

Ansley leaned over the bucket and retched. She heard another chuckle over her shoulder as she wiped her mouth with the kerchief she had borrowed. Although she had rid herself of the wine, Ansley felt that warm sensation move up her spine once more. *His laugh is worse than the wine!* Ansley thought exasperatedly.

Rhyn's hand patted her on the back gently. "There you go. Now, this." He said as he thrust a jug of water into her hands. Ansley took a small sip and rinsed her mouth. She frowned as she realized the water made her stomach feel even more treacherous.

"Yes. That wine will do more to you than these seas. Maybe you can try it again once we land?" Rhyn asked, giving Ansley a smile. She knew he was teasing her, but her stomach suddenly rolled so violently that she could not think of a good comeback. She rested her hands on her face once more and tried to breathe through her nose. Suddenly, the sickness filled her again, but instead of reaching for the bucket, Ansley felt herself falling…falling…falling into darkness.

*

Ansley now stood in a crowd of people in a large room. The room was very noisy, and the sounds echoed off the stone walls and floor. She looked around desperately for the source of the dream, but Ansley had to admit, she had no idea how she had gotten here.

Ansley moved out of the crowd, trying to see what was happening around her. She glanced up ahead and saw three figures waiting at the end of an empty aisle. It dawned on her that she was in a throne room. A sudden movement behind her caught her off-guard, and she stumbled out of the way of a man and woman who walked directly towards her, seemingly unaware of Ansley blocking the aisle.

The pair walked in tandem to a slow tune that was being strummed on a stringed instrument in the corner of the throne room. The woman's face was covered, and the fabric reached all the way to her feet, where it was lined with precious stones of every color Ansley could imagine. Relieved that she could not be seen, she realized that this must be a memory instead of a normal dream.

Ansley slipped back into the crowd and walked alongside the pair as they moved up to the front near the extravagant thrones. When she drew closer, Ansley could make out the priest's features, and she saw that the man in front of him was wearing a crown. But that was not what drew Ansley's eye. Her gaze immediately shifted to the man standing to the left of the king.

He stood there with a bored expression on his dark features. His wavy brown hair was combed and cut into a style that seemed to be one of a man of high standing. He wore a black tunic that was trimmed with gold threading at the sleeves, and he boasted several large golden rings on his right hand and one small, thin silver one on the left. He twisted these rings, in obvious annoyance, as the procession continued. His scowl had given him away immediately. His face had filled Ansley's nightmares since she had discovered the truth about him.

Ansley watched as the king looked to Magnus to see his expression. Magnus's face shifted so quickly that the king never saw his scowl. His look was now one of pride and love. That look would deceive any man, even a king.

The memory dragged on and Magnus's patience grew even thinner. He stared off into the rafters of the chapel as the king's ceremony was performed. At the end of the ceremony, when the marriage was announced, Magnus patted the king on the shoulder in congratulations. He actually patted the shoulder of a king!

Ansley's shock grew as the lines around her smudged and melted away to reveal the sea and the rickety boat she sat on.

*

As Ansley sat up, she noticed that Rhyn had pulled her to lean against his legs. He pushed the stray hairs off her forehead and cupped her cheek in his hand. "There you are! I thought that wine had gotten the better of you after all!"

"No, Rhyn. It was a dreamvision."

"What happened?" Rhyn asked quickly. His expression changed from playful to serious as quickly as a raindrop would run down a pane of glass.

Ansley gasped as she recalled the memory she had just seen. "It was him. *Magnus*. It seems we have grossly underestimated his influence."

CHAPTER TEN
Deryn

King Deryn paced back and forth before the heavy iron doors that led to his dungeons. He nervously twisted the giant rubies on his fingers as he stared at the door, trying to imagine what was happening behind them. He should have never agreed to this. His advisors would be furious! He knew when Dominic walked into his throne room that anything he suggested would be madness. Gods above! *How had Dominic convinced him to allow this?*

Suddenly, the king's anxious thoughts were interrupted by the doors swinging slowly open. A guard stepped out through the doors and moved to the king's ear to share his information. Though he spoke in a soft whisper, the words he shared twisted the king's stomach in horror.

"He did what?!" The king bellowed. The guard jumped in surprise and bowed his head to the king who lunged through those massive doors. The king strode quickly around the corners and by the few prisoners who still remained in his dungeons. His purple cape whipped around his legs as he walked. He had always prided himself on finding more suitable options for those that broke his laws. What good would a man do behind bars? If he had two strong hands, that man would be better use if put to work for the good of the country. His thoughts raced as he turned the final corner and entered the room where stronger forms of persuasion were used, the torture chamber.

Immediately, he spotted Dominic leaning over a man

who had been strapped to a stone table. The man's eyes rolled in his head, and his skin had deep wrinkles.

"You!" Deryn shouted. All of the men's heads whipped around to see the king, shock playing over their features upon noticing he had entered the dungeon. He had been asked to wait outside, but none of the guards seemed eager to ask their sovereign to leave his own dungeons.

Dominic looked up at the king, and a cool smile swept across his face. "Your majesty! How kind of you to join us! Please, come in, and take a look."

Deryn's hands tightened into fists by his sides. He suspected his face was starting to turn that dark shade of purple that his queen, Mirena, always teased him about. "How dare you experiment on the elder prisoners!" Deryn spat at Dominic. "We had a deal! You were only to speak with them. The young ones were yours. Not the elderly!"

Dominic's smile faded as quickly as it came. He gestured back to the old man lying on the table and said, "Him, an elder? Oh no, Your Majesty. You are mistaken, my friend. We have just finished here. He is the result of our experiment." Dominic finished, avoiding Deryn's other accusation.

"Do not assume to call me friend!" The king bellowed as he stomped around the table to look at the prisoner. The man's hair was white and his skin looked like it had seen decades of sunlight. He gestured to the man and asked, "How dare you claim that this is not an elder? He is clearly aged and does not deserve this mistreatment. I don't know where you are from, but in Arvenia, I do not do things like this to our people, even if they *are* prisoners."

Dominic shook his head and held his hands open in front of him. "Your Majesty. I understand you are disturbed by what you see here, but truly, this man is only of twenty and two years, and he is *not* just a prisoner. He is a dreamwalker."

King Deryn glanced back at the man on the table and then up to the guards standing over him. "Jyskar?" He barked at his captain.

The captain stood to attention and replied, "My king. He speaks truth." He placed his hand over the left side of his chest and added, "On my honor."

Deryn turned back to look at Dominic who had that stupid smile plastered on his face once more. Deryn was a head shorter than the man, but he had never let taller men intimidate him. He was, after all, a king. He gestured to the table. "If this is true, prove it. Let's see this *work* you claim to be doing with my prisoners."

Dominic nodded coolly and gestured to the guard nearest to the hall. The man hastily retreated and returned several moments later dragging one of the men the king had passed on his walk into the dungeon.

The man tried to resist entering the room, and it was clear that he knew something the king did not. The prisoner was young and still had many years ahead of him. His face drew forth a memory of the king's from the previous year. *Murderer*...this man had killed his neighbor. If Deryn remembered correctly, the neighbor's lands had access to a creek that the man had desperately sought to add to his holdings. After his death, the lands had been put up for auction, and they were purchased within the hour. Other neighbors suspected that the man was guilty of murder, so they tipped off the guards in hopes of seeing justice served. Life in prison was given as the crown's judgement.

The man saw the king standing near the table and fell to the floor, "My king. Please do not let them harm me!"

The king stepped forward to the man and said, "Your choices have landed you here."

"But, your majesty, I heard you say that Arvenia does not allow this type of treatment to its prisoners!" The man frantically appealed to Deryn. Deryn pressed his lips together and furrowed his eyebrows. "Consider this the price you pay to the crown." Deryn said to him gravely.

The man buried his beardless face in his hands that were crusted with filth. He whimpered as the guards removed the now motionless and wrinkled man from the table and prepared to lay the distraught prisoner in his place.

The guards heaved the man up by his arms, and it seemed to Deryn that all the fight had left him. He allowed the men to lift him onto the table as he whispered prayers to the gods. The king felt a pang of sympathy upon seeing the man's fear, and he looked to Dominic to see his response. Dominic was calm and did not seem bothered by the man's reaction. He waited silently until the man had been strapped down. Then, Dominic turned to a box on a nearby table where he removed a single crystal. The crystal shone white in the dim light of the dungeon.

Dominic said nothing but nodded to the guards, who moved to hold the man's head still. The king felt uneasy as Dominic placed the crystal to the man's forehead. A few moments passed before the crystal began to emit a greenish-yellow glow. The light was bright enough to illuminate the entire room. Then, the man began screaming. His screams echoed off the walls and inside the king's head. The king forced himself to watch what he himself had allowed.

As Dominic continued to hold the crystal to the man's forehead, a faint shape appeared. The outline of a circle with horizontal lines filling the bottom half of it glowed in the darkness of the chamber. The shape looked like that of a lake with gentle ripples moving across the surface of the water. Light poured from the symbol into the crystal that Dominic held against the man's brow. As the light left his brow, the man's face began to change. Wrinkles appeared along his mouth and at the corners of his eyes. His hair was leeched of color, and as the skin wrinkled and shrunk around his skull, the scream died in his throat. The man's eyes were still open, but it appeared to Deryn that no life was left in him.

Dominic drew the king's attention to the crystal in his hand that now glowed that same greenish-yellow color. He held the stone out to Deryn who took it by the string and held it up to look closer. The light whirled around inside the crystal and glowed more brightly as he held it closer to his face. Deryn was drawn to it, and he pulled the crystal very close to his eyes to inspect it further. The crystal had a pull on him and seemed drawn to him too.

Suddenly, the crystal was ripped from his hand by Dominic. "My King. Please, be careful. We have not studied its effects on…typicals yet."

"Typicals?" The king asked, the spell of the crystal broken.

"My name for those that have no skills." Dominic responded as he lifted the crystal.

"How did you know he had these…skills?" The king asked as he gestured to the now lifeless and motionless man.

Dominic merely smiled and gestured to one of the younger guards in the room. "Salvo is skilled as well. He has been most helpful."

Deryn nodded and turned away from this scene, finding that he now felt a rising nausea.

"Your Majesty?" The captain inquired.

"Yes, well, continue on then. We will meet at the end of the week to discuss implications for use of these *skills*."

"Yes, yes. Your Majesty." Dominic uttered as he bowed, probably eager to return to his horrifying studies.

Deryn never saw him bow. His cape brushed the bars of the door as he hastily forced his way out. A cold sweat had covered him. Months ago, Deryn had not known dreamwalkers existed; however, this wasn't the thought that tormented him. The thought that made him the sickest was that he was not sure who the real monster was here: The madman he now employed or Deryn himself, the one allowing that madman's work to continue.

CHAPTER ELEVEN
Damon

The winds were brutal as the boat moved slowly through Otto's Pass. Damon had asked the captain just moments ago where exactly they were. The captain said he thought they were near the city of Karlow. This city was one of four that stretched up the east coast of Calvenia to Bolivar, which was the closest coastal city to the capital of Dunbar. Currently, they were headed towards Deniz. They could stay at any of these ports, but it was safest to move on to Dunbar as soon as possible. Arvenians were not welcome in Calvenia because of the growing tensions between the nations. If Damon got them to Dunbar, he would be recognized there as a local. They would be safe in Dunbar.

The winds blew the waves into rolling giants as the boat traveled through the pass. To their southwest, they could see the outline of Alyanna's Thumb, the strangely shaped mountain peak named for the first princess of Arvenia. Damon remembered the story from his childhood. The first true settlers of Arvenia came from the north, where the ocean waters remained frozen year-round. These explorers had settled in between the Spruce Mountains and the Dream Hollow mountains. It was said that the princess Alyanna was the second child of the first king of Arvenia. She was not yet a woman, and her spirit was still reckless. She sought adventure where she could find it. One day, the weather was clear and beautiful, and Caeli, the god of the winds, was restless. Caeli was always thought to be one of the more troublesome of the gods, and he often interfered with Matrisa's children.

Caeli saw Alyanna as she walked through the outskirts of the Spruce Mountains, enjoying the beauty that surrounded her and listening to the birds call to one another. He sent a whisper of her name on a breeze to her from the mountain to the north of the Spruce Mountains. Alyanna was drawn to the voice, and she decided to find its source. She traveled through the valleys between the mountains and eventually reached a strange peak. The voice continued to call to her, so she climbed the peak and finally found who it was that was calling her. Caeli waited for her on that mountain peak that day, and when she arrived at the top, disheveled and exhausted from her climb, he could only admire how bold she was to follow his call. They spent many hours there getting to know one another, and afterwards, Caeli begged her to return to him soon. Alyanna continued to travel to the peak for the next several months to visit the one who had whispered her name in the winds.

Caeli eventually asked her father, the king, permission to wed Alyanna. Once wed, they made their home on the mountain where their children, the god and goddesses of the storms, rain, and lightning played and brought storms to life. It was said that a small, abandoned cottage still remained on the mountain's peak. Damon looked back at the Thumb and saw lightning streak across the sky. He smiled and wondered if the god of lightning sent that as a tribute to the memory of their mother's story.

Damon's thoughts returned to Arvenia and the life he had there. It had been so easy once. But then, Damon's mind drifted to when he was first exiled from Arvenia. What a horrible embarrassment it had been. But over time, that embarrassment had faded to relief. Damon did not think he could bear to stay in Arvenia after what had happened between him and Rory. His parents would never forgive him, and it was futile to even seek their forgiveness. Rory had been their firstborn, so after Damon's betrayal, his family refused to even see him. They would never forgive him for what he had done.

Damon had moved on to Calvenia, the more interesting of the two neighboring countries. Tortia was mostly desert lands, and Damon had no interest in that. He moved to Deniz in hopes of finding a run-down ranch to repair. He had always loved horses too, and when he was exiled, horrible as it was, it gave him an excuse to seek a life spent training horses. Calvenians were "horse-people". They had the land, the space, and the experience to excel in horse breeding and training. So, this was where Damon had decided to live his life, and it had not been a bad choice. He had relocated to Dunbar, shortly after a bar brawl in Deniz. Damon had been recognized for his Arvenian features and was beaten to a pulp by local nationalists who held grudges for the wars of the past between their two nations. Damon couldn't blame them. Thinking back, he wished he had understood the anger of those Calvenians better, but at that time Damon was focused on his own self-preservation. Their poor country had been turned upside down only three decades later.

Damon had stumbled out of that bar desperate to find passage to safety. He was pleasantly surprised to find a ship preparing to leave the dock at that very moment. Damon shook his head as he realized he was traveling the same course now that had ultimately brought him to Dunbar those many decades ago. He hoped that it was going to be as pleasant of a reception at the docks as it was the first time. Damon knew from that previous experience that Calvenians harbored many grudges against his people.

He may not always understand why they held grudges prior to the rebellion, but he knew the Calvenians had the right to hold them now. Arvenia's leaders had betrayed the Calvenians, resulting in the death of Calvenia's royal family and the rise of a new ruling power.

Damon looked out to the stern and saw those dreary dark clouds chasing them to Calvenia. He frowned at them and muttered curses under his breath.

"What was that?" The young captain yelled in Damon's direction over the roar of the waves.

Damon shook his head in response. "Just telling those clouds that they need to turn around if they know what is best for them."

The captain looked at Damon and frowned with confusion but let the conversation drop. He returned to adjusting the sail to better catch those southern winds that were whipping them so strongly. Damon leaned back in his seat and tried to enjoy the trip, knowing his family would be there when he finally arrived. His ease was disrupted by a loud thunk near the middle of the boat.

When Damon turned, he saw the new kid, Rhyn, holding Ansley up by her arms as her head lolled around. "What happened?" He shouted at him.

"She's had a little too much to drink I think!" Rhyn replied with a chuckle. Hair whipped around his forehead and obscured his eyes for a moment, making him look like even more of a stranger to Damon. Damon looked back to Ansley and realized her eyes were moving beneath her eyelids. Surprise and concern led him to stand carefully and step over the few benches that lay between him and the kids.

"Wait!" The captain yelled. "You'll throw the weight off!" He threw his arm out quickly and motioned for Damon to return to his seat. Damon sat hesitantly down and noticed that Ansley had awoken from her dreamvision. She spoke a few words that Damon lost to the sounds of the furious waters, but he did notice the surprise on Rhyn's face as he listened to Ansley speak.

This had to be important. Damon stood once more and began crawling over the benches to reach them. Five more to go. Four. Two.

"Wait! Sir, I told you…" The captain began once more, but he never finished his sentence. The boat lurched suddenly with the movement of the waves and Damon's shift of weight until it flipped over in the water, breaking the small mast that held the raised sail. The deafening crunch, like the sound of splintering bones, echoed in Damon's ears as he was thrown face-first into the rolling waves.

Damon surfaced quickly but gulped down a mouthful of water as he tried to call to the others. His thoughts finally calmed, and he began to push himself away from the pull of the small boat. The hull rocked slowly back and forth in the water. Damon stopped treading water long enough to allow his head to sink below the waves. In the darkness, he could see their belongings sinking to the depths of the Pass. Damon lingered for a moment below the surface, trying to decide if he should chase their supplies but knew he could wait no longer for a breath. His lungs burned, and he longed to draw in clean air. His vision grew spotty from his hesitation in the water, so he finally kicked furiously to the surface. At last, his head broke the waves, and cool air rushed into his mouth. He sputtered as he swam to the boat to help attempt to flip it.

Damon spotted a wet and angry Kenna swimming towards him. She muttered a few words in his direction, which he assumed were curses. She was right. Damon was to blame. He had shifted the weight unevenly. The captain had already reached the boat and was directing Kenna on how to help. Above, the storm raged on, and blinding streaks of lightning appeared suddenly in the clouds. Damon turned in the water as he heard movement behind him. Rhyn's head broke the waves, and he frantically screamed to the rest of them, "Where is she? I can't find Ansley!"

Damon turned in a circle in the water, panic flooding his thoughts. His body responded instantly. *Thank the gods my father taught me to swim!* Damon scanned the rolling waves in all directions while treading water. He could not see Ansley. He took a deep breath and dove under the water, thankful for the calm environment below. The waves from the storm above were battering him to fatigue. Using his arms to push him deeper beneath the surface, Damon moved as quickly as he could. He scanned the water around him but saw nothing but a few scattered fish and seaweed. Struck by an idea, Damon glanced above him to the capsized boat. He had been right! Ansley was under the boat, desperately trying to pull her bag free from one of the benches they had been seated on when the boat flipped moments before.

Relief flooded his chest, and Damon swam quickly up to her. But he noticed she wasn't actually trying to free the bags. She was trying to free her foot. It was tangled in the straps of the bags. He grabbed the strap she held in her hands and noticed that her eyes started to glaze over. Damon drew a knife that he kept strapped to his belt, cut the strap, pushed Ansley away from the bag, and motioned towards the surface. She squeezed his hand in reply and kicked herself out from under the boat to the open waters. There was a small pocket of air under the boat that suited his needs at the moment. Damon swam upward to take a short breath. He thanked the gods for sparing him and that nobody else had been hurt from his silly mistake.

Damon took several breaths before sinking below the surface once more. Damon cut the straps of the bag that had tangled on the bench and grabbed a few of the other bags still dangling from the capsized boat before quickly kicking himself up for that precious air. Once he broke the surface, Damon heard the captain yelling to the others and watched as they flipped the boat back over. The boat rocked unsteadily for a few moments, but it finally settled into a rolling motion. Damon swam towards the boat, pulling the heavy and water-logged bags along. When he reached the side, the captain and Kenna grabbed his arms and heaved him into the boat. Unfortunately, at the same time a large wave also rolled over the boat. Damon had no time to warn the others even though he knew what was going to happen. The waves crashed onto them, washing them all from the safety of the boat once more.

Damon swam slowly beneath the surface, trying to get his bearings. He tied the straps from their gear to one of his arms before trying to reach the surface. When he did, he saw Kenna, Rhyn, and the captain trying to re-enter the boat once more. Damon yelled at them, but his voice was lost in the roar of the waters. A streak of lightning hit the tattered sail where it hung from the broken mast, and the flames began to move towards the hull of the boat. Rhyn and Kenna jumped into the safety of the waters, but the captain remained on the boat, trying to stomp out the burning embers. Damon heard his exclamations as the fire began to engulf him as well. Damon turned away in shock and horror. He found the others and motioned in the direction he knew the shore to be. Then, he began swimming while also trying to block the sounds of their poor captain's screams from his mind.

After what seemed hours of swimming in the darkness as the waves still pursued their endless tirade against them, Damon and the others finally dragged themselves onto a sandy shore. The shoreline was dark, and no houses or docks were in sight. Damon clung to the soft sands eagerly, resting as the waves continued trying to reclaim him. After catching his breath, he sat up and shook water from his face and hair. He saw Kenna to his left and Rhyn to her left, but where was Ansley?

Damon stood with effort and walked to the others. "Where is Ansley?" He asked softly, his voice hoarse from the seawater he had unwillingly ingested.

Kenna coughed violently and shook in the cold air blowing in from the rough seas behind them. She shook her head. "I haven't seen her since she surfaced earlier. You went under to find her, and then she came up. When I looked back, she wasn't there anymore."

Damon felt colder as those words sank into him. He sat on the sand and tried to stop shivering. Then he looked to Rhyn. Rhyn held his head in his hands silently. "Rhyn?" Damon asked, afraid of what he may have to report.

Rhyn raised his face to the others, and they saw he had paled in the moonlight. "We must find her, Damon. We must." He said sadly. Damon nodded.

"Let's make a fire and try to put together a shelter near the shore. If she can see the fire, she will be able to find us." Kenna and Rhyn nodded eagerly. Then, they all rose, exhausted from the long swim to the shore in the storm. Damon looked out again at the dark waves and watched them roll angrily, as if taunting him. "Give her back to us, Ondo," Damon whispered softly, in hopes that the god of the sea could hear him and would head his words. Then, he turned and followed the others into the cover of the trees to gather firewood.

After several hours of shuffling in the dark brush, three failed attempts at lighting a fire, and one fire being blown out by the winds that continued to roll off the Pass, they finally had a comfortable fire burning. They all fed the fire slowly and finally began stripping off their soaked clothing to try to warm themselves. Kenna took on the task of emptying out the contents of their remaining bags. Everything was soaked. Thankfully, they had enough foresight to pack dried meats and cheeses wrapped in waxed papers. The food was soggy but sufficed.

Rhyn hung their wet clothes, blankets, and cloaks from nearby limbs. The rain had stopped, but the winds continued to angrily claw at them, trying to take back what the ocean had lost. Damon hoped that these winds would die down soon, but he anticipated at least several more hours of fighting them. This must be a big storm.

Unfortunately, there had been no signs of Ansley or the captain. The others did not speak of the captain, and Damon avoided that subject as well. They all could guess what had happened to him. *Poor soul.* Damon muttered prayers to Ondo and Matrisa, the mother and comforter. He hoped that they would allow that young boy to find rest in those treacherous seas. Damon turned his thoughts away from this disturbing thought and continued to scan the waters. Nothing moved around them, and the coast was quiet except for the howling of the winds. Even his companions sat in heavy silence, chomping on small pieces of the dried meat they had heated over the fire.

Desperately, Damon closed his eyes and called to Ansley using her tether. As her mentor, Damon had shared blood with Ansley, connecting them with what the dreamwalkers called a tether. He had this direct link to her dreams from the moment they began their training. If he summoned her using the tether between them, she would hear and hopefully answer if at all possible. He waited for a few moments but sensed nothing. His anxiety grew, but in the darkness, there was nothing for them to do but wait. If she had not found them by morning, they would plan to search for her. Until then, Ansley would have to fend for herself.

CHAPTER TWELVE
Damon

The three had taken shifts keeping watch. Damon had volunteered to start, eager to continue looking for and trying to summon Ansley through his dreams. When Damon took another shift after Rhyn, it had been difficult to convince the boy to go to sleep.

"She is out there…alone!" He had yelled at Damon in response to being told to "try not to fret". "She is easily at risk of being captured by the Arvenians, found by Magnus, who is gods-knows-where at this point, or eaten by a wild creature in the night! And you want me to sleep?" Magnus had turned away from Rhyn back towards the fire in response, deciding not to engage his anger. Rhyn had waited a moment before finally throwing himself onto the hard ground under a still-damp blanket. A sigh of exasperation had echoed in the dark. Kenna, laying across from where Damon sat, stood and reached for another of the damp blankets from a tree limb. She frowned at Damon and shrugged her shoulders as if saying, "What else can we do?". Then, she laid down and tried to make herself comfortable once more on the uneven and wet ground.

Damon had kept watch for at least six hours before waking Kenna again. Nothing had disturbed the silence that had settled over them as the winds died down throughout the night. The sun began to rise over the now-calm waves, and Damon felt himself struggling to stay alert. He finally relented and allowed Kenna to take over.

When he woke once more, the sun was much higher in

the sky, and he guessed at least four hours had passed. The sun warmed their chilled bones and gave them some hope for finding Ansley. After eating a meager breakfast of a few bites of meat and cheese each, they searched for clean water to drink. Finding none, Kenna suggested they drink the rainwater that gathered on the plants' leaves. They had done so, but their thirst was not sated. They packed their gear and sought a stream or pond, knowing if they did not find water soon, they would also be in danger.

Rhyn asked Damon as they walked if they should approach a local village. "No. We don't know exactly where we are, and regardless of where we are, you two are distinctly Arvenian. You will be turned over to the authorities and jailed, if not hanged." Rhyn's face had frozen in fear. "Hanged? For what? Asking for water?" Rhyn had asked angrily.

"For being Arvenian. I told you prejudice is high here, Rhyn. What did you think I meant by 'Calvenians hate Arvenians'?" Damon responded.

Rhyn was quiet for a moment before finally whispering, "Well, I did not expect you to say they would kill us just because of where we are from."

"The world is a hateful place, my friend. The sooner you learn that, the easier your life will be." Damon replied casually. This had ended all talk between them for the next several hours.

*****

The day dragged on as if the sun was intent on watching them for as long as possible. Damon could not be certain how far they walked, but he kept to the thick woods near the shore to avoid attention from the locals. The land here was not heavily populated, but there were some local ports and piers used for fishing. Whenever they spotted one in the distance, Damon pushed them further into the trees to avoid being seen.

As the day wore on, their tempers grew shorter. The thirst was getting to them, and Damon worried that if they did not find freshwater soon, they would have a more difficult journey the following day. But even more than that, he worried for Ansley. Where she had gone and what happened to her haunted him, and at times, he was thankful for the distraction of their search.

After making their way through some large boulders, they happened upon a small stream. Kenna and Rhyn eagerly dipped their canteens into it. Damon dropped the bags he carried and suggested they take a short break here to rest. Kenna took advantage of the stream to wash the salt from her belongings that had been submerged in her pack last night. Then, she washed her face, braided her hair, and chewed on some dried meat. Rhyn sat under the shade of a large oak and rested with his feet in the stream. When Kenna had washed her hands and filled her canteen once more, she approached Damon where he attempted to light a bundle of sage. He felt that Ansley was safe somewhere, and even if they could not find her, perhaps he could find some answer with a dreamvision.

Kenna squatted near him and gestured to the now-smoking bundle he laid on the dirt in front of him. "Does that bring on your visions?" She inquired. "Why don't you scry for her?" She added quietly.

Damon looked at Kenna with surprise but thought meaningfully about her suggestion. "You know what it does to me. Scrying takes years off my life and can kill me if I am not careful because of the power it requires. Besides, scrying usually draws attention from any nearby dreamwalkers. I think they would be more accepting than the Calvenian typicals, but I do not know this area or these people well enough to bet our safety on it." Damon paused. "But regardless, if we do not find her soon, I will use any tools I can to locate Ansley and return her safely to us."

Kenna nodded quietly and maintained the quiet for a moment before she was unable to bear it any longer. "But Damon, what are we doing now? We need to find her, and we need to find her quickly. How are we supposed to linger here and search for her at the same time? Rhyn has tried looking for her in his dreams, and he cannot find her there either. I am at a loss." Kenna put her hands over her face and groaned. "Our whole reason for journeying here in the first place, and we lose her in less than a day's travel on the sea."

Damon broke off some of the herbs and munched on them, hoping to give himself more of the scent to bring forth his visions. "She isn't *lost*. Well, she *is* lost, but not in that way. She is alive. I can sense it." Kenna did not respond. Damon added. "Besides, we did not just journey here for her. We came looking for answers about this Magnus, and while we wait for her, we may as well continue that search. When we do find her, we may need those answers much more than we do now."

Kenna sighed. She looked up at the now-dying sun. "I wish I had your patience, Damon. I find myself restless and consumed by thoughts of giving up this...*mission* we have started. Why did I need to come here anyway?" She asked him softly. Damon turned to her, surprised to hear her say such things.

"Kenna, maybe you did not come for Ansley at all. Did you consider that you came with us because the answers you seek about your own life reside here also? Maybe that uneasiness draws you to it? And please don't give up hope so easily! Your mother, Vida, was relentless, and you are very much her daughter."

Kenna's face melted into a soft smile. "I suppose. I hope Calvenia will give us all the answers we seek here. And I also hope that it will allow us peace, Damon. We still have not spoken of what happened with Dane. Those things...those things you said about my mother." When Dane had trapped them, he had spoken of Damon's involvement in her parents' deaths.

Dane had learned these things from Jameson who was the leader of Kenna and Dane's tribe. "A tribe is like a family, and there is no room for secrets within ours", Jameson had always told them. Kenna had shared with Jameson that Damon was the one responsible for Vida's death. But when Dane had confronted him about this in front of Kenna, Damon had said something that he knew had confused Kenna. He supposed that she had not yet felt the time was right to speak to Damon about her mother, but apparently, now she had finally found the strength.

Damon stiffened and made a point to avoid Kenna's eye. "I know those things are difficult for you to talk about, just as they are difficult for me to think about. I just want you to know that I don't blame you anymore for their deaths." Kenna said. "What happened changed the course of my life, and if it had not happened, I may never have met Edric. I could never imagine my life without him. I suppose that is why I am struggling to be here when I feel so disconnected from him."

Damon stiffened again. He nodded but said nothing as those words of forgiveness melted over him. He felt himself breathe again and relax. Kenna placed her hand in his for a moment, and he squeezed her fingers. They sat in silence as the sun fell below the trees, letting their anger disappear with the last rays of light.

*

Damon had been sleeping, but now he felt that familiar

tug. He followed it eagerly, trying to find Ansley. Instead, he found something else.

*

Damon could barely see in the dark, but he could hear the horses. They rushed past him, and he heard familiar voices screaming a warning.

Then, he caught a glimpse up ahead of three riders moving quickly into the night. To the side, a figure sat on horseback, waiting for them. Then the figure drew an arrow and let it fly. Damon awoke with the sound of Kenna's screams echoing in his ears.

*

When Damon sat up, he was relieved to see Kenna sleeping under a blanket to his right. Rhyn waved silently, and Damon was glad someone had thought to keep watch. Damon walked to the stream and splashed cold water onto his face to clear the terror brought on by the vision.

He decided not to trouble Kenna with it for now. He never knew when his visions would come to pass, and sometimes they were easily avoidable. For now, they needed to look for information about why the attack may happen. Until he was sure she was safe, he would stay close to Kenna.

*****

Damon casually walked from the brush into the town of Talteo. He timed his entrance when he thought no one was looking, and he did his best to appear casual. People moved around sluggishly trying to start their day. They carried goods to the market or tools to begin their work, and some carried their friends from the streets after the long night spent at the bottom of a glass.

Damon moved through the crowds as if invisible. No

one spared him a glance as they started their day. Damon was dressed in the attire that most Calvenians in this area favored, so he blended in well. He wore a white short-sleeved shirt, with buttons down the front, and linen pants that were belted at the waist. The weather was humid and hot here, so clothing was suited to the temperatures and the high chance of rain. If you were caught in the weather, you needed clothing that would dry easily and quickly or you would spend your day miserable.

As he walked, Damon took care to not appear as if he hurried or was looking for someone in particular. He knew that these harbor towns followed a slower pace than the towns closer to the capital of Calvenia. Extra attention was not what he needed, and although he considered himself a Calvenian, Damon was still an Arvenian. He doubted that these people would pause long enough in their prejudice to ask questions about his change in nationality. So, he walked through the town until he saw the market ahead. Damon entered the market and bought fresh supplies of dried meats, cheese, bread, and, just for himself, whiskey. He also bought a new cloak. His was badly torn from the efforts of pushing through the brush close to the shore.

He allowed himself a short glance around, hopeful that he may spot Ansley among these people, but that hope died quickly. He knew that if she was indeed here, she would stick out horribly. It would take little effort to find the poor girl in a town full of Calvenians. He just hoped that if he did find her here, she wouldn't be at the mercy of the Calvenian locals.

*****

It had been four days since Damon had ventured into Talteo. He and the others sat forlornly around a campfire, silently considering their plan. Rhyn gloomily poked a stick into the dying embers of the fire. Damon had just suggested that they consider moving on towards Dunbar. He knew Ansley was young, but she was resourceful. If she had gotten to shore, he was hopeful that she would continue on her journey and look for them in the capital. Rhyn and Kenna had disagreed.

"We cannot possibly leave her here." Rhyn had argued, his voice barely louder than the crackling fire.

"But what if she isn't here? She may already be hundreds of miles ahead of us, and we wait here for her like lost children. We do her no service in lingering, and we only increase the likelihood of being caught and imprisoned as suspected spies." Damon countered.

Kenna shook her head in frustration. "Oh, give it a rest, you two. I grow tired of hearing your bickering. Damon has a good point, but Rhyn, you do as well. There is no easy answer. I say we…" Kenna trailed off midsentence as loud footsteps were heard in the bushes behind them. Damon gave her a look, and as he did, he unsheathed the knife from his belt. Rhyn reached for his knife as well, and Kenna moved to the fire to grab a piece of smoldering wood. All turned in the direction of the footsteps, but they did not have to wait long for their guest to approach.

A shadow stumbled out of the brush and tripping, fell onto all fours in the dirt. Rhyn rushed the figure with Damon trailing close behind him. Kenna lingered, unsure of where she was most needed. No others followed the figure out of the bushes, so Rhyn leapt to the shadow and grabbed a handful of the stranger's cloak. As he yanked the person's face upwards, Damon let out a relieved sigh.

"Ansley!" Rhyn exclaimed, quickly letting go of her. Ansley fell back face first onto the dirt and slowly lifted herself upwards. Damon and Rhyn crouched nearby, and

Kenna joined them after tossing her branch back into the flames. Ansley grimaced as she moved herself into a seated position. "Are you hurt? Did I hurt you?" Rhyn asked her softly, reaching towards her shoulder. Ansley lifted her hand to dissuade his touch and shook her head.

"Not badly. My feet are very sore, and I'm hungry though. Do you have any food? Water?" She asked tentatively. Kenna rushed to their bags and retrieved a canteen and a bundle of dried meat for her. Ansley sat for many moments and chewed the meat. Damon found the waiting torturous. When she had washed down one piece of meat with several long gulps of water from the canteen, she looked back up at the others.

"How long have we been separated?"

Kenna glanced at Rhyn in alarm. Damon answered. "Nearly a full seven days, Ansley. Where have you been? What happened to you? You were in the water, and then you weren't. We waited for you, but we had no idea if you were even still alive!" Ansley frowned and covered her face with one hand.

Rhyn touched her shoulder gently. "Come sit by the fire. Rest, and eat a little more. We can talk in the morning. You look exhausted." Ansley looked up at him, and she shook her head firmly.

"No, you deserve answers." Ansley paused for a moment before continuing. "I was there, and then I wasn't." Damon's confusion must have shown on his face. "You look as confused as I feel. One minute I was in the waves trying to make it to the shore, and the next I was on dry land. I have no idea where I was, but I somehow...*moved* myself from the water. I have been walking since then. Avoiding towns, snatching food where I could, and drinking from streams. I did not think I would ever find you. For all I knew, I was on another continent."

"How *did* you find us?" Rhyn asked her. She shook her head in confusion.

"That's the weirdest part. I was walking in the dark, and suddenly, I had moved myself again. When I opened my eyes, I saw your fire ahead and heard your voices. I don't know how I found you or where I came from." Ansley finished with a whisper. She started to shake with the stress of all she had endured, so Rhyn pulled her to her feet and settled her near the fire.

Damon sat near her and returned Kenna's anxious look. "What does it mean?" She asked him quietly.

"I don't know, Kenna. I think the most disturbing part is that she did it while awake. No dreamwalker wields their skills in the waking realm. Whatever this was, it was not her skill as a seer that allowed her to do that." With that statement, they all fell quiet and looked at Ansley. She sat leaning against Rhyn's shoulder, her head nodding in sleep already.

"Do you think it was the 'transference' Alden mentioned that she had used in the dream with Josilyn?" Kenna asked softly. Damon shook his head uncertainly. "I can't be sure of anything except that we need more answers before this happens again."

Damon offered to keep watch that night, but Kenna did not attempt to sleep. He assumed she was thinking exactly what he was and trying to find answers that neither of them had. He could only hope that Dunbar would bring them answers to all of these questions and not any more mysteries to solve.

CHAPTER THIRTEEN
Kenna

The morning brought warmth but no rest for Kenna. She had sat awake with Damon all night in silence, contemplating the strange conditions of Ansley's disappearance and reappearance. After eating a meager breakfast, the four began packing their gear. Ansley seemed relieved to find her bag amongst the recovered gear from their now-sunken boat.

"What happened to the captain?" Ansley asked uneasily. "I thought I saw a fire before I…well, before…*you know*."

"He didn't make it." Rhyn answered sullenly. "The lightning lit the sail, and I don't think he made it off the boat."

Damon grunted. Ansley looked at him. "Are you angry with me, Damon?" Damon softened his face but looked away from her as he responded.

"No, I flipped the boat. I feel that I was somehow to blame."

"We won't get anywhere trying to place blame for a sunken ship and a dead captain on anyone other than the gods. Besides, the storm was the real cause of the trouble." Kenna added. She pulled her pack onto her shoulder and nodded that she was ready to travel.

"Wait. There was something else though, Ansley. Right before I flipped the boat, you had a dreamvision. Didn't you?" Damon asked her in a rush. "That's why I was moving and why the boat tipped in the first place. What did you see?" He asked her.

Ansley's face paled. She shook her head and replied, "Damon, I finally know something about Magnus. He must be very close to the king."

Ansley described the vision she had and stopped once she saw the look on Damon's face. "What?" she inquired.

"Ansley, that is not King Orlan you are describing. That is King *Finley*. King Orlan is Finley's son, and Finley has been dead for over twenty years."

"What? No...that would mean that Magnus was older than Finley. That would mean that..." Ansley started.

"That Magnus is *at least* a century old, and he may be even older." Damon finished for her. "It seems we are out of our depth here. No more mistakes! When we land at Dunbar, we must seek answers quickly. I fear that Magnus may be an advisor to the king or worse."

"What would be worse than that?" Ansley asked quietly.

"If the king is his puppet." Damon replied.

CHAPTER FOURTEEN
Bianca

Bianca took her cup of black coffee from the bar and navigated to a table in the back of the tavern. The place was loud and noisy, too distracting for the business that brought her here. She moved a worn, wooden stool toward the table and sat down, thankful to have a place to rest her aching legs.

Bianca had not ridden this far in quite some time. She forgot the strain it took to maintain a good seat on her horse for that long. She took a small sip of her coffee and looked around the tavern. The tavern was dark on the inside, and the light from a small window barely lit one corner of the place. The air was musty and smelled of ale and sweat. Even the sign in front hung crooked and read Tavern of the Seven Stags with several of the letters missing. Strange place to meet, but she had let Josilyn decide on the location.

She had sent her letter with a messenger almost a week ago, just a few days after Ansley's departure, to ask Josilyn to meet with her. Bianca did not like to boast, but she knew her family. Ansley had seemed disturbed when she departed from Terra, and Bianca had a bad feeling about this so-called training she was going to receive in Calvenia. She had been there once herself visiting her son, Ryker, and she knew it was not a kind place for Arvenians. Bianca took another sip of coffee as she glanced at the door. Nothing yet.

A full-figured woman wearing an apron approached

Bianca's table. She was carrying a tray holding several empty flagons. "Anything else over here?" The woman asked in a husky voice. *Sounds like she has spent years using a pipe.* Bianca thought to herself.

She smiled at the woman and answered, "No, thank you." She held up her coffee cup and added, "I'm all set."

The woman nodded and turned away. Bianca watched her go and wondered why Josilyn had wanted to meet in such a dark and dreary place as this. The door swung open loudly, and Bianca saw Josilyn walk in. Looks like I am about to find out why we are here after all, she thought.

Josilyn waved to the woman who had approached Bianca. The stern-looking lady gave Josilyn a full smile and held up a finger to ask her to wait a few moments. Josilyn paused by the bar and saw Bianca sitting by herself in the back. She waved whole-heartedly as the woman brought out a steaming cup of something and placed it in front of Josilyn. Josilyn said something to the lady and laid a few silver coins on the bar. The woman smiled at Josilyn, kissed her on the cheek, placed the coins in her apron pocket, and wiped her eyes on her sleeve. Josilyn patted the woman's arm to comfort her and then started walking towards Bianca.

Bianca did not know what to make of this exchange. She waited with one eyebrow raised, trying to determine who the woman was that Josilyn had spoken with. Josilyn walked briskly to her table and grabbed a stool to sit on.

"Mrs. Black! So nice to see you! How are you?" Josilyn asked joyfully. She flipped her long blonde hair over her shoulder and took a small sip of her hot drink.

Bianca's other eyebrow raised. "Oh this? Just tea!" Josilyn responded, her eyes sparkling with laughter. "Mrs. Seicar is my landlord! I rent my house from her. Cheaper than buying, and I know her family has been in a pinch since her barn burned last month during a lightning storm. I've been trying to come here every chance I have to give them more business. The poor lady needs the money, and she refuses to just take it. I have to get crafty!" Josilyn winked at Bianca jovially as she asked, "What brings you to my part of town?"

Bianca smiled at Josilyn. It was impossible not to when in the young woman's company. Bianca had been disappointed when Josilyn's family had moved away from Ansley's. Kind people like her were too few in this unhappy world. "Well, Josilyn, I hate to admit this, but I need someone's help. Out of all of my options, I decided you were the best one."

Josilyn raised her eyebrows. "Oh? Need help with the farm? I'd be happy to after you helped me with that incident two weeks ago." Josilyn fingered the grey streak in her otherwise blonde hair. "Still here. I doubt it will ever go away, but I try to think of it as a statement instead of something ugly. Something that represents that whole ordeal." Bianca watched her sadly, remembering when Rhys and Ansley had brought Josilyn's unconscious form into her kitchen. She had been terrified for her, but thankfully, Alden had saved her life and returned her skill with the crystal. Fear lingered in Bianca's heart as she imagined Ansley's unconscious form in much the same state as Josilyn had been. She hoped that Josilyn may be willing to help her prevent Ansley from doing something that may endanger her life.

Brushing aside those horrible thoughts, Bianca returned to the conversation, her goal at the center of her attention. "How are you, Josilyn? Feeling better?"

"Yes, very much! I am back to my tribe and shifting each night with no difficulty. In the beginning, you know, after Alden transferred my skill back from the crystal, each shift was exhausting! It took me some time to gain my strength back."

"I can imagine. Gods bless you, child. You never deserved that."

Josilyn's face fell into a frown, and Bianca noticed for the first time the small wrinkles around Josilyn's eyes. She wondered if those were from the attack too, but something told her that they may instead be a result of the emotional trauma the girl had dealt with from the ordeal. "Let's get down to it. I need help with Ansley, and I think you are someone that can get the truth from her."

"Ansley?" Josilyn asked. She took another sip of tea. "Sure! What is she up to now?"

"Not what you think. She traveled to Calvenia to complete her training." Bianca responded.

"Calvenia? With the boy? What was his name? Rhys?" Josilyn asked.

"No, no. With Damon, Kenna, and Rhys's brother. I believe his name is Rhyn." Bianca looked at Josilyn who was finally starting to understand her request to meet. Comprehension spread slowly across her face. Her eyebrows lowered, and she frowned knowingly.

"You think she is up to something, don't you?" Josilyn asked softly.

"Yes. She told me she was going for training with Damon, but it does not seem reasonable that he would need her to travel out of Arvenia for that. I just worry that she has gotten herself into something that she is too afraid to share with me." Bianca replied. She held her coffee cup in both hands and rubbed her thumb along the rim. She hesitated before adding, "She is all that I have left of my son, Josilyn. I cannot bear to think of losing her." The grim image of her son, daughter-in-law, and grandsons' dead forms lying on the floor of their home flashed before

Bianca's eyes. It had been around a month since they had been attacked, and Bianca had barely begun to grieve them. She could not imagine something happening to Ansley as well.

Josilyn's green eyes met Bianca's with sympathy. "Of course, you can't. Bianca, I will do whatever you need me to do to help Ansley. You know she has always been like a sister to me. I would not want to see anything happen to her either."

Bianca placed her hand over Josilyn's on the table and squeezed it gently. A tear rolled down her cheek, and she hastily wiped it away with the back of her hand. She took a deep breath in and blew it out before smiling at Josilyn. "Thank you." She whispered

"So, what is your plan?" Josilyn asked with a smile, her green eyes sparkling this time in anticipation of an adventure.

CHAPTER FIFTEEN
Kenna

Even in her wildest dreamwalking experiences, Kenna had never imagined or experienced the deep ache she felt now. Her arms felt as heavy as lead and seemed ready at any moment to detach from her body. She was overjoyed at the sight of that dock in the darkness up ahead of them. They had finally reached their temporary destination, Bolivar.

After Ansley had arrived back at their camp, the group had decided to rent a boat to travel by water the remainder of the journey. Unfortunately, there was no sign of wind on that beautifully clear day. They had been forced to use oars to row the entire journey. Kenna had volunteered, but she grew to regret her eagerness to show her strength. Minutes became hours, and the journey grew into what felt like one long, endless night. Kenna had overheard Damon telling Ansley that at this rate, they may have to dock, make camp, and risk interacting with the locals. He worried that there was no way they would make the journey in one night. Kenna rubbed her tense shoulders and forearms, hoping that sacrificing two working arms was worth whatever answers they sought here in Calvenia.

Kenna was sure that Damon had not meant to delay them, but after Ansley had shared her dreamvision, he had insisted on remaking camp and picking apart each detail of her vision. When they had finally journeyed to the closest port, the sun was already high in the sky. The harbor master told them that they were just outside the town of Deniz. That left them two hours of travel by sail, which apparently equated to four hours by oar, when the winds were blowing in the right direction and there was a good current. Kenna dropped her oar for a moment to wipe her brow. They were nearing the dock now, and she was eager to place her feet on land once more.

They had been lucky though. Another storm developed to the south, but it had turned to the west in the last few moments and missed them entirely. Kenna was thankful for that, but she was unsure if it was a sign that this journey was going to be a successful one. Her thoughts continuously lingered on Edric and their last conversation about Calvenia. She frowned as she remembered how he had pushed her away. Kenna hoped to have enough time to sleep and speak with her husband tonight. She felt that there was something about Edric that she needed to uncover, but for now, she would have to settle for a hot meal.

"Woah, there!" A man yelled as he ran down the dock and reached for the rope Damon had helped Rhyn toss up to him. "You have reached Bolivar. Is this your destination?"

"It is." Damon said. "Passage for four Calvenians into the country."

"Twelve silvers, sir." The man replied with his hand held out for payment.

Damon removed his money pouch from inside his cloak and counted out the coins to give to the man. The man tipped his hat and tied the rope to the dock. "Welcome to Calvenia."

"My thanks, sir." Damon responded as he turned to the others. The harbormaster did not wait to hear Damon's answer, but turned and walked back up the dock to the port as soon as he had placed the coins inside the small bag he held in his hands. So far, Calvenia was not as unfriendly as Damon had said it would be. They seemed more eager to fill their pockets than to investigate the origins of the incoming travelers.

"Gather your things." Damon said. Kenna could read the exhaustion in Damon's face. *At least he feels uncomfortable too,* she thought. Damon turned to Kenna as if he had heard her thoughts. He stared at her for a moment before nodding to her. Even though Damon lived here, he was also uneasy about entering Calvenia with the rising tensions towards Arvenians. Nevertheless, he was the first to climb the rope ladder onto the dock.

Kenna reached for her travel bags that Rhyn held out to her. Again, she was thankful that they had recovered them from their overturned boat. If they had not been found, she would have no supplies and no clothes. The wind bit at her as she walked around the benches in the boat towards the dock. It would be a cold winter. Winter clothing was always expensive this time of year, and in short supply. She had brought the cloak lined with rabbit fur that Edric had given her after their wedding as a gift. That would have been something she would have grieved over if it were lost.

Kenna glanced at the young ones on the boat as they moved in front of her. Ansley was thinner than when Kenna met her around two weeks ago, and her face seemed bleak. *That girl needs some grit if she is going to fight her battles and win,* Kenna thought sadly. Ansley had many that were counting on her, and she was not even a fully-trained dreamwalker yet. Ansley had so much to learn about her skills. *Maybe that one can help her?* Rhyn walked beside Ansley, not comforting her but modeling a strength that Ansley needed. He seemed very conscious of never being too close to Ansley, but it was clear to Kenna that he had feelings for her. *There must be a story between them I'm missing.*

Kenna's thoughts quieted as she finally stepped onto the dock. Firm wooden boards echoed her steps as she walked towards Bolivar. Bolivar was a place that most foreigners knew very little about. Just outside the capital of Calvenia, Bolivar was a warm and lightly populated coastal town. It boasted a well-kept dock, an inn for travelers, and a community of fishermen. Kenna supposed that the inn was always busy. From where she stood, she thought she could make out many lights burning in the distance. She wondered if that was the inn up ahead.

Bolivar had a good reputation too, which was not surprising in Calvenia. Kenna had always heard the Calvenians treasured their peace, but she had never experienced it. Arvenia was known to be a place where criminals lurked, and the capital was too far from the east side of the country to do much about the dangers there. The people had developed their own ways of handling these issues, and Kenna had never truly approved of them. She had always loved the idea of a place she could trust to be safe. A place she could walk freely without concern for harm. The small town ahead of her filled her with a comforting feeling as the lights glittered in the darkness. Despite Damon's concerns of Calvenian prejudices, Kenna hoped that Bolivar would be a place they would find rest as well as answers. Kenna pulled her cloak tighter around her neck and began walking faster in anticipation of the hospitalities waiting for her.

*****

The inn was bigger than any Kenna had ever visited. This amazed her because of her recent travels with Dane across Arvenia in search of Terra. They had stayed at many inns on the way, but nothing compared to the luxury that was laid out before her eyes. The floor was made of stone, not wood like most places she had stayed before. The stone had been stained a beautiful rust that sparkled as if recently cleaned. The walls were whitewashed wood, and the air was fresh with the smells of the sea air. Windows lined the back walls of the inn's kitchen and dining area. It was dark now, but Kenna wondered what that view would be like when daylight broke. Her heart ached with the beauty of this inn. She wished that she could share this with Edric. Instead, he was hundreds of leagues away sleeping in their flat by himself. Kenna felt her face grow hot with emotion and tried to swallow it down as Ansley approached her.

"Isn't it lovely?" Ansley breathed as she motioned towards the wall of windows. "I've never seen anything so elegant."

Kenna smiled. "Yes, it is very beautiful. Even Avendale does not have such charmingly decorated inns."

Ansley nodded. "When I traveled to Avendale, the inns did seem bare to me. But they had electric lights and running water! Do you think they have those here?" Ansley asked, her eyes lighting up with anticipation.

Kenna laughed quietly. "My dear Ansley, we have those in Willow too."

Ansley eyes grew wide. "You must come visit me sometime once we return." Kenna added. Ansley did not speak but simply nodded in awe. The young girl turned away from Kenna and continued to look around at the inn.

Suddenly, Damon approached with an older man, "They have our rooms ready for the night. We will lodge here tonight, and in the morning, we will eat breakfast before we continue on to Dunbar."

Kenna nodded her approval. "Which way?" She asked,

heaving her bag back onto her shoulder and ignoring the ache in her arms and shoulders.

Damon motioned with his head to the left and began leading her down one of many long hallways with doors on each side. Ansley had noticed them walking away from the dining area, so she fell into step behind Kenna. Kenna counted at least eighteen doors they walked past on the right and left before Damon stopped. He pointed to two rooms facing each other and said, "These two. You can choose the room Ansley and you prefer." Damon added considerately.

"This one is fine, Damon." Kenna responded, pointing to the room to her left. "Come on, Ansley. Let's see what the rooms look like." Damon handed her a small brass key and turned to go back to the dining area. Rhyn was presumably talking to the owner of a tavern across from the inn they were lodging in. Their inn's kitchen had shut down for the night, so they could not eat there until the morning. At the owner's suggestion, Rhyn had walked over to the tavern to request food to sustain the weary travelers until breakfast was served at the inn.

Kenna swung the heavy wooden door inward and walked inside the room. One large bed filled the space with two small benches on either side. Kenna walked in and lit the candles with matches laying nearby to brighten the space before inspecting the rest of the room. No windows or electric lights, but their room had an adjoining wash room. No running water either, but there was a large metal tub for baths. Ansley eyed it eagerly.

"Go ahead. I suspect someone from the kitchen can give you water to bathe. You better hurry though. I know they are cleaning now, but I am sure they will retire soon too."

Ansley's face betrayed a nervousness before she bolted

out the door. Kenna laughed again. She set to unpacking her bag for the evening, pulling out clothes that were dry and would be more comfortable to sleep in. After Kenna had removed her clothing and placed it in a neat stack on the bed, she reached in to see if she had missed anything in her pack. Her hand closed around a small, damp item. She removed it, curious to learn what she had found.

It was oddly heavy and wrapped in a kerchief. Kenna did not remember packing this. She turned the item over in her hand and unwound the kerchief. In her palm rested a colored glass about the size of a coin. Kenna touched it and noticed the edges were smoothed as if fingers had rubbed all the harshness from the stone. It was green. Bright green with a turquoise tint. Kenna was still unsure about where or who this came from. She picked up the stone and saw a damp piece of parchment under it.

Kenna sighed and set down the stone before trying to open the parchment without tearing it. Around the wet smudges, it read:

"……ry. Please don't be…. with me. Take my…. and know I am with you wherever…. It was my favorite souvenir from my childhood……deep in the sands of Bolivar…. from my father's people."

Kenna picked up the stone once more and was thankful for this peace offering from Edric. Maybe she had misinterpreted his motives in staying behind. Surely, she had misjudged him. She held the stone and prayed to the gods that it would bring her luck in the mission that had brought them here.

Suddenly, Ansley appeared at the door flanked by a woman only a few years older than Kenna. The woman was wearing an apron and carrying a large bucket of steaming water slowly, to avoid spilling it. Ansley smiled at Kenna and gestured towards the water. "Don't worry! I think there is enough for us both to use! I'll leave half in the bucket for you!"

Kenna nodded with a half-smile at Ansley's kindness.

"Ohh! And you should go out there before you turn in. Damon's wife has just arrived to meet us. She brought us some extra clothes and food for our journey to their home. She is such a nice woman!" Ansley added, walking towards the washroom where the serving lady had deposited her bath water.

Damon's…. *wife*. Kenna whipped her head around, but Ansley had already swung the washroom door closed for privacy. Kenna glanced quickly at the open door of her room. Hastily, she tucked the stone away in her pocket for safe-keeping, and she walked out the door towards the dining area.

Damon stood up ahead with a woman a head shorter than himself. Kenna could only see the woman from behind, but she noted the sunset-red hair that flowed down the woman's back all the way to her waist. Damon saw Kenna approaching and spoke a few words to his wife, who turned to greet Kenna. Kenna held out a hand to meet her but was surprised to see a look of disapproval on her face. Kenna let her hand drop, and a blush burned her cheeks under the woman's glare.

"You must be Kenna, *Vida's* daughter." The woman said sharply. Damon glanced at Kenna from over the woman's shoulder. His uneasiness ensured Kenna that this was the response that he had expected. "Unfortunately," the woman continued, her dark brown eyes glittering angrily, "Damon has told me nothing about you or your mother until just now.

Kenna glanced at Damon, still confused. "Why, yes. Damon and my mother were…together when I was a young child. I do not remember anything about it, but I know he was there when she died."

The woman soaked this information in and nodded. Then she turned to glance sourly at her husband, who lowered his gaze in shame. "Did you think I would never make the connection, Damon?" She asked. Instead of anger, her voice now portrayed the hurt she clearly felt. She turned back to Kenna and said, "Excuse me," before walking back out of the inn.

Kenna glanced at Damon expectantly, waiting for his explanation. "I named our daughter *Mila*vida." Damon almost whispered to her. Understanding flooded through Kenna in a cold rush.

"You knew better than to name your daughter after another woman, Damon. Especially *my* mother. Haven't you taken enough of her from me already?" Kenna replied before turning away from him too and returning to her room. *Damon certainly has a knack for angering the women around him,* she thought crossly, as she slammed her door shut to drown out the hurtful memories of her past.

CHAPTER SIXTEEN
Magnus

"My lord, the people received our summons and have gathered, demanding that you speak." Dane whispered hurriedly into Magnus's ear. Magnus was suddenly and deeply annoyed. He sighed.

"Can it be postponed?" He asked, frustrated that he was being disturbed. He had just sat down at his desk to glance over the most recent letter from King Orlan.

Dane shook his head and swallowed quickly. "Forgive me, but you have postponed twice already, my lord."

Magnus glanced up at Dane who bowed his head rather than look him in the eye. Seeing Orco's mark, a circle with an arrow beneath, tattooed on Dane's brow only further whetted Magnus's fury. Magnus sighed once more and stood from his chair. "Very well then."

Dane waited for Magnus to put his black cloak over his shoulders once more, and then Dane led the way down a long corridor into the dining hall of the castle. The benches and tables had been moved to the back wall, but they were not visible to Magnus as he walked into the room. All he could see were the hundreds of people that were packed in the room and that now stood shoulder to shoulder, eagerly awaiting Magnus's words. The restless crowd murmured quietly among themselves until they spotted Magnus at the doorway. Then, utter silence descended on the room.

Magnus felt the weight of the peoples' stares as he walked forward and stood where he could be seen by all. He was not intimidated by them. This type of power was his destiny.

"My dear friends," Magnus began, opening his arms wide in welcome, "welcome to my home. I hope you are comfortable here and are not weary from your travels." Magnus paused for a moment to glance around, feigning genuine concern. "I have summoned the followers of Orco because we face a trial, and we must be united in our plan. My plan will not work without the help of each and every man and woman in this room. We must work together as a single fist, demolishing our enemies and grasping the power we know is ours for the taking."

A single shout echoed out in the room, and Magnus raised his hand to silence the man.

"Let us not forget that these dreamwalkers have had the advantage for hundreds of years and used it against us when we are at our most vulnerable. How are we supposed to protect ourselves when we sleep? We are not equally armed, but we will be! My brother and sisters, the time has come for us to ascend! We must take that power that we were wrongly denied and seek justice for ourselves and all those who came before us. Let us remove this danger from our world and become guardians of this dream realm so our children shall not live in fear as we have! Let us purge our country of these outsiders that have been branded with these weapons and deceived us all! Let us regain control of our own minds and thoughts and push out those who have intruded where no other is welcome!"

Magnus stopped here as his voice reached a crescendo. The crowd exploded into cheers and shouts of agreement. Magnus smiled at them and nodded. These were his people. A proud few, but the numbers would grow. *Yes, the numbers will multiply once I have the girl.* He turned back to Dane who stood behind him silently. Dane nodded and looked at Magnus with adoration in his eyes. Magnus clenched his jaw, glancing once more at the mark of Orco on Dane's forehead. Then, he looked through Dane and moved towards the door to return to his study. The peoples' cheers continued long into the night, even after Magnus had retired.

*****

The next morning, Magnus's trusted advisor, Gyan, came to him with news. "My lord." Gyan bowed at the waist before delivering his message. Magnus nodded at him to continue. "My lord, the crowd was pleased with your speech. I believe they are willing to fight."

"Do you think they are ready?" Magnus asked Gyan thoughtfully.

"Not yet, my lord, but perhaps with…time and training." Gyan frowned. "We are lucky to have as many as we do. It is difficult to spread word when one is suggesting regicide."

"Yes, unfortunately Gyan, you are right." Magnus rubbed his face and tried to smooth the stress away. "We are moving faster through our plan than I am prepared for. We have not even had word about Ansley's whereabouts. Are there any updates?" Magnus asked hopefully.

Gyan shook his head. His small, black spectacles reflected the disappointment in Magnus's face. "No, sire. Our spies are searching, but they have not seen her in Terra in over a week. I fear that she has eluded us. Can't you use your connection to locate her?"

"No. If I use the connection from the blood oath, it will leave my mind vulnerable to her as well, so, we must continue with our plans until she surfaces once more." Magnus replied grimly. "Orlan is a fool, but he knows the tensions are growing towards him. Calvenia has struck against him once more. Openly this time."

"Oh?" Gyan asked, shocked to hear this most recent

and top-secret detail.

"Yesterday. They sent ships and tried to breach Avendale. Just like I warned the bastard." Magnus said as he tossed the letter he had been holding onto the table. "Now he tries to beg for more guidance. What does he think I am? A necromancer?" Magnus rose suddenly. The legs of the chair dragged noisily along the stone floor.

"Well, my lord, you are almost six hundred years old." Gyan added, sheepishly.

Magnus laughed viciously. "Old age doesn't translate to magical talents, Gyan. Even you know that. Besides, Orlan knows my secrets. He knows that I am no god or spirit sent here to change the world. I am simply flesh and bone that is preserved in time. That is precisely why we will have to find Ansley and make our move against the king quickly, Gyan."

"Because you are growing older, my lord?" Gyan asked. Magnus walked over to his advisor and friend. Gyan was growing older as well. He was bald, so he had no gray hairs to show his age. But the tiny lines that dug deep into his forehead from the years he had spent thinking over Magnus's aspirations for power gave others a hint of his age. Magnus patted his friend on the shoulder. "No, good man! I am as young as I was five hundred and fifty years ago! We will move quickly because Orlan is the only one other than you that knows all my secrets. These are secrets that are best drowned, along with our king, deep in the ocean."

"Yes, of course, my lord." Gyan responded. Magnus knew that although Gyan did not openly show his emotions, he desperately wished to see Magnus rise to the throne. Gyan had been with him a long time, and Magnus knew his secrets as well. "Enough heavy talk for this morning. What news of the dreamwalkers?"

Gyan nodded, acquiescing to the topic shift. "There are no changes in any tribe we are watching, sir. But it seems that the girl's grandmother has been seen with that shifter you met. We believe that she knows where Ansley is hiding."

"Good. See that she is treated to our hospitality, Gyan. And quickly. I will not let Ansley evade me for long. She is the key to all of this, and I need her in our safekeeping as soon as possible."

"I'll see that it is done, my lord." Gyan responded and bowed once more, leaving the room empty, quiet, and peaceful once more.

Magnus leaned back in his chair and folded his hands behind his head. He looked out the windows at the tree lines drenched in morning light and pictured himself rising in the morning in a different palace. *Gyan is a trustworthy man. I will appoint him to chief advisor once this mess is all behind us.*

CHAPTER SEVENTEEN
Ansley

Ansley had decided Bolivar was where she wanted to live. After a mere night, Ansley had fallen absolutely in love with Calvenia, its people, and this lovely small town on the sea. They had opted to stay at the inn by the dock where they landed, which Ansley had discovered was named *Ondo's Tavern and Lodge* for the sea god. Damon's poor reunion with his wife had soured his mood. She had left that night after having a row with him in front of the inn, so Damon was reluctant to journey home after her. In response to the revelation that Damon had named his only daughter for her mother, Kenna had decided to avoid Damon at all costs. This had left Ansley and Rhyn in an awkward position, caught between two feuding dreamwalkers with hostile moods, both in the daylight and in dreams.

Ansley was not sure how they had all linked themselves, but they were constantly dreamwalking together now. It had started the day they had set sail for Calvenia, and each night was the same. Ansley and Rhyn were always together initially, and eventually, Kenna and Damon would join. Ansley supposed she should be thankful for the extra protection, but it made avoiding those two very difficult.

The morning after that momentous meeting, Rhyn had eagerly suggested over breakfast that Ansley and he go out in search of locals who may have useful information about the history of dreamwalkers or Magnus. Damon, who had been stuffing sausage into his mouth, looked up at Rhyn as if this was the stupidest idea he had ever entertained. "You cannot just ask around, boy. That will get you killed."

"Maybe in Arvenia, but is Calvenia not different? Are they not more tolerant here?" Rhyn inquired.

"Yes, but they do not offer care packages to dreamwalkers just because they come to Calvenia!" Damon exclaimed, causing bits of chewed sausage to spew over the table between Rhyn and himself. "You have to be stealthy! Try not to get your head mounted on a spike. Bolivar is a good place to start, but please, in the name of the gods, do *not* ask strangers where the dreamwalkers keep their records here, especially when you are so clearly *Arvenian*."

Rhyn looked at Ansley and rolled his eyes. "Fair enough." He responded to Damon. "Any suggestions, then, oh wise one? I thought you knew exactly where we were supposed to find these records after all, or was that just a ploy to drag us to Calvenia, where we are more likely to get killed by the locals every day than to actually accomplish our goal of finding answers?"

Damon looked up at this jab and glared in annoyance at the young man seated across from him. "I know of a hall of records, but I will have to pull some strings to gain admittance. The record-keeper is old and retired. Until then, I will send you to Braddock, and he will set you on a good path. He is a dreamwalker I have done dealings with in Bolivar who is discrete but reliable. He seems well-known in this area, so he should have contacts in the capital as well that may prove useful."

"Sounds like a good place to start." Rhyn added. He turned to Ansley with an easy smile and said, "Looks like we are ready to start an adventure, eh?" Ansley just smiled back at him and took another bite of oatmeal.

Kenna, who had been quiet throughout breakfast, finally spoke up. "I think I will rest today. It was a difficult journey, and I need to see if Jameson has any updates for me regarding Willow. I will catch up with you two tomorrow." She rose from the table, noisily pushing back her chair.

Damon watched her walk away, and he sighed deeply, rubbing his hand over his face. He glanced in Ansley's direction as if wanting a comment about the situation he had landed himself in. Ansley raised her eyebrows at him and turned to Rhyn. "Well, I guess I will go wash up and prepare for our adventure, Rhyn. Damon, we will leave you to your…dilemma." Damon looked at Ansley with irritation, but he stayed silent. Rhyn rose from the table as well and walked with Ansley back towards their rooms. They parted ways in a rush to prepare for the day. There was much in Calvenia they had to uncover if they were to have a chance against Magnus.

*****

It had been five days since they had set out to find Braddock. Damon had been right, Braddock had connections, but his connections had not been helpful thus far. Braddock had directed them to a recordkeeper who had completed his inheritance ceremony only a few months ago. The poor boy had no clue where or when any person named Magnus may have existed. Ansley used the information she had learned from the dreamvisions about Magnus to direct the recordkeeper's search for answers. Unfortunately, they found nothing of use.

After that, Braddock had insisted that they meet with the chief elder in Bolivar. Apparently, Bolivar had a separate set of elders than Dunbar, but these elders were also in charge of the lands south of Bolivar to the Karlow region. The most southern part of Calvenia, near Otto's Pass, was ruled by a third set of elders. It was common to separate the different regions thus, and Arvenia did this too; however, it made it very difficult to search historical records because each region had a different set of elders and a different records-keeper. The sets the Bolivar elders had were all out of chronological order, and each keeper often had only small pieces of information about the surrounding regions. Thinking of all of this gave Ansley a pounding headache. She was trying desperately to stay patient, but she knew that many lives, including Rhys's depended on the answers they were seeking.

Kenna had stuck to her word and joined Ansley and Rhyn's search after resting the first day. She had no news from Willow or Arvenia in general, except that there was unrest in the parishes. The people knew that raids were occurring off-shore, and they knew the Calvenians were to blame. Nobody knew why though, so this had only enflamed a long-standing hatred for their neighboring country. Making it even less of an opportune time for Ansley and her friends to be there.

The three of them spent hours searching for letters, scrolls, and dreamwalkers they had never laid eyes on. It was tedious work, and by the end of each day, all of them were exhausted by it. They would drag themselves into *Ondo's*, fill their rumbling bellies with a late dinner of stew or roasted meats, and force themselves to walk the last few feet to their rooms. Damon had not joined their search yet, but Ansley believed that his role was undeniably the most important. Damon slept during the day, either casually dreamwalking or inducing a dreamvision to maintain their safety. He then remained alert at night to guard their rooms from any that may attempt attacks on them in the physical realm. Thank goodness he had discovered no threats so far.

Today had started the same as the others. First, they had breakfast at the inn, and then, they began traveling to meet with another dreamwalker just outside Bolivar who was over a hundred years old. Ansley had to admit she was intrigued when Braddock had mentioned her. She was the only local seer, and Braddock had suggested her as a last resort before sending the group to Dunbar to search for information more formally. Ansley had never met a seer from another country. Ansley had only just learned she herself was a seer, and her experience with other seers thus far was limited to an old and angry drunk and a boy held as a prisoner and forced to gain her trust. The prospect of meeting another seer, especially one that was normal, intrigued Ansley, so her excitement was barely contained as they pushed their horses north of Bolivar to where the woman lived.

The countryside in this area was flat and lush. Although Bolivar was north to Arvenia, the country was still warm in the summer and fall seasons. When Yule, the winter solsitice, neared, the lakes and rivers in the northern-most part of Calvenia would ice over, but there were many lands even further north than Calvenia that Ansley had heard remained icy all year. She had always wanted to travel to see those places. In her mind they existed as a glittering and lovely dream, crisp and clean, sparkling when the sun hit them. But she doubted the ice was as beautiful as she dreamed it would be. So, Ansley journeyed with the others away from Bolivar's coast, enjoying the crisp winds that blew through tall grasslands of Calvenia. She could see for miles, and the greens of the fields were as vibrant as they must be in high summer. Ansley breathed deeply and tried to soak in that wind that had the first bite of winter in its touch.

Ansley noticed Rhyn watching her and blushed. He had continued to be respectfully distant, but she felt at ease in his company and had begun to develop an easy friendship with him. Ansley tried to avoid looking at Rhyn because she knew she would only blush deeper. The wind soothed her warm cheeks as she recalled the hours they had spent over the past week together. She had never been around anyone who seemed so…comforting to her. She initially thought that he only reminded her of how she had bonded with Rhys before coming to know it was really Magnus, but this was different somehow. Ansley felt that Rhyn had seen a piece of her soul that was buried so deep inside her that even she had not seen it yet. He *knew* her. It was comforting but also a bit unsettling at the same time.

Ansley's horse threw its mane back, and this pulled her away from thoughts of Rhyn's mysterious connection with her. She noticed that to the west a small, wooden cabin sat nestled between a few tall pines. The sun was starting to drop from the sky, but there was still plenty of daylight to allow them to reach the cabin. She looked at Kenna who nodded avidly, pushing her own black mare onward. The group broke into a gallop and reached the house before the sun disappeared below the horizon.

*****

Ansley sat at an old wooden table in the small cabin. Her hands held a warm cup of coffee, and she was grateful for the warmth that broke the chill she had fought during her last hour's ride to this destination. The walls of the cabin were unfinished wood, but they kept out that wind that had grown crueler since the sun had set. Ansley glanced at the large fire behind her that added a warm glow to the cabin. She tried to relax her tense shoulders as she turned back to look at the woman who owned the cabin.

She was a small woman, shorter than Ansley, but she seemed spry for her age. Her hair was reddish blonde, like the rising sun. No wrinkles were visible on her face, but she did not look young. Her wisdom was revealed through her gaze, which lingered longer than expected on Ansley. Her fathomless eyes were a light grey but spoke of many experiences and years spent dreamwalking. It made Ansley nervous to imagine herself seated on the other side of that table one day, sitting in this woman's place and sharing her seer's knowledge with young ones like herself. If she lived that long.

The woman had introduced herself as Darby, and she had greeted her guests jovially, stating that she had seen them in a dreamvision a few days earlier. She hastily sat them at her table, poured coffee, and added logs to the fire to warm their frozen hands. Darby was light-hearted and friendly, but those eyes gave her away. She knew things. Maybe the things they also needed to know. Ansley hoped that they were finally in the right place to have their questions answered.

After they had settled down and had relaxed, Darby asked, "So, what brings you young ones to my lands?" Her grey eyes twinkled perceptively, but she gave no hint of what she knew of them already.

Kenna answered for their group, "We come in search of answers, and we need them quickly. Our people are in danger, and we fear that the evil that terrorizes Arvenia is older and stronger than any of us."

Darby nodded thoughtfully, but then she looked at Ansley. "Well?" She asked softly.

Ansley sighed, knowing that Darby had read her correctly. "I have entered into the blood oath with a man I should not have trusted. We are unsure exactly what it means for him or me, but I had a vision and was told it was a connection that could lead all dreamwalkers to danger. His name is Magnus, and he is the evil one that my friend speaks of."

Darby nodded, taking in this information. "My dear, it will not lead us to danger. We are already there." She paused looking to Kenna for a moment. "You have come to me too late; I fear. There is nothing that can be done to break the oath. It is made and unreversible. Besides, dreamwalkers have not meddled in necromancy for years. I know no walkers now living who know anything about it."

Kenna gasped. "Necromancy!" Then, she looked at Ansley in horror. Ansley, unaware of this implication simply asked, "What does that mean?"

Darby swallowed before responding, "It is magic of the gods, dear. The necromancers change fate, and most often, their intervention is not amicable. But let us wait to discuss this further. From my visions, I have seen no danger of this connection being used by Magnus. We have some time before we need to worry about that. But do tell me about your friend, the one that is being held."

Rhyn's eyes widened, but he started, "He is my brother, wise one. He is being kept as a prisoner of Magnus."

"And he is the reason that you agreed to the oath?" Darby inquired.

Ansley pursed her lips. "Not exactly. I was deceived."

"There may be a way around this magic then. Please, continue." Darby added, folding her hands together. Her eyes bored into Ansley's, searching for any dishonesty there. Ansley was happy that she had always been so terrible at hiding things. She supposed that it made her more trustworthy.

"Magnus is using Rhyn's brother to ensnare Ansley,

and he is somehow connected to the attacks that have been happening across all of Arvenia. They are stealing skills of dreamwalkers and using those skills to enter into dreams where they can harm other dreamwalkers. We thought we had found the source of the trouble, but I fear we were mistaken." Kenna responded.

Darby finally turned her full attention to Kenna, and her eyebrows lifted in surprise. She had a revelation that she did not share, and a knowing smile played over her face once more. "You must be...*Kenna*."

Kenna nodded, visibly uncomfortable. "If this is about my mother, then…"

"It isn't." Darby said briskly, cutting Kenna off. "I have dreamed of you. Very often." She smiled at Kenna, and Ansley saw excitement in the old woman's eyes. "Welcome." She finished, inclining her head to Kenna. Kenna looked around at her friends uncomfortably, and then she fell silent. Ansley knew she was trying to determine why this strange seer from a different country had dreamed of Kenna in any way. Her comment had certainly given Ansley goosebumps. Ansley took this opportunity to change the subject back.

"So, can you help us?" Ansley asked desperately.

Darby turned her eyes away from Kenna and back to Ansley. She paused for a moment before answering. "I can give you information, but that is all. You know as well as I the limits of my skills, young one."

Ansley nodded in agreement. "Information is all we seek."

"Then you are in the right place." Darby answered.

*****

Darby moved the empty plates from the table. She had offered to cook her guests a meal before they continued talking, and they were very thankful for this after their long journey to her cabin. They had relied on jerky and cheese to stave off their hunger on the journey, but that meager sustenance only delayed it. The meal Darby prepared was warm and filling. Goose with roasted potatoes and vegetables Ansley had never seen before. Darby wiped her hands on her apron and sat back down in her chair heavily. She noticed Ansley watching her closely, and she said, "Even though my face is young, my joints are not. The cold bothers my old bones." She chuckled and added, "You will understand someday."

"If I live that long." Ansley responded.

"Yes, indeed." Darby added sadly. She took a deep breath and faced the others. "Shall we continue?"

They all nodded eagerly. Their stomachs were full, and they were ready to listen.

So, Darby started and continued talking well into the night. Her guests were engrossed in the conversation and in no danger of falling asleep because they felt the information she shared was so crucial to their success. Once Darby had finished, the room fell silent for some time as they processed all she had shared with them.

"But how is he alive?" Rhyn asked, breaking the silence.

Darby responded, "That I do not know. He is obviously employing necromancers," she said, gesturing to Ansley, "so it would be wise to tread carefully. He is a dangerous man."

Ansley looked at Darby in fear, unable to understand where she fit into the equation.

Kenna spoke up, "But he is only a man, right? He is not a dreamwalker?"

"No. He is not, but do not make the mistake of believing that matters in this situation. He has magic on his side and has access to unlimited dreamwalkers' skills until he is ready to use them."

"Use them for what?" Ansley finally asked.

The room grew quiet once more. "I do not know, young one. I do not know. That has never been revealed to me in the visions. I have only seen you, what has happened between you, and his past. I cannot ask for information. I only receive." Darby frowned.

"It is enough." Rhyn added, closing the subject. "We will make a plan to save Rhys and protect Ansley with the answers you have given us. This information is invaluable, and I am very grateful to you for opening your doors knowing the danger we bring with us."

Darby simply inclined her head to Rhyn. "I have opened my doors to many dangers and closed them to others when I shouldn't have. I am old now, so I try not to make the same mistakes as my time grows shorter. I am thankful that you were sent to me."

Rhyn frowned. "Sent? Nobody sent us here aside from Braddock."

Darby smiled again at Rhyn. "Of course, they did. Do you think Vito would leave you to fight Orco on your own?"

Rhyn's face changed, but Ansley was unsure if he was confused or angered by what Darby said. Darby noticed this too, so she added, "The gods watch you whether you will it or not, young man. Enough of that, though. Let's make pallets for you to stay the night." She glanced out the window at the single ray of light breaking through the clouds. "I mean the day. You have traveled and now have been troubled by the details of my visions for long enough. Come! Let's gather some blankets to keep you warm. Even the days are growing colder now." Darby ushered Kenna and Ansley towards the only small bedroom in the cabin and handed them a stack of blankets that were hand-knitted or crocheted. Ansley felt her muscles ache with relief as she took them. Within minutes, she had made her bed on the floor and laid down to sleep away her worries. She found it easy to prevent herself from dreamwalking this night. Her exhaustion buried all attempts she may make to leave her own mind in search of others' dreams.

CHAPTER EIGHTEEN
Ansley

Ansley slept deeply the rest of the day until the noises in the cabin finally roused her. She noticed sheepishly that she had been the last one to wake. The others were dressed and had just finished eating more of the leftover goose from their last meal with Darby. Ansley's stomach rumbled jealously, so she rose from the floor. Darby met her at the table and placed a plate of hot food in front of her. Ansley tore into it quickly, and Darby chuckled at the sight. When Ansley had finished the last bite, Darby scooped up her plate and heaped more food onto it. Ansley took the second course slower, but she still easily finished everything that was given to her. At last, she leaned back in her chair and wiped the grease off her fingers and mouth with a clean cloth.

"Good?" Darby asked.

"Very. Thank you again for allowing us to stay. We have coin if you would let us pay you for your trouble." Ansley started to reach into her pocket to dig out a few silvers, but Darby closed her hand over Ansley's and shook her head.

Then, Ansley noticed that Darby's smile faded. "I fear for you, my dear. Magnus is a formidable opponent for any grown dreamwalker, and you have barely begun to learn your skill. If you let him, he will destroy your entire country through you."

Ansley's confusion was evident. "But how? I am just a seer..."

"Not just a seer. You are a Black. You are a descendent of Rosalie Black, and she was special too."

"Yes, I know. She was Magnus's mother." Ansley added, eager to get to the point of this discussion with Darby. She was growing uneasy again.

"No. That is not why she was special. *Is* special. She is something more, and I think you know that you are too." Darby looked knowingly at Ansley before releasing her hand.

"You mean…my *transference*?" Ansley asked uncertainly.

Darby nodded and put a finger to her lips. Ansley quickly responded, eager to continue their conversation, "The others know. They have seen me…", but Darby interrupted Ansley by shaking her head. She pointed to the window that showed the flat lands surrounding Darby's cabin.

"We do not know who else may be listening." She responded quietly.

"So, what does it mean?" Ansley whispered, eager to receive all of the answers at once.

Darby smiled. "Your impatience betrays your age. I do not know, but this is *why* he seeks you. You must tell the others. Tell them somewhere that you are certain is safe from listening ears." Darby rose to end the conversation, but Ansley was not finished with her.

"Wait!" She whispered angrily. "Are you saying it is bad that I can do that? Our head elder knew what it was, so I thought it must be common among seers. Should I *fear* it?" Ansley asked quietly.

Darby turned back to Ansley and placed a hand on her shoulder. "Ansley, my dear. Nothing about you is common. You must start to accept that now, and all that being uncommon implies." Darby turned away from

Ansley at last to go retrieve their horses from the tiny barn that stood behind her cabin. Ansley sat silently, pondering what Darby had said. She was so confused. Suddenly, her temper flared. *Why does everyone only give me half answers? How is any of this supposed to be helpful if I don't know everything?* She thought dejectedly. Rhyn must have sensed her irritation, so he came over to her.

"Are you okay?" He asked her softly.

Ansley shook her head and felt hot tears roll down her cheeks. Rhyn gently wiped one away and waited for her to speak. "Later." Ansley managed to choke out. "Later." She turned away from Rhyn and wiped her face before Kenna noticed. Darby returned from the barn, and she gestured towards the front door, "All is ready when you are prepared to travel."

"Thank you." Kenna responded, and she was the first to leave the cabin. Ansley had a feeling that she wasn't the only one who felt uneasy around Darby. Rhyn placed his hand on Ansley's arm, nudging her to follow Kenna towards the horses. Ansley turned away from him to glance in Darby's direction once more. The woman smiled at her, and she said, "Good luck to you, Starlight," before giving her the dreamwalkers' salute of lifting her forefinger to her brow. Ansley simply nodded to her, shocked once again by her knowledge. *Only my family calls me that*, Ansley thought to herself. Then, she glanced at Rhyn as awareness dawned on her. And he had called her that too…earlier…when they had been in the boat and she was drinking his wine.

He looked at her with a questioning glance. "You…you…" Ansley sputtered, as she walked alongside Rhyn.

"Yes?" He asked, as he mounted his horse.

"You called me *Starlight*. Why did you call me that?"

Ansley questioned, frozen next to her horse who whinnied in anticipation of their journey.

Rhyn frowned. "I..." he paused, unsure of how to continue. Ansley waited impatiently for his answer. "I fear I have not been totally honest with you, Ansley. I know you believe that Rhys was the one bound to your dreams, but that has never been true. It was *me*. I was the one who shared that connection with you." Rhyn said, averting his eyes from Ansley's gaze.

Ansley shook her head in confusion and finally mounted her horse in a single motion. Her mare moved eagerly forward before she pulled the reins gently to stop her. She tossed her head angrily at the restraint, but Ansley was too lost in this newest revelation to acknowledge the horse. "Why would you keep that from me, Rhyn? I feel like you *lied* to me." She said, looking accusingly at Rhyn.

"I am sorry you feel that way, Ansley, but this situation was bigger than you or me. My brother's life was in danger, and I needed to focus on that instead of you. Plus, I have to admit that I feel a great deal of guilt about Rhys being captured. It was my fault Magnus took him in the first place." Rhyn added, continuing to avoid Ansley's eye.

"What do you mean it was your fault, Rhyn?"

"Magnus took the wrong brother when he captured Rhys. You know the reason he took Rhys was to get to you. He was misinformed that you were connected to Rhys, so that is who he captured. If he had known that I was the one connected to you, Rhys would have never been involved in this mess." Rhyn added quietly, so that Kenna could not overhear him.

Ansley swallowed her frustration at Rhyn's dishonesty. "Yes, but if he had taken you instead, you would be in his dungeons and Rhys would likely still be with me, looking for you. I don't think the situation would be much different, Rhyn. Don't blame yourself for Rhys's capture. Magnus wanted me, and he would have found a way to get to me regardless of the consequences. I'm glad that you are here. Our connection is…special, and it may give us an edge over whatever Magnus has planned. I just wish you had told me the truth instead of keeping it from me."

Rhyn nodded his head sullenly. "Yes, I do too, and I am sorry for making you mistrust me when you have endured so much deception lately. I will make this up to you, Ansley, but for now, let's focus on getting back to Bolivar tonight. We have learned many things from Darby, and I am sure Damon will be eager to consider them as we plan our next step."

Ansley nodded and prodded her horse into a trot. Kenna had just mounted her own mare and was securing herself in the saddle. Kenna looked at Ansley as she moved past her and spurred her own horse on too. Rhyn followed behind both of them at a distance. The sun set slowly, and Ansley pulled her shirt collar up to shield her bare neck from the cold air. The wind bit almost as harshly as the thought that Rhyn had lied to her. She urged her horse on, eager to escape this thought and quiet her unrest. Could she trust anyone anymore?

Suddenly, a rider appeared ahead of Ansley to the left side among the trees. The rider approached their group at a gallop, and as Ansley looked in that direction, she noted that the rider's face was hooded. Ansley wondered about this for a moment before she saw the stranger raise a bow. Ansley instinctively reached back towards her own, which she had slung across her back, as usual. She had no time to draw an arrow before the stranger's arrow hit home. Kenna let out a cry, and the rider disappeared in the distance just as quickly as he had arrived.

Ansley turned in her saddle and was distressed to see a shaft protruding from Kenna's left shoulder. Alarm filled Ansley as she realized this could be a deadly wound. Ansley anxiously looked at Rhyn who had pulled his horse alongside Kenna's to inspect her wound.

"It looks like it just hit your shoulder. You're lucky it was not a few inches lower, Kenna." Rhyn said, pointing to Kenna's heart. He turned to Ansley, "Keep riding, and let's pick up the pace!" He shouted, and Ansley nodded in agreement.

Ansley felt her horse fly beneath her as the wind whipped her braid behind her. She galloped across the fields towards Bolivar in hopes of reaching a healer before Kenna lost too much blood. Kenna was still behind her, and Ansley heard her speaking to Rhyn, ensuring him she was alright. Suddenly, Ansley felt a sharp sting from her left ear, and Kenna let out another cry of pain. Ansley touched her ear gingerly and was shocked to see blood covering her hand. She felt her eyes unfocus as she looked at it on her hand. A familiar feeling began to pull her away, and Ansley was unable to resist it. The sounds of angry shouts and the pounding of horses' hooves echoed in the background as Ansley entered the dream realm to find the source of her vision.

CHAPTER NINETEEN
Ansley

Ansley stumbled around an empty room and shouted into the darkness, trying to find the source of her dreamvision. Nothing emerged.

She turned around and was surprised to see Rosalie standing in front of her once more.

"You! How did you...? You realize that you chose the worst moment to meet with me?" Ansley roared at her ancestor. Rosalie waited patiently for Ansley to take a deep breath.

"I have come to warn you." She said simply.

"Well, you are too late! We are already being attacked, and you pulled me away to warn me?" Ansley continued angrily.

"No. I came to warn you again about Magnus." Rosalie answered.

"Too late for that too! Where were you when I needed answers? Hanging out in the dream realm and ignoring me? Having a vacation up here?" Ansley yelled at Rosalie who flinched. Ansley saw Rosalie's expression change from one of urgency to sadness.

"I cannot always bring you here. It is not an easy feat for me to do." Rosalie answered quietly.

"Why not? Aren't you all-*powerful and special?" Ansley asked, throwing her hands up.*

"Because you are growing in power, Ansley." Rosalie responded sadly.

Ansley froze in her spot and turned to look at Rosalie.

"Yes, you heard me correctly. It is your turn now. Once you have taken on my responsibility fully, I will cease to exist in this realm."

"But…" Ansley started.

"No, listen closely to me." Rosalie began again, placing her hands on Ansley's shoulders. *"He is strong, and your time is running out. Do not tarry in Calvenia long, or you will lose your chance to catch him off guard. You are the one who must destroy him now, Ansley. But as we speak, he plots, and your friend fades quickly. You are wasting time."*

Ansley had a strange recollection of her ancestor saying these words to her during her trials. She swallowed down her fear and stared into Rosalie's dark brown eyes. She noticed, with surprise, the tears that had begun to fill Rosalie's eyes. *"I am so sorry, young one. This was never a burden I wanted to pass on to anyone, but by the time I realized what he had become, it was too late for me to intervene."*

Ansley placed her hand on Rosalie's cheek in a comforting gesture. *"I will defeat him. I promise you that. But please, tell me,* why *I am so important to him? Why does he seek my skills, and why is he so dangerous? I do not understand."*

Rosalie remained silent for a moment before she responded. *"He knows that you are developing the skill of transference. It is a skill that was long gifted to women of our line, including me. It is how I saved Rhael from Magnus's wrath by moving him out of Magnus's reach. I transfered Rhael to safety at the same time, in both the dream realm and the physical realm. I had never used the skill in front of my boys, and I didn't even know that I had it until after they were born. I hoped that I would never need to use it. It is not a skill that is used lightly, and it should only ever be used in the most dangerous of situations. After Magnus saw me use it to save Rhael, he went to great lengths to learn exactly what transference was and what it can be used for, and now he seeks to take it from you to use it for his own purposes."*

"But what can it be used for? I mean, other than allowing me to move things to new places?" Ansley asked, desperate for answers.

"Ansley, you are the key to the dream realm. There is only one seer that has this skill at a time, and now that I am fading, it is yours. Vito gave us this skill to keep the dream realm intact. Your existence ensures that our dreams never become reality. Your transference moves objects, but it also keeps dreamwalkers and their skills in the dream realm."

A horrible thought dawned on Ansley. "He wants to break *the dream realm? Why would he want to destroy it?" She asked, frightened by this possibility. Rosalie's edges started to blur before she could answer.*

"I must go now, Ansley. I may be able to reach you one more time before I fade, but I cannot be certain. I must go." Rosalie replied.

"No!" Ansley cried, as Rosalie disappeared.

*****

Ansley woke in the middle of the night to the sound of galloping hooves all around her. She still sat on her horse, but Rhyn rode to her right with Kenna sitting in front of him on his horse. He had tied both of their horses' reins to his, and the group galloped as one. He saw Ansley stir, and called to her, "Hurry! Let's get back before the attacker returns!"

Ansley glanced at Kenna, who now had two shafts protruding from her left shoulder. She moaned as the horses picked up speed, and her eyes remained closed. Blood soaked through her light-colored, fur-lined cloak. Ansley was afraid, but she wasn't certain if her fear stemmed from the attack or the news Rosalie had just shared with her.

*****

Kenna opened her eyes, holding her shoulder in anguish but feeling no pain at the moment. She looked the hand covering her shoulder, but it was clean. No blood? Then realization hit her. She must have fallen unconscious. She had never dreamwalked when she passed out before. Not that she passed out often, but…What an odd feeling…she thought to herself.

Kenna sat up from where she lay on the ground, which she now noticed was covered by sprawling grasslands as far as she could see east or west. Wild horses galloped in the distance, playfully tossing their manes. She stood gingerly and watched them canter around one another. These were colts. Probably under a year old. The raced and played happily in the warm sunshine. Kenna glanced around, looking for an older horse or someone who must be tending to the horses, but there was no one. She sighed happily, enjoying the calming view of nature, trying to push away thoughts of the injury that still awaited her once she awoke.

She heard steps behind her, so she turned to see the source. She smiled as she watched Edric circling a mare in the distance. She was not saddled or bridled, but she listened eagerly to Edric's soothing voice. Kenna listened as well, but she couldn't make out his words. They must be another language, perhaps one spoken in Calvenia? Edric moved closer to the mare and stroked her neck gently, murmuring softly into her ear. Then, he swung gracefully onto her bare back, as if it was something he did every day. Kenna's mouth hung open as she watched him ride as if he had been born to do so. Edric was looking towards the young stallions, but once he saw Kenna, he urged the horse into a trot in her direction. Kenna was perplexed by his frown.

"Kenna, my love. What are you doing here?" Edric asked as he slid easily from the horse's back. His horse cantered off happily in the direction of the colts. Kenna noticed that several other mares had joined the young horses and were grazing in the fields with them.

Kenna smiled at Edric. "I don't know. I woke up here. I believe I passed out." Edric's eyebrows lifted in concern. He approached Kenna, and she noticed the shadows beneath his light green eyes. Creases wrinkled his forehead. Many more than he had before she left Willow several weeks ago. Edric placed his hand on Kenna's cheek.

"Are you ill?" He asked her, worried for his wife. Kenna dropped her gaze. "I've been wounded, but the others are with me and are tending to my injuries. Besides, I have to admit that this is a pleasant escape from that *reality." She added, gesturing to the calming scene before them. "Where are we, Edric?"*

Edric glanced at the horses in the fields and sighed. He waited a long time before answering her. "A place that has long since disappeared. But, no matter." He said solemnly. He grabbed Kenna and pulled her into his strong arms. "I have missed you desperately." Kenna closed her eyes, and she soaked in Edric's familiar scent of saltwater.

"I found the stone you tucked into my bag," Kenna whispered into Edric's chest. "Thank you for putting it there."

Edric smiled. "It is called seaglass. I used to dig for pieces of it with my sisters and brother when we would visit the shores of the Glass Sea. Rumor had it that was why it was called the Glass Sea, but I always thought those were silly stories my siblings and I told each other to encourage our continued searches for seaglass. To us, it was a buried treasure that would make us wealthy." Edric chuckled and paused, his smile fading. He sighed and added, "I hope you are not still angry with me for not going with you. I still think it was best that I stayed in Arvenia."

She searched his face and sensed his unease. "What has happened? You are not yourself, Edric." Edric released Kenna and turned his back to her. His silence only worried her more. She placed a tentative hand on his shoulder, but just as he turned, Kenna felt the familiar pull of herself regaining consciousness. She felt the wound grow in her shoulder until the pain blinded her. She touched her shoulder and looked at her fingertips, surprised to see them smeared with warm blood. Edric reached out to Kenna, worry etched across his face. Then, Edric's features began to blur, and he watched helplessly as she disappeared before him. Kenna hated herself in that moment for not escaping the pull, but dreams were only dreams. She could never hold onto them for long.

*****

Kenna was surprised to find herself here, but she shouldn't be. The shore rolled along the pier, and birds called in the distance. Kenna smelled the familiar bite of the salt in the breeze as she glanced out at the pier. Her pier in Willow. *Jameson and Sophie stood in front of her, blocking her path down the pier, both of their faces betraying their concern.*

"What has happened?" Kenna asked eagerly, approaching the pair. Jameson shook his head angrily, his face red.

"We are here to ask you the same question. We sensed danger." He responded, his face a mask of worry.

"And...pain." Sophie added hesitantly.

"Oh." Kenna responded, turning from them. She reached up to her shoulder and found that she was still bleeding. She must have called them to her in her distress. There truly was nothing that a tribe could hide from one another.

"'Oh' is right." Jameson said with frustration. He reached forward and grabbed Kenna's uninjured arm, pulling her to face him. He examined her injury without touching it. *"This looks like an arrow wound. Were you shot?"* He asked urgently.

Sophie had moved down the pier to where Laurel now stood. The pair quickly approached Kenna together, trying to hear her response to Jameson's question.

"Yes...but..." Kenna began. She was cut short by Jameson's irritated sigh.

"Kenna, what am I to do? I am hundreds of miles from you, and here you are with an open wound! Are you unconscious?" He asked suddenly.

Kenna frowned. The truth was that she wasn't sure. *"Umm..."*

James shook his head before turning to Laurel. *"Can we help her here?"* He asked desperately. Laurel was the most experienced member of her tribe with caring for wounds, so they always looked to her for guidance in these situations.

Laurel shook her head. *"She got the wound while awake, so we can't treat the source. We just have to hope she finds help there. Kenna, are you with anyone?"* Laurel *asked her.*

Kenna nodded, "Ansley and Rhyn. They will take me to Damon. But wait...tell me of Edric. Where is he? I just saw him in a dream, and he seemed...troubled."

The three exchanged glances before Jameson finally spoke. "Kenna, we have been trying to reach you for a few days, but I guess you have been distracted. Edric left Willow."

"He left?" Kenna asked, her heart dropping into her stomach. "But why? Where *did he go?"*

"He didn't tell us or leave us a message. We just woke one morning, and he had left Laurel's place. We assumed he was at your flat, but when we went to look for him, it was empty. We were hoping you may know where he was." Jameson said softly, sensing the distress he was causing Kenna, who was already injured and suffering enough already without him adding to it.

Kenna shook her head, feeling that in her heart something was wrong. "I must..." She started, but her shoulder pain intensified sharply, until her vision blackened. When she came to again, she was on the ground with the others around her.

"That isn't all, Kenna. We have heard whispers. Dreamwalkers are still being attacked, but now, all the attackers are claiming they are in the service of "Orco's Cult". Their symbols, an arrow below a circle, are always at the sights of the attacks. Tensions are rising, and dreamwalkers in Willow are being forced to keep a low profile. We need you to keep yourself open to our calls. Whatever is going on must be connected to this Magnus *and all the events that took place in Terra." Laurel said quickly. Jameson touched Laurel on the shoulder gently.*

"Now isn't the time, Laurel. Look at her. She is barely hanging on to this dream." Jameson smoothed Kenna's

hair and cupped her cheek in his hand. "Rest easy, my friend, and come to us when you are healed."

Kenna drifted from the comfort of Jameson's arms into a world of pain, wishing she could have lingered in her tribe's company where she did not have to face what lay ahead of her.

CHAPTER TWENTY
Damon

Damon looked around himself in confusion, unsure how he came to be here. He sat in a darkly-lit tavern that had an air of familiarity to it. He turned in his chair, trying to look for anyone he might know, but there were only strange faces around him. Damon sighed and took a sip of the ale that sat in front of him on an abandoned table. If he was to be here in a dream, he may as well enjoy himself.

Suddenly, a figure walked in from the noisy street. The doors opened to reveal a face Damon had not seen in years. It was his friend Ciaran. Ciaran was a school mate of Damon's when he was only a young one. Ciaran was from another family of dreamwalkers and shared the joys of learning his family's trade with Damon when nobody was around to hear his stories. Damon almost raised a hand to wave at his old friend before noticing himself walking in after Ciaran. Damon drew in a quick breath as he watched his younger self, brimming with youth, walk to an empty table near the bar. Ciaran and he ordered food and ale. Damon glanced around the tavern again, but nothing gave him any hint as to why he was reliving this memory. He downed his ale to drown out the painful thoughts associated with this night. Then, he stood and walked to sit at the bar, making it easier to find another abandoned ale and overhear the conversation he was obviously meant to remember.

Damon, with his back to their table, caught a piece of the conversation Ciaran had started as he sat down.

"...yes, it was. They have already scheduled my ceremony. Father says I should prepare for the trials. I will either inherit or die trying it seems." There was a nervous melancholy to Ciaran's statement that Damon recalled. He could not blame his old friend. Looking at the trials from that side of the inheritance was very intimidating.

"But it is so soon! Can they not give you more time?" Damon heard himself ask in a whisper.

"No. My grandfather passed so quickly. My father says that the elders were able to save his skill, but they are unsure if their attempts to preserve it will last more than a few days."

The table fell silent for a moment. The barmaid approached the younger Damon as she wiped out a mug with a clean cloth. *"More ale for you?"* Damon watched from the corner of his eye as his younger self nodded and pushed his glass forward. He had not been eager to drink ale back then, but Damon had also never turned away a mug that was offered to him. Those habits probably contributed to his drinking problems over the years.

Then, he heard his own voice speak up once more, starting a conversation he had long tried to forget. *"It is a shame that we have such few skills to go around. You would think we could preserve them better and even share them with multiple members of our family instead of waiting for the old to die or tire of their skills. I'm sure you know that Rory will inherit first? He could care less about inheriting and rarely ever prepares for his trials."*

"Do you think he will inherit from your grandparents, Damon?" Ciaran asked.

"No. Our grandparents have been dead for many years. Their skills went to other grandchildren in the family. No, if Rory is to inherit, it will be from our mother or father."

Damon heard a gasp. *"But that could take years!*

Decades!" Damon heard Ciaran whisper, "And if he has to wait that long to inherit, how long will you have to wait?"

Damon frowned, listening and wishing that the conversation would turn from this. Anything but this! *"Yes. I suppose I must be patient, but it seems ridiculous that I must wait so long when my training was complete years ago. Besides, Rory does not even seem eager to be a dreamwalker." Young Damon finished pathetically.*

The table fell silent once more as the boys contemplated death and how short a typical lifespan could be compared with a dreamwalker who had inherited. "Damon, you are my friend, and I know this troubles you. Can I not help in some way?"

"Actually Ciaran, I think you can, but it won't be pleasant." Damon's stomach knotted as he remembered the plotting his friend had helped him with. How he wished he could step in and end this conversation!

"I have a tough stomach, Damon. I know what a solution would mean."

"Very well. Then, cheers to our future!" Young Damon exclaimed. Hatred echoed in his younger self's voice. Damon closed his eyes in pain and anger with himself. When he opened his eyes, the scene had changed to a different and more dreadful one.

Another young Damon, only a few years older than the one in the tavern, was climbing the sheer rock face of a small, unrecognizable mountain. His brother, Rory, was climbing above him, and he did not realize Damon was below him. Damon watched himself gain ground on Rory, who seemed to be taking it slow to avoid injury. Rory stopped for a moment to see how much higher he needed to climb to reach the ledge. Damon closed his eyes, knowing what came next. Then, Damon heard a familiar shout.

Damon ran forward, unable to stand back and do nothing. He watched as his younger self held on tightly to Rory's ankle. Rory, still above Damon, was struggling to maintain his grip on the sharp rocks. Damon winced as he saw Rory try to kick Damon's grip off. Damon knew the emotions playing out on his brother's face. Confusion, fear, hurt, betrayal. And then, horror. Rory's fingers finally slipped free of the rocks, and he fell, in slow-motion, into the crevice of sharp rocks below the rock face. Young Damon turned back to the cliff and began climbing again, eager to find his escape from his brother's trials. The trials he had disrupted and essentially stolen.

"NO!!!" Damon shouted and ran towards the cliff face, but he knew it was hopeless. This was only a memory. It could not be reversed. He closed his eyes but still heard the loud crash of his brother's body breaking on the stones, more than a hundred feet below where young Damon now climbed over the ledge. He watched young Damon wipe his hands on his trousers and leave the cliff face without ever glancing down at Rory's body. Little did he care at the time that Rory's blood would forever stain his unwrinkled hands. Damon shouted once more and fell to his knees on the rocky, dusty ground. He felt his trousers tear and a sharp object cut his knee, but he did not notice it. Damon covered his face and wailed into his hands. Living with the memory of his treachery was one thing, but reliving it was another.

Damon heard footsteps behind him and turned in surprise. His face was streaked with tears that he hastily wiped away to find a blurry Kenna staring at him in horror. She clutched her left shoulder in obvious pain from a wound that Damon could not see, but she said nothing to him. Her eyes were wide, and she shook her head silently. She started to back away from him but fell onto the ground. She hastily scrambled away from this perceived monster in front of her as she held the wound in her shoulder. When he noticed the blood soaking through her shirt, Damon stood and ran to Kenna. Then with horror, he realized there were actually two big stains of blood on Kenna's shirt. Kenna's eyelids fluttered as she tried to scoot herself further away from Damon.

Damon reached out to her, but Kenna put up her right hand, which was covered in blood and said, "No! You…. stay away from me."

Damon stopped walking and realized that Kenna had seen everything he had seen. He lowered his head shamefully, but a gasp had him glancing at Kenna once more in concern. She had collapsed on the ground and blood continued to seep from her wounds, into the dusty, dry ground beneath her. Damon knelt beside Kenna and gently lifted her head into his lap. Kenna's eyes were still open, and she gulped with effort.

"Kenna, what happened?" Damon asked desperately.

"Damon. We are coming back. Please, help me.*" Kenna said softly, barely strong enough to speak in a whisper, before her eyes closed.*

Shocked, Damon closed his eyes too and placed his hand on Kenna's forehead. Just a small scry. He knew the danger of it, but this was an emergency and choosing to scry may make a difference in saving Kenna's life. It would not take much effort with her here with him in his dream… Damon felt the familiar spinning sensation, and then… There! He had found her! Damon stopped scrying and focused his attention on leaving this place.

*

When he opened his eyes, Damon was sitting at a table

in the room he shared with Rhyn. He had been reading a pamphlet about recent events in Calvenia when he had fallen asleep. He shook his head but was unable to get rid of the headache that pounded behind his eyes from his scrying. Damon stood suddenly, remembering his dream. He grabbed his cloak and hastened to find a healer. He ran, afraid that he may be too late to save Kenna.

CHAPTER TWENTY-ONE
Kenna

Kenna opened her eyes, instantly aware of a deep ache in her shoulder. She groaned and tried to sit up, but gentle hands kept her in place.

"Please, rest. You will need it." A strange voice said. Kenna rubbed her right hand over her face as she heard that same voice say, "No moving the arm. Keep her in bed for the next few days, and if the stitches rip, send for me. Here is a vial of milk of the poppy to help with the pain. And before you ask, Damon, no. You will get no more of this."

Kenna opened her eyes again and blinked the brightness away as she watched the strange woman leave the room. Rhyn and Ansley sat on one of the benches next to the bed where Kenna lay. Kenna now realized she was in her room at the inn in Calvenia. After the healer left, Damon turned back and looked at Kenna with much concern on his face. Kenna took a deep breath, then gasped from the pain that spread down into her chest. She took a shallow breath and found that this was much less painful. Then, she said to Damon, "Don't worry. I'm still alive."

"Edric is going to have you killed." Damon said, pointing a finger accusingly at Rhyn. Rhyn looked at Ansley who shrugged her shoulders in response.

"You *idiot*. They don't know who you're talking about." Kenna croaked. She laughed a bit before a memory struck her. Damon climbing a cliff face. A struggle and another man falling to his death. Kenna's eyes widened at Damon, who seemed to perceive her thoughts.

Damon cleared his throat and asked Rhyn and Ansley to go get extra blankets from the innkeeper. The two rose and made for the door. "We will go look for some food too. Kenna?" Rhyn asked kindly.

Kenna shook her head. "No, thank you, Rhyn. I think I am too nauseous to eat." He nodded and led Ansley out of the room. When Ansley passed, she smiled reassuringly at Kenna. Kenna noticed a small wound on Ansley's left ear, but it didn't appear to be bleeding anymore. When they left, Damon shut the door behind them and turned back to Kenna.

"Kenna, I..." He started.

"No, Damon. I do not want to hear your bullshit. Tell me the TRUTH! What *was* that? *Who* was that you killed?" Kenna snarled back at him.

Damon stopped speaking and bowed his head as if the words caused him pain. "He...was my brother."

Kenna gasped again, even more repulsed by him. "How *could* you?"

Damon sat on the edge of Kenna's bed and put his head in his hands. She heard him take a few shallow breaths, but he remained silent for a few moments. She guessed that he was trying to calm himself. Kenna found that she actually felt pity for him. This revelation surprised her when only moments before she had thought Damon a monster.

Damon finally lifted his head. "I was young and stupid. I prized my own achievements over my brother's life, but I have paid *dearly* for it."

"Damon, I think he was the one who paid dearly for it." Kenna responded with frustration.

"No. Don't you see?" Damon began again. "This is why I was exiled. They knew what I did and made me leave. He died in the trials, and I took his skill. I killed my own brother for his skill and my family had me exiled for it. My *family*. Not that I fault them for their actions."

Kenna nodded, acknowledging what Damon had said. It finally made sense. *I knew he was a horrible person, but I didn't imagine he was a murderer*, she thought to herself in shock. *And even worse: a kin-slayer.* Damon took her silence for judgement and decided to fill the silence with his own thoughts.

"I thought at first that exile would be better than being there to live with their scorn. I was actually happy to leave. But, after many years, many dirty deals, and many cold nights spent trying to keep myself alive with no fortune or lands, I realized that I had been punished not only by my family but by the gods. They gave me this," he said as he pointed to his forehead where his mark of a seer would have been after the trials. "This *skill*! Ensuring I lived much longer than all those that I loved, even the other dreamwalkers. Ensuring I could always see and never be able to take action. I was in a dark place for so long."

"So, how does my mother fit into this story, Damon? She would never choose someone so…" Kenna could not find a good word to finish her sentence, but Damon read her meaning.

"You're right. And she *didn't* choose that monster. She saw through my act and knew that I was a different person on the inside. She was my only friend for some time. I had chosen to go to Willow for a deal, in hopes of avoiding notice. There was a time that I helped persuaders find dreamwalkers whose skills could be taken easily, and I was paid a hefty sum for each victim of ours. Your mother intercepted me one night when I was on a mission. She knew what I was doing, and she still let me go instead of turning me into the elders. She found me again the next night, and she followed me every night after that for over a month. She made me change, Kenna. She told me if I didn't, she would turn me into the elders, but not before she 'beat some sense into me'." Damon chuckled. "I never realized someone so beautiful could be so fierce."

Kenna smiled half-heartedly. She reached up and touched Damon's shoulder. "I never knew." She said softly.

Damon nodded, his black eyes glistening with such emotion that it surprised Kenna. "She saved me, you know? I have her to thank that I am no longer that version of myself. But even redemption will never change what I did to Rory, and I know that I will have to face him someday in the afterlife. I can only hope he has watched me try to change knowing that I wish I could take back what I did." Damon turned back to look at her. "Kenna," Kenna looked at Damon more closely, taking in the new streaks of grey in his hair from his scrying just a few weeks ago. She tried to quiet her anger towards him to accept what he was about to say. "I never meant to hurt your father. I know that saying these things can never bring your parents back to you, but I just want you to know that I am truly sorry. If I could…I would…"

Kenna closed her eyes and pinched the bridge of her nose with her fingers. "Damon, I know. You are right though. You can't bring them back, and you are forever linked in my mind to their absence. You can never change what you did that led to their deaths, but I do accept that you never wanted things to happen that way."

Damon nodded sadly. He rose from the bed. "You were lucky tonight, Kenna." He said, pointing to her shoulder. "You had lost so much blood when you got here that you were unconscious. How did you manage to find me in my dreams if you were so badly hurt?"

"I'm not sure. I just knew we needed help, and you were

the only one I could find. It felt...it *really* felt like I reached you with a tether, but that wouldn't make sense. We have *never* been tethered, unless you count when you joined our tribe. But this tether felt...I don't know...*deeper*." Kenna replied, confused by her own thoughts.

Damon nodded as he reached into his cloak and removed his flask. He unscrewed the top and took a long drink. After several moments, he responded softly. "That would actually make sense. We are tethered and have been since you were three years old."

Kenna gasped angrily. "What are you talking about, Damon?" She growled at him, fury rising in her chest to replace the ache of her wound. She tried to pull herself up but a deep ache forced her to relent.

Damon avoided her gaze and sighed. "Your mother insisted. She worried about you being so alone, and she wanted someone to be there for you if you needed them. Someone who could keep you safe if anything happened to her or your father."

Kenna scoffed. "And *you* were supposed to be that person? How could my mother be *so*..." she started, but Damon interrupted her.

"Don't speak ill of you mother's choices. It's in the past, and today it helped save your life. Maybe one day you can sever the tether if it bothers you that much, but for now, I think it is in all of our best interests to keep it."

Kenna's cheeks burned. She was furious with Damon and her mother. How could they do this to her without her consent? Even if she was a baby at the time, a tether was such a personal connection, and it was one that could only be undone with extreme difficulty. She shook her head and sighed. Her mother had definitely *not* been a seer. Her mother would have had no idea what would happen to

Kenna's father and her in the next few months that would leave such a hatred in Kenna's heart for Damon. Kenna swallowed her anger for now as best as she could, putting it away until she could think about what to do with it.

"Did you find out any information on who attacked us and why?" Kenna asked Damon finally, changing the subject to a safer one. Damon replaced the top of his flask and stowed it back inside his cloak before answering.

"No. But it seems that someone had followed you to the seer's home. I suppose we are not welcome here after all."

"What do you mean?" Kenna asked. "I know we were attacked, but I doubt they knew why we were meeting with Darby."

Damon handed Kenna a piece of paper, "This was wrapped around the shaft of one of the arrows you were hit with."

Kenna unrolled the paper and read the short message. She looked up at Damon with fear in her eyes. "Do you think it was Magnus?"

Damon shook his head. "No. I don't think he knows where Ansley is, so it couldn't be him. I guess we will have to wait to see if these people strike again. In the meantime, I think it is finally time for us to leave Bolivar. We leave for Dunbar tomorrow. Hopefully my absence has given Lya room to consider forgiving me. We can continue our search for information about Magnus there."

Kenna nodded and laid the paper on the bed. The words were few but powerful.

KEEP LOOKING, AND YOU DIE.

CHAPTER TWENTY-TWO
Ansley

Ansley sat across from Rhyn at the kitchen table in a home she never expected to visit: Damon's. Ansley looked to Rhyn who was watching Lya, Damon's wife, clean up Ansley's wound from one of the arrows that had also pierced Kenna's shoulder. It had been almost two days since that attack, and Ansley was still trying to digest all that had happened afterwards.

Damon had met them a few miles from Bolivar, and his timing could not have been better. Kenna had been unconscious for the last stretch of their journey, and Rhyn was concerned that Kenna may have lost too much blood. When Damon approached them on horseback, Ansley had been relieved to see that he was not alone. A stranger rode with him, and they soon learned, to their great relief, that it was a healer. *Gods bless Damon!*

They had let the healer tend to Kenna before continuing their journey. The woman removed the arrows, and she wrapped Kenna's wounds to prevent any more blood loss. When she had deemed Kenna safe for travel again, their party had mounted their horses and finished the trek to the inn that had become their literal 'safe haven'. Ansley offered to help with Kenna, but Damon and Rhyn refused, insisting that they could carry Kenna to the room easily enough. Once they arrived, Ansley had sunk onto one of the benches placed in the room for traveling bags and tried to reason through all that had occurred on their trip.

Darby's and Rosalie's words echoed through her mind.

You are the key. You are running out of time. She had been lost in thought when Rhyn had touched her shoulder in a comforting way, breaking her trance. He had guessed her thoughts and seemed concerned for her. Ansley stood and followed him to the bed where Kenna lay unconscious. They sat closely while the healer finished rewrapping Kenna's wounds with clean bandages.

"Are you okay?" Rhyn asked Ansley softly, a wrinkle appearing between his eyebrows.

Ansley sighed. "Kenna is in more danger than I am." She replied but touched her wounded ear to see if the blood still flowed.

"You know that is not what I meant." Rhyn responded. Suddenly, Kenna groaned. They both looked in her direction and were pleased to see she was awake. Their conversation died as they listened intently to the healer's last comments.

"Can you get some extra blankets from the innkeeper?" Damon had asked Rhyn. Ansley was confused but eager to escape this room. It seemed to have shrunk in the last few moments, and Ansley felt that her breath was not coming easily enough. Fresh air would help.

Rhyn and Ansley stood and left. Rhyn mentioned food, which prompted Ansley's stomach to let out a low growl. Rhyn looked at her and chuckled, grabbing her hand and pulling her towards the inn's tavern. Ansley's heart leapt when he touched her hand, and she felt the blood rush into her cheeks. She was glad that Rhyn was not looking at her. *What is wrong with me?* She thought to herself.

When they had ordered two heaping servings of the special, Ansley and Rhyn sat at a table and waited for their meal in silence. Ansley stared at her hands as she began to think through the events of the day again.

Rhyn cleared his throat, in an attempt to start

conversation, but Ansley did not say anything. She remained adrift in her dilemma, thinking of all those who were in danger because of her poor decision to tie herself to that…monster. Their food finally arrived, and they both dug in without a word. Ansley guessed that Rhyn sensed her need for space and chose to honor it. A few moments after they had finished a second helping of their meal, a steaming beef stew with potatoes and carrots, Damon had joined them and announced their plans to leave Bolivar. Because of the fondness she had felt for this place, Ansley should have felt more disappointed, but the attack had left her feeling empty and restless. She had hurried back to her room to pack and was happy to find Kenna asleep once more. Ansley did not feel like talking to anyone.

And now they were in Damon's home. Damon's wife was not initially pleased to see her husband, but as soon as she learned of the danger he was evidently in, Lya dismissed her anger. She had ushered her guests in, put Kenna to bed in her daughter's room, and begun cooking a hot breakfast while also mending Ansley's wounded ear. Ansley felt at ease with the woman, but her curiosity was drowned in her worries.

"You seem troubled, young one. What's wrong? Are you in pain?" Lya asked Ansley, gesturing to her ear. She laid the bowl of warm water aside that she had been cleaning the wound with and picked up a bowl of some sort of poultice to apply to the wound next.

"No. The pain is…bearable." Ansley paused as Lya began to smear the poultice on her ear. The wound burned, but the poultice was cool on it. She let out a breath of air in relief and continued, "We have had a strange week, and honestly, I am beginning to wonder why we continue wasting our time here in Calvenia."

Lya smiled. "Calvenia has a deep history. Damon said

you search here for answers about the man who is attacking dreamwalkers in Arvenia. Are you still looking for information?"

Ansley opened her mouth to speak, but Rhyn took the opportunity. "We do. We have only learned *who* our enemy is but not what he is capable of or what he is planning. Most importantly, we have not learned how to defeat him." Rhyn added grimly.

"We have not even learned anything of my abilities." Ansley added.

"Damon mentioned that he would like you to try meeting with an old record-keeper here. He keeps an extensive collection of dreamwalker records." Lya offered. *Great*, thought Ansley, *more record-keepers*.

"No, but our informer in Bolivar told us not to expect to find any information on Magnus." Ansley said, wincing from a sudden jolt of pain when Lya placed a bandage over her wound to seal in the poultice.

"No, but there may be some answers about your skills. That is what you need now, after all. You just said so yourself." Lya said, matter-of-factly. Her eyes were kind but sparkled with a laugh at Ansley's and Rhyn's thick-headedness.

Ansley turned and shared a look with Rhyn, who also seemed surprised at how direct Lya was with them. "She's right, Ansley," he said, shrugging. "It's worth a try."

Lya nodded. "I will take you to this see this collection of records tomorrow. Rest today. Your ear will need more poultice in the morning." She rose and went to the kitchen to store the poultice in the ice box.

Ansley felt a spark of hope fill her at the prospect of finding more answers. Hopefully these answers would not lead to more questions like the others had.

*****

Lya had been right. There was a huge collection of papers, scrolls, and books that had been saved by the dreamwalkers in this area. The record-keeper in Bolivar, who had passed on his skill before Ansley had been born, was almost seventy-eight and extremely ornery, but his knowledge of the history of their people was legendary in Calvenia. So, this is who Lya took them to see the following day. Kenna was still recovering and in need of rest. Damon, who was gone yet again, had stopped by for a few hours' sleep only to leave again at dawn. Lya said he was trying to find the perpetrators by investigating the site where they had been attacked on their way back from Darby's home. He hadn't had any luck so far. Ansley hoped wherever this hall of records was, would be safe.

When they had met the old record-keeper, Ceorl, he greeted them with a frown. Ansley was surprised by his manner, until Lya explained that she had told him where his visitors were visiting from. I guess the prejudice here is stronger than I knew, Ansley thought to herself as she examined the former dreamwalker. He was tall but stooped over in his shoulders. His hair was mostly gone, but he had two white tufts on either side of his head above his ears. What hair had disappeared seemed to have relocated to the man's eyebrows, which were extremely bushy. The man shuffled when he walked and mumbled to himself as he had led them to a massive oak door with brass handles.

"...probably don't even appreciate history..." Ceorl complained.

Ansley frowned and looked at Rhyn who was smiling. He leaned down to Ansley's ear and whispered, "Reminds me of my grandfather." Ansley had returned his smile and wondered what Rhyn's family was like. She knew of Rhys and recognized his face and features on Rhyn, but she felt that she had never truly met him. She could not separate which encounters between them had been with Rhys and which had been with Magnus. The memory of Rhys made her angry, and hot tears welled up in her eyes. Ansley gritted her teeth and swallowed down those thoughts for later. They *were* here to help him. *We will not fail you, Rhys!*

They had followed Ceorl passed rows and rows of shelves. Some shelves reached almost to the ceiling, but others were short enough for Ansley to reach the top. The shelves had lettering on the sides, and Ansley noted with surprise that these were descriptions of the texts shelved there. They passed "Dreamwalker Beginnings", "Famous Dreamwalkers", "The First Battles", and "Evolution of Skills". Ansley was intrigued. She had looked up at Rhyn happily, but he had been absorbed in searching for a section that would best serve their purposes.

Interrupting Ansley's recollections and amusement at all the volumes surrounding them in this dusty room, Lya tapped Ansley on the shoulder and said, "I will return when the sun drops just below the horizon. Will that be enough time for today?"

Ansley nodded. "Thank you for bringing us here."

Lya inclined her head. "Damon asked me to. He has been trying to get Ceorl to agree to your visit since you arrived in Bolivar, but the old man has been...*difficult* to bargain with. Damon and I both believe whatever resources you need to defeat Magnus may be here somewhere. I am sorry to leave you here, but Damon asked that I keep a close eye on Kenna. I will come for you this evening. Good luck." Lya turned away from Ansley and walked back towards the door. She was a direct and intelligent woman. Ansley was thankful that Damon had found someone to make him happy in his exile.

Ansley turned to see Ceorl seated at the desk in the center of the room. "Go on! Find what you need, but don't mess up my books!" He said harshly, gesturing wide with his arms. He leaned back in his wooden chair, which creaked loudly. Then, Ceorl crossed his arms and closed his eyes. Ansley shook her head but could not wipe the smile from her face as she turned away from him to explore the texts. Rhyn had already left her and was walking down the center aisle reading the descriptions. He found something interesting and walked onto the aisle to see what was available.

Ansley began walking in the opposite direction from Rhyn. She walked past Ceorl and towards the front of the library. Each description on the shelves sounded intriguing, but it was not what she needed. "Dream Missions", "Dreamwalkers in Tortia", "Dreamwalkers in Arvenia", "Betrayals and Exiles", and "Totems". *What are totems?* She wondered as she continued.

Finally, when she was nearing the end of the aisle, Ansley found a shelf that looked promising. "Genealogy of Dreamwalker Families". She stepped onto the aisle and began looking through the volumes there. After finding one marked "Arvenia" with her own family crest of The Bear on the cover, Ansley left the aisle with the heavy book to see if it mentioned anything noteworthy.

Rhyn met her at a table near Ceorl who was now softly snoring, his head lolling towards his chest. Rhyn dumped a stack of volumes on both his right and left sides and then sat, plucked one from the top, and opened it to the first page. He slid his finger along the dusty page and absentmindedly scratched his nose with the same finger. A trail of dirt remained on the bridge of his nose as evidence. Ansley giggled, causing Rhyn to look up at her.

"What?"

"I…you just…you have dirt on your nose…" Ansley started, but her giggles made it hard to finish what she was trying to tell him.

Ceorl let out a low growl, "Do you know how lucky you are to be allowed in here? This place is *sacred*! Do not make me throw you out for your insolence!"

Rhyn raised his eyebrows at Ansley and returned to his volume, dirt still streaked down his face. Ansley giggled again but opened her own book to begin reading.

*****

Ansley suppressed a yawn and walked to the windows to check the sun's position. "It looks like we still have another hour." She informed Rhyn and Ceorl.

Rhyn replied, "Good. I am almost finished taking notes on this book. I will leave the others for tomorrow."

Ansley glanced once more out the window at the flat farmlands around the large building the library was inside. Horses and cattle moved slowly ahead of her. She let herself breathe in the peace. It had been too long since she had felt peace. She closed her eyes and let herself sink to the floor.

*

Ansley opened her eyes to see Damon sitting ahead, with his back to her. They were outside his home, a humble cabin built from wood that had been treated to prevent rotting. Damon held his whiskey flask in one hand and had removed the top. He took a short sip and wiped his mouth with the back of his hand. Ansley thought for a moment how Damon looked very different from when she had first met him. It was hard to believe he was the same person without the long hair and scraggly beard.

Ansley started walking towards Damon, but suddenly,

she fell to the ground, pushed aside by a fast-moving shape that could not see her. Ansley then noticed the dark shape moving closer towards Damon. Damon was still facing the opposite direction, and the shadow began sneaking up on him. The person drew a knife which gleamed in the moonlight for just a moment before he held it against Damon's throat. The person uttered a warning, "You have been asked to leave. Your guests are not welcome. Make them go back before you regret them staying."

Damon dropped his flask and held his hands up in submission in the air. The attacker did not lower his knife. Damon stayed motionless for a moment before quickly reaching back to grab the person's arm. Damon shifted his weight and pulled the attacker over his head and onto the ground by his arm. The knife clattered to the ground, and Damon kicked it away.

Damon drew a knife from his belt and rushed at the attacker just as a new shadowy figure stepped out from the tree line. This figure had a knife drawn as well. When the first attacker saw the second figure approach, he tried to rush Damon. He lunged at Damon, but Damon dodged his attack. The second figure snuck around behind the first attacker and stabbed a knife into the person's back. The stranger crumpled to his knees, blood gurgling from his lips. Ansley heard a groan as the first attacker fell face-forward onto the ground.

Damon rushed at the second attacker, unaware that this person had actually helped him dispose of the other attacker. Damon made quick work of his knife. The second attacker gasped loudly and fell to the ground with Damon's hilt protruding from his chest. Ansley stepped closer to see who the wounded person was. She covered her mouth with her hand as she realized it was a girl, and not just any girl. It was a young girl with black eyes.

Damon's *black eyes. She reached towards Damon as blood soaked through her dark tunic. "Father...," she groaned softly. Damon kneeled at her side and called her name loudly, cradling his daughter's lolling head in his arms.*

*

Ansley opened her eyes in shock. She found herself lying on the dirt floor of the library. Rhyn and Ceorl had not seen her fall. She stood and ran to Rhyn.

"Rhyn! Damon is in danger! We have to go. *Now!*" Ansley bellowed. Ceorl jerked awake once more and stared at her as if she were mad.

"You just had a dreamvision, didn't you?" Rhyn asked her.

"Yes. Damon will be alright, but...he...he..." Ansley sputtered.

"Well good. Maybe we have time to finish these last texts?" Rhyn responded, turning back to the book in his hands.

"No! He will be okay, but she won't! We must go. *Now!*" Ansley said as she grabbed Rhyn's shirt collar and pulled until he stood from the bench he was seated on. She had to warn Damon before his daughter appeared, or he would have to live with her death on his hands. Ansley could not let that happen.

CHAPTER TWENTY-THREE
Magnus

Magnus rolled the crystal around in his palm. It emitted a soft glow that looked almost blue in the darkened chamber. He sat in a chair across from his prisoner and sighed. It had been years since he had thought about his first encounter with these crystals. He was honestly lucky to have found them at all.

Magnus had been a young man the first time he had met King Deryn. That was just a few years after his attempt to steal Rhael's skill in his trials. He was extremely bitter about losing track of his brother, but his mother's capture had been a small consolation. He had bound her to the dreamworld by removing her spirit's link to her body. Well, he had actually hidden her body. So, if Rosalie had tried to come back from the dreamworld, she would die. She was buried in a stone tomb near the cabin she had raised him in. Years after he had trapped her body there, Magnus had returned with his necromancer to lock the tomb with magic. She was not going anywhere. Unfortunately, Rosalie was still alive and could apparently visit Ansley's dreams, making it difficult for Magnus to control Ansley's actions and coerce her to make decisions that furthered his goals.

Even though he had been successful in capturing his mother, Magnus could not let go of his desire to find his brother. He had tracked Rhael to the distant reaches of the Spruce Mountains in Arvenia, but his brother had evaded him again.

Musing over his frustrations, Magnus had happened across a castle. The *same* castle he now lived in. *Destiny will always find you*, he thought to himself. The crystal in his hand glowed with power as he remembered what he had found there. King Deryn and Dominic, his servant, were in desperate need of help. It was thanks to that encounter with them at the king's castle that Magnus was forever linked to the Arvenian crown and along with that, these crystals.

Magnus looked up at his prisoner. His handsome face had sunk in around his eyes and was smeared with dirt. The man's hands were still in shackles, and Magnus could see wounds around his wrists where he had strained against them too often. The skin was cracked with dried blood in spots. Magnus had let his healer look at the man to make sure he was healthy, and his healer had confirmed that nothing was infected or broken, except perhaps his spirit.

"Rhys…. Rhys…." Magnus called softly, trying to wake him. Rhys's eyelids flittered, and he looked up at Magnus's face. Magnus smiled at him. "Ready to play?"

"You *monster*. When will you ever leave me alone?" Rhys answered in a soft tone, too tired to show emotion.

"Someday, but you should hope that I still have use for you for many, many years. Otherwise, you will die." Magnus said matter-of-factly.

"Just let me die then." Rhys responded.

Magnus laughed deep in his throat. "We are not done with our waltz quite yet. So, while we wait for our guests to join us, perhaps we should spend some time planning for their arrival?" Magnus lifted the crystal to show it to Rhys. Rhys simply glowered at Magnus and turned his face away. Magnus stood from the chair and walked for a moment into the next chamber.

"Regin!" Magnus called. A man stepped forth out of the shadows to greet Magnus. He threw his hood back to greet his master. Regin was a short man, but he exuded an undeniable air of power. Magnus had always respected him, especially because of the wisdom Regin possessed that had helped Magnus reach some of his more difficult aspirations.

"Yes, lord?" Regin responded. His dark green eyes looked to the crystal held in Magnus's hand. "Are you ready?"

"I am. Let's begin." Magnus responded and walked back towards Rhys.

Magnus sat down in his chair once more and waited as Regin approached Rhys. He was a necromancer. Some called him wizard or sorcerer, but he was not that grand. Regin was a man of mystics and science. He knew what ingredients to use to make things happen. Regin grabbed Rhys by his hair and pulled the man's head back, to expose his neck. He inserted a long needle into his neck and drew blood from him. Rhys winced in pain, but Regin was done quickly. He then emptied the blood into a vial and handed this to Magnus. From his cloak he produced a separate vial, one that was filled with a dark blue liquid. He handed this to Magnus too.

"You remember how to use them?" Regin inquired. "It has been a few weeks since you entered the dream realm as a jinn, lord."

"I remember. Thank you, Regin. You may go." Magnus responded. Regin turned and left the chamber to resume whatever work he had been doing. Magnus opened the vial of blood and poured the blue potion into it. He drank the mixture of blood quickly and tried to suppress the urge to spit it out. Magnus may be evil, but he never rejoiced at the metallic taste of blood. He was more civilized than that. Magnus then took the crystal and placed it at his brow.

Suddenly, Magnus's brow glowed with a mark shaped like an eye. Rhys's forehead glowed with the same mark, and his eyes had turned from blue to black as the potion took effect. Magnus closed his eyes to begin his work.

*

When Magnus opened his eyes again, he was in a dream. He looked around at the people walking nearby, and he realized that he was once again in Avendale. Rhys's dreams always started that way. Magnus began walking down the street and felt the struggle inside of him. Rhys's dreamself did not easily submit to Magnus's presence. He struggled against Magnus's every movement, making it as unpleasant as possible each time Magnus possessed him.

Magnus continued on, eager to find the right tavern. He saw the carving of a lion's head on a door ahead, and Magnus knew this was the place. He pushed through the doors, eager to meet the dreamwalker elder inside. They had work to do.

CHAPTER TWENTY-FOUR
Damon

Damon sat on the porch outside his home looking at the stars. His wife, Lya, had left in their wagon to retrieve Ansley and Rhyn from the hall of records for the night. He was pleased that she had taken them there and hoped they found something useful. His own searches had been fruitless.

Damon removed his flask from his cloak and unscrewed the top. He thought of Rory as he looked to the stars and wondered if his brother would have been more capable of handling this situation. Damon took a short drink that burned all the way into his stomach. As he felt the liquid warm his chest, he thought to himself, *I need to stop drinking so much*. His breath showed in the cool night air, and Damon pulled his cloak tighter around his arms. It wasn't his fault really. The events of the last few weeks had really been difficult to handle, even with the added alcohol. The winter solstice was fast approaching. It was hard to imagine that he had left Calvenia only a few weeks ago. The events had made time pass so slowly that Damon was having a difficult time returning to reality.

He had not heard from Bianca, Alden, Daro, or Quinn. Damon hoped they still believed that he was here in Calvenia training Ansley. But, some part of Damon knew that it would have been better to include the elders in their plan. They may have helped them find Magnus's weakness and dispose of him sooner. Damon shook his head as he thought of the man. How could someone who has mastered the mystery of death be killed? These thoughts turned over in his mind until he was interrupted by a noise behind him. A sharp blade was placed at his throat, the hand holding it covered by a black glove. "You have been asked to leave. Your guests are not welcome. Make them go back before you regret them staying." The voice growled at him. It sounded like a man's voice, but Damon could not be sure.

Damon had no idea who this was and didn't try to guess. He just hoped they knew very little about him. He grabbed the person's wrist, wrapping his entire hand around it. Then, he pulled as hard as he could, forcing not just the arm but the person to roll over his shoulder onto their back. The knife fell, and Damon kicked it away. He reached for his own knife and prepared to strike just as someone jumped on him from behind.

"Arghhh!!" Damon yelled. The new attacker grabbed Damon's knife-hand and pulled the weapon from his clenched fist. Damon turned to face this assailant, wrestled his knife away from the stranger, and punched him in the stomach. The person sank to the ground, and Damon turned back to his first assailant, who had gotten to his feet once more. He lunged at Damon, and Damon sunk his knife into the person's chest, narrowly avoiding being struck by a large blade that now dropped uselessly to the ground from the wounded man's hand. Damon finally glanced back at the second attacker-the person he had punched. The second assailant lifted his head from where he still crouched in pain on the grass, and Damon felt the blood drain from his face.

"Ansley? What in the *gods'* names are you doing!" Damon shouted at her. His voice roared over the empty fields around him, and he was sure it could be heard for miles. "I could have *killed* you!" Damon roared in frustration as he looked at Ansley's face in the moonlight.

Ansley replied hoarsely in between gasps, "I was...trying to...from hurting her." She pointed in the direction of the tree line, where a second figure emerged now, with a short knife in hand. Damon tensed, readying himself to fight off another attacker, until he recognized his daughter's voice calling his name. "*Mila*?" Damon asked tentatively.

Mila let out a sob as she ran towards her father. She dropped her weapon and wrapped her arms tightly around Damon. "Father, I am so glad I got to you in time. I was worried I would be too late." Mila said, her concern lacing each word. Damon hugged her fiercely to his chest. As Damon held his daughter tightly, thankful that no harm had come to her, Rhyn walked over to Ansley and pulled her to her feet. Damon could still hear Ansley's wheezes, and he felt shame creep over him.

Once he released his daughter, Damon stared dumbstruck at the scene before him. Ansley, Rhyn, Mila, and he stood in a circle around the bloody body of Damon's attacker. "What happened here?" Damon asked, trying to make sense of everything that had happened. His head thrummed with confusion and fear for his daughter's safety. If she had arrived before Ansley and Rhyn, he may have...Damon rubbed his hand over his face to clear the disturbing thought as he turned back to look at his daughter.

Ansley spoke first. "I had a dreamvision, Damon. I didn't see anything in my vision other than what just happened. Who is he?" She asked him, pointing to the crumpled form on the grass. Damon shook his head.

"I don't know." He answered softly. Then, he knelt and began rifling through the pockets of the motionless man, hoping to find something that would answer their questions. Unfortunately, Damon did not find anything.

"Why don't we go inside?" Damon suggested softly, as he motioned to the door. As Mila, Ansley, and Rhyn moved past him, Damon removed his flask once again from his cloak. *I thought I only had to worry about Magnus killing us. Now we have assassins in Calvenia looking for us too?* Damon took a long sip from the flask and hoped it would erase the shame and fear that lingered in his chest. He turned and walked inside his home, worried what other dangers may await them in Calvenia.

CHAPTER TWENTY-FIVE
Ansley

Ansley dropped into a chair at the table in Damon and Lya's kitchen. She was exhausted, and her legs ached. After her dreamvision, Rhyn and she had run to the nearest house and demanded to borrow horses, leaving Ceorl alone, complaining loudly in his chair. She was thankful they had arrived in time to stop Damon from harming his daughter. Ansley didn't want to imagine what would have happened if they had not made it to the house before Mila. She shuddered to think of how Damon may have reacted if he had hurt his only daughter.

Ansley glanced up at the girl seated across from her. Though Mila's face was pale with fear, it was alarming how closely she favored her father. Dark, wavy black hair flowed to her waist. Ansley remembered seeing the girl's familiar black eyes in her dreamvision. Those were Damon's eyes. It was still so strange to imagine him having a family. She watched Damon pace behind his daughter's chair, and she realized that Mila was likely close to her own age. *How odd...* she thought, watching Damon more closely and wondering how someone who had treated her so coldly at first could be such a loving father.

Silence hung awkwardly in the room until Damon finally spoke to Mila. "You should have been home before now, Mila. Where were you? You know our rules. What were you doing in the woods, and *why* did you have a weapon?" Damon asked, his voice growing in volume. He stood next to Mila's chair awaiting an answer. She opened and closed her mouth without making a sound. Ansley thought she had decided it was better not to say what she was thinking at the moment. And she was probably right...Damon did have a temper.

Mila finally sighed and turned to her father, meeting his gaze without flinching. The color had started to come back into her cheeks, and Ansley thought she could detect some of the fire Damon had deep inside him. "I was out visiting my friends, father. Yes, you have rules, but I am an *adult* now. I have inherited, and I am no longer a child." Mila paused as she glared at her father. He did not respond. Obviously, he was used to this sort of response from his daughter. "As I walked down the path to our home, I saw a dark figure dart into the trees. I didn't know who he was, but it's much too late for anyone to be visiting, let alone skulking outside our house." Mila added.

"Including you." Damon added, disdain dripping from his words. Mila rolled her eyes, choosing not to address Damon's comment. "Anyway, I decided to follow him and see what he was up to. Unfortunately, he had a head-start, and he was much faster than me. By the time I reached the clearing in front of our home, he was already laying on the ground."

Damon's face turned bright red and then to a dark shade of purple. Ansley looked anxiously at Rhyn, unsure if Damon was going to actually explode. Slowly, Damon released a breath, and his face returned to a semi-normal color. He finally responded to his daughter's explanation, and Ansley was shocked at his restraint. "It seems as if you were trying to protect us from this...stranger. For that, I must commend your bravery, Mila; however, you are never to do anything like that again. Understand?" Mila hmphed at her father and ignored his question, eager to be considered one of the adults in the room. Ansley looked at her hands, embarrassed at witnessing this conversation between Damon and his daughter. She wondered what her own father would have said to her if he had been here. Likely something similar…

Rhyn stood behind Ansley's chair with his arms crossed behind his back in thought. Damon shook his head at his teenage daughter's reply and turned to Rhyn and Ansley, "Thank you for rushing to my aid. I…I would have…" he finished quietly. Unable to say the words, Damon closed his eyes in pain.

Ansley nodded silently, and Damon finally sat down beside his daughter. His face was pale, and the silence drifted over them once more. Ansley was not sure how long they sat there. Each of them was so lost in the intensity of what had just happened that no words seemed appropriate to fill the emptiness between them.

Finally, Damon pushed back his chair and stood stiffly. "We should probably…" he said uneasily, gesturing to the door. Ansley felt a shiver run over her as she remembered the form lying motionless outside the house. "Rhyn?" Damon asked. Rhyn nodded in agreement, and the men walked out of the house to dispose of the body. Ansley shuddered as she thought of what that may mean. She and Mila sat quietly at the table, unwilling to comment on what had happened, both eager to move past it.

*****

When the door was thrown open just a few minutes later, both girls jumped in surprise. Ansley was shocked to see Damon and Rhyn coming back inside already. She was not sure how long their task would have taken, but she had expected it to take longer than that. She was even more concerned when she noticed the look of bewilderment on both of the men's faces.

Damon walked over to the table and said softly, "He's gone." Ansley looked up at him in confusion, but before she could ask her questions, Damon dropped a letter on the table. "Read it."

Ansley hesitantly picked up the letter and read through it quickly. Her breath caught in her throat as the words sunk into her.

You have been warned. Do not make us come again.

She looked back at Damon and opened her mouth hesitantly to continue. "What is this?" she finally sputtered. Rhyn spoke this time, moving closer to where Ansley sat. "When we went outside to move him, there was no body there. This note was lying on the bloodstained grass where we left him when we came inside." Rhyn cleared his throat. "We were pretty convinced that he was dead when we came into the house, so this either means that he was still alive, or that someone else moved him." Ansley felt her stomach churn.

"That would mean that someone else was out there...watching and waiting for us to leave him." She responded quietly. Rhyn and Damon nodded silently. Mila also sat silently staring at the note Ansley had laid back on the table after reading it. The girl's eyes were wide with the terror Ansley herself felt and, Ansley assumed, the thought that another attacker could have intervened, possibly killing all of them.

*****

Ansley was not sure how long they sat at the table after this revelation. Her mind felt hazy as the others talked around her. After a few moments, she suppressed a large yawn. Knowing the importance of the next decision they made, Ansley turned her attention back to Damon, who was now speaking, and tried to focus. He talked for some time and moved his hands as he spoke, emphasizing the point he was making. Then, he lifted the letter again and held it out to Rhyn, who took it slowly, nodding at what Damon was saying. As they talked, Ansley found it excruciatingly difficult to hear anything they were saying to one another. Her vision got blurry, so she blinked. She was surprised to find that when she blinked, her eyes almost felt too heavy to open. *What is happening to me?* She thought to herself, frightened of this deep fatigue that was overtaking her.

Ansley narrowed her eyes to focus on Damon and his words, but she could not hold her attention there. Her eyes continued to blur, and she stared at his lips moving without hearing anything he was saying. Finally, Ansley took a deep breath and let her eyes close. It felt so...*needed*... as if her body was begging to be released from consciousness. She fell blissfully into a deep sleep at the table, unaware of the disturbing news Damon had just shared with Rhyn.

*****

Ansley felt as though she had slept for decades. Finally, when she "awoke", she was here. *She was not sure where "here" was, but she knew it was dark and cold. She shivered and walked around the place in search of clues as to why and how she had come here.*

Suddenly, the darkness molded into something different. The images were blurry at first, but when the shapes grew clearer, Ansley noticed that it looked like the outside of her grandmother's home. It was still dark, and she guessed that it was mid-morning. Ansley could not understand what was happening. This is not a dreamvision, *she mused, looking around at each distinct part of the dream.*

Then, a heavy hand fell on her shoulder. Ansley jumped, terrified to find someone here with her, and when she turned, her fears were realized. Rhys stood before her, his face no longer friendly or pretending. Magnus knew that she knew who he was now. He smiled menacingly at her.

"How good of you to finally join me here, Ansley." He said softly. His voice felt like ice in her veins, and she swallowed nervously as she started backing away from him.

"Hi...Rhys. What are you...Why did you bring me here?" She replied, eager to give herself some time while she tried to discover how to flee from him. Magnus took two steps towards Ansley to make up the distance she had placed between them.

"Oh, please, Ansley. Do not toy with me. You know my true name now." He answered her. "Say it." He added with a snarl.

Ansley swallowed again, but she found her throat as dry as sand that had soaked up the midday heat in a desert. Her voice stuck in her throat, and all she could manage to do was to take another two steps away from Magnus.

"Say it." He said again, growling with each word, as he stepped closer to her once more.

"Magnus." Ansley whispered. Her voice came out soft and hoarse in comparison to his voice. His confidence in their situation was maddening to her.

Magnus smiled. "And you must know what I am capable of. Yes?" He took another step towards her. Ansley did not reply, but she glanced to her right and left, trying to find somewhere to hide herself or some weapon she could use.

"Oh, my dear. Do not even try. You cannot escape this

place. We are…bonded." Magnus lifted his hand to show her a white-glowing scar on his palm. Ansley gasped as she realized that scar was from the "blood oath" she had taken with him. She glanced at her own palm to find hers glowing as well. "It is amazing what magic necromancers can work. I shall reward mine when I see him again. I admit that I did not think this trick would work, and so it has!"

"What trick?" Ansley asked in confusion.

"Our bond, my dear. It is what brought you to me. Did you not find me easily enough?"

"You cannot be here! You are no dreamwalker!" Ansley yelled at Magnus. His eyes narrowed in anger at her comment.

"Not yet. But I will be, and you are going to help me. One way or another, but for now, I have Rhys to assist me." Magnus replied. Menace dripped off each of his words, and Ansley felt suddenly colder. She wrapped her arms around herself. "Why did you bring me here?" She asked Magnus, trying to distract his attention from her constant attempts to move away from him.

"Ahhh! Finally, a good question! I brought you here to witness the next step of my plan. You see, I knew you would never come back willingly to me, so I decided I needed a little…leverage." Magnus said happily, gesturing to the cozy home ahead of them in the dark. Dread filled Ansley's stomach and rolled over her, making her nauseous and even colder.

"No. You will not." She said in response.

"I already have, my dear. You see, I am here with you in the dream realm while my people are also at your grandmother's cabin. You cannot stop me. It is done." Magnus smiled at Ansley. "I will keep her until you decide if her freedom is worth your cooperation. If you come

quietly, she will be freed. If not, well, I'm sure I can find some use for her." Magnus laughed coldly. "Then again, what use would I find with an old woman, long past her time? Perhaps, I will dispose of her instead?"

Ansley's eyes widened in fear for Bianca. A vision of her family, lying motionless and covered in the blood of her brothers, flashed before her eyes. "No, please. What do you want with me?" She asked with anguish. "Why are you doing all of this?" Ansley fell to her knees in front of him, and she dropped her head into her hands.

"I want everything, and just as I said before, young one, you will help me attain it. Come to me, and I will not harm her. Ignore this warning, and you will find her body waiting for you when you return home." Magnus growled again.

Ansley shrieked in fear and anger at Magnus's threat. Suddenly, the wind blew fiercely, and Magnus's eyes lifted to look behind Ansley. "You? But how can you be here?" He asked in confusion. "What...?"

The wind's fury increased until Ansley could barely see her hands held out in front of her. Her hair lashed around her face like a whip. Ansley blinked away tears and tried to stand. She could see Magnus covering his face with his arms and shouting, but she could not make out his words. She stumbled away from him, and only looked back once, seeing that the wind had turned into a cyclone and whirled angrily between Magnus and her. Ansley took her chance and ran in the opposite direction, to the house. The wind continued to whip her hair and clothes angrily. She breathed heavily as she tried to outrun its fury.

A hand grabbed Ansley's wrist, vicelike. Ansley shrieked in fear and pulled her arm desperately trying to free herself. Despite her efforts, the hand pulled her closer to its source, and Ansley found herself against a warm chest, protected from the vicious winds. She closed her eyes and smelled the masculine fragrance on the shirt under her nose. When she looked up, she saw Rhyn, holding her with one arm and extending his other arm towards the cyclone, which ravaged the land between Magnus and where they stood. She noticed with surprise that Rhyn had two curved, parallel lines glowing on his brow. He did not look at her. It seemed that the cyclone required all his efforts and attention to control. Ansley closed her eyes and concentrated on leaving this place.

*

Ansley sat up from the table, where her head had been resting. She rubbed her forehead and turned to look at Rhyn, who she noticed had slumped against the wall when he had entered into the dream realm. Damon, Lya, and Mila all sat before her with fear written across their faces. Ansley waited until Rhyn opened his eyes, to break the silence. "How did you find me?" She squeaked, as he suppressed a yawn.

He smiled weakly; his energy spent. "Magnus may share a bond with you, Ansley, but you and I also have one. There is nowhere you can go that I cannot find you." Rhyn reached towards Ansley and placed his hand on her shoulder in an attempt to comfort her. "Are you alright?"

Ansley sighed. "No. I am afraid that we have run out of time."

CHAPTER TWENTY-SIX
Ansley

Ansley held her head in her hands and covered her face with her fingers. It was useless! She had tried to send a dream summons to her grandmother five times already with no answer. The others sat silently around the table watching her, and Kenna stood in the doorway, looking around in confusion.

"I can't reach her!" Ansley groaned into her hands. "He was telling the truth I suppose..." She added unhappily. Ansley felt a hand rest on her shoulder in a comforting gesture. She turned to look up at Rhyn, whose face was lined with worry.

"We knew he was biding his time, Ansley, but that doesn't mean he has won. We will save her. I promise you this." His eyes were earnest and displayed his determination to defeat Magnus.

"But you can't promise that! We don't even know where they are! How are we supposed to help her and Rhys if we cannot find them?" Ansley replied hopelessly.

Damon frowned, but said, "I can scry for them." At this, Lya reached over from where she sat and covered Damon's hand with hers. "I have done it before, and I am willing to do it again, if it is needed."

Ansley looked at her mentor and took in his appearance. Age lines marked that once smooth face, and his hair now had streaks of grey from his last attempt at scrying for Kenna. Ansley's gaze fell to her own hands. She knew she could not ask this of Damon. It was too dangerous.

"I do not think that is necessary, Damon." Kenna replied, turning everyone's attention to her presence. She walked slowly into the room, holding her shoulder in pain. "It's true that Magnus is conniving and manipulative, but he also seems determined to make his actions known. I believe he will find a way to draw Ansley to him when he is ready for her."

Damon nodded silently, and Ansley wondered if he was trying to formulate a new plan. Silence fell heavily on the room once more, and Ansley felt suffocated by it. Tears caught in her throat, and her chest grew tight. Suddenly, the room felt too small for her. She rose, pushed her chair back, and walked to the door. "I need some air," she said tightly.

Ansley stepped outside into the darkness and let the cool breeze fill her lungs. Rogue tears fell from her eyes, but she made no effort to conceal them. Instead, she sat down on the steps of Damon's porch and looked up at the night sky. There was a full moon tonight. The light was so bright that it looked the moon was trying to challenge the sun. Stars winked at her from distances she could not comprehend, and she searched vigilantly until she found a small, familiar group of them. Even in Calvenia, her family's constellation, the Bear, guarded over her.

"Father, Mother…" she started, unsure of what she was trying to say. "I am lost here without you." She finished truthfully. Emotion flowed from her eyes and dripped down her chin. The breeze blew once more, chilling the tracks of her tears. A sob rose in her chest, and Ansley, unwilling to fight it anymore, let it take over.

She was not sure how long she sat there or how long she cried, but when she began to settle down again, Ansley noticed someone standing behind her. She wiped her face carefully and turned, expecting to see Rhyn. She was surprised to see Kenna instead. Kenna smiled warmly at her and gestured to the spot beside Ansley in question. Ansley nodded and moved to give Kenna room to sit down.

Kenna sat silently and looked up at the stars like Ansley had done moments earlier. Ansley watched Kenna search the sky, wondering what she was looking for. Finally, Kenna pointed up and said, "There. You see those stars near the Hunter? That is the Fish. My family's constellation. Most dreamwalkers agree it is the most difficult to locate, even on a night as clear as this one." Kenna paused and looked at Ansley. Then, she turned back to the sky again and added, "My mother and father wait for me in the afterlife also."

Ansley looked at Kenna in surprise. Kenna dropped her head, saying softly, "Ansley, I know you feel so alone now, and it is truly a tragedy you have been forced to endure, losing your family. I too lost my parents, but I lost them at a much younger age than you. I always felt...*unsure* of myself and of who I really was without them around." Kenna paused, twiddling with her fingers for a moment as if trying to decide on the right words to say. "I do not pretend to know you or your grandmother, but she is a lovely and bright woman. Please do not lose hope for her. She has not left you yet, and you know she won't if she has a choice." Kenna placed her hand on Ansley's and squeezed reassurance into her fingers. Ansley simply nodded in reply.

"You are not alone here," Kenna began again. "You have Damon, Rhyn, Lya, and me. We may be a wayward group, but Ansley, we will not abandon you. You can count on us, so don't be afraid. We will face Magnus together."

Ansley squeezed Kenna's hand in return, and Kenna stood and turned back towards the door of the house. "When you are ready, come back inside. Damon found something else on the note left by the attackers. We hope that it may give us more information about who is hunting us. At least, who is hunting us in Calvenia." Kenna rolled her eyes, and Ansley reluctantly smiled as she watched her friend walk back inside.

*****

Ansley walked back into the house a few moments after Kenna left. She heard the others' voices, so she entered the kitchen quietly, trying not to disturb the conversation. Lya stood behind Mila's chair, trying to take in the information Damon imparted to her.

Damon held the short note in his hand and pointed to one of the corners. The others leaned forward in their chairs to see what he was pointing out, but Ansley could not make out anything from where she stood. Ansley stood next to Rhyn, where he leaned against the wall. He turned and smiled at her in response before turning his attention back to Damon, who had continued speaking in a hurried tone.

"…it has to be them! This proves it!" Damon finished excitedly.

Lya and Mila frowned and looked at Damon questioningly. Lya spoke first, "Damon, dear, it is an *imprint*. I can't even see it." At that, Damon moved closer to his wife and thrust the note into her hands.

"See! There!" He pointed to the corner, and Lya lifted the note closer to her face to look for the imprint Damon had pointed out.

"I don't see why it matters if it is their symbol or not. We still don't know who these people are." Kenna said, as

Lya examined the paper. Lya turned to Damon in surprise and said, "You're right. It's their seal." Damon smiled at her and kissed his wife quickly on the cheek.

"What seal?" Kenna asked in frustration. Damon moved over to her and handed her the letter to let her examine it herself. "The seal of the Calvenian government." Damon responded.

Ansley felt puzzled. "Damon, why would *they* have anything to do with this?" She asked angrily.

"Well, I think that is the big question. But we are obviously digging in something that they don't want us to learn anything about. Maybe they are invested in keeping it quiet too?"

"Keeping what quiet?" Rhyn asked. Ansley glanced around at the others and wasn't surprised to see that they were all struggling to follow Damon's reasoning. Damon sighed heavily.

"Information about Magnus! They do not want us here digging because they have some investment in his well-being. *Or*…they have something else they are trying to hide from Magnus themselves." Damon finished suspiciously.

"But what would the government want to hide from Magnus?" Ansley asked exasperatedly.

Damon smiled mischievously at Ansley. "My dear, the government always has something to hide. It isn't the "what" we need to wonder about. We should focus instead on the "why"." Damon responded slyly.

Ansley held her head in her hands. All the questions seemed to multiply, and they seemed just as far from answers to the questions that had brought them to Calvenia as they had ever been.

"So, what do we do now?" Rhyn asked, eager to form a plan.

"We need answers, and the only way we can find those is to keep digging." Damon said, looking at his wife, who nodded her agreement.

"When do we start then?" Ansley asked, pushing for their plan to be set.

"Tomorrow morning." Lya answered her. "We will return to the hall of records and stay until we find something to answer at least one of the questions we have."

Ansley nodded and said, "Good. Then I will see you bright and early." Ansley moved from the kitchen in the direction of one of the small rooms she was sharing with Kenna. She did not wait for an answer or for the others to reply. She walked straight into that room and shut the door on all the thoughts, worries, and endless amounts of confusion that seemed to be circulating in this house tonight.

CHAPTER TWENTY-SEVEN
Bianca

Bianca opened her eyes and found herself in a dark chamber. Her thoughts were fuzzy, and she felt disoriented. Bianca wondered if she had been drugged. Her temple also pounded, so she reached to her temple to check for blood. Her arm wouldn't extend fully, which confused Bianca further. Using her fingers to investigate in the darkness, she realized her hands had been chained to the floor on a metal ring near her feet. The chain clinked as she moved her hands, trying to stretch them towards her face, but the chain was too short. Baffled, Bianca blinked her eyes as they adjusted to the darkly lit chamber.

When she looked to her right, a young man sat about ten feet from her with his hands chained also, but his dangled from a ring above his head. He was silent, and his chin drooped onto his chest. His hair was long and obscured his face, making it impossible for Bianca to identify him. Bianca could not be certain the man was still alive.

She turned to her left and saw another man chained in a similar fashion. But this man she recognized. Bianca scooted herself along the floor closer to him until her chain was taut. "Hey! Wake up!" She hissed at the man. "Alden! Are you alright?" She asked in a whisper, trying not to draw attention from her captors. Alden did not move, but suddenly, Bianca heard the young man's chain jingling. She turned to look back at him and was astonished by how much blood covered his face. Dried blood was caked from his forehead to his chin. Bianca shuddered at the thought of how much this man had been through and also what her near future may hold.

"-s no use," the man said, slurring his words around lips that were swollen. "He has been out since they dragged you both in here."

Bianca hastened a glance back at Alden who remained motionless. "Do you think he is dead?" She asked quietly.

"No. I heard the guards talking. They had to drug him to get him to cooperate. He will likely wake up with a bad headache and no idea how he got here." The man replied. He spat on the floor, and Bianca was not surprised to see that he had spit out blood.

"Who are you? Where am I? And how did I get here?" Bianca asked in a rush, as she scooted herself away from Alden and towards the other man.

The stranger remained silent for a moment, as if gathering his thoughts. Bianca was almost worried he had fallen asleep, but then he lifted his head, looking at her with defeated eyes. "Two guards brought you in with a bag over your head, but you were unconscious. I suppose they drugged you too. My name is Rhys of the Brooks, and I am sorry to say, Bianca, but you have been brought to Orco's hel." The man shuddered and continued, "and there is no way out of here. Trust me. I have tried."

"Orco's hel? What do you mean? Why would anyone bring me here, and who would want to hurt Alden and me?" Bianca asked, flustered by Rhys's answers. "Wait a second. You said your name is Rhys? You are *not* Rhys... I have met him, and he looks nothing like you."

"Well, you *thought* it was me when you were actually meeting our captor, who could be confused for Orco, the god of death himself. Magnus Black." Rhys answered softly.

"Magnus of the Blacks?" Bianca asked, confusion filling her thoughts. "But that means that he is a relative of mine? What would he want with me that would lead to this?" Bianca asked, lifting her chained hands to gesture around the chamber.

"Absolutely nothing. But when it comes to Ansley, that's a different story." Rhys answered.

*****

Magnus walked slowly down the corridor leading into his dungeons. Three sets of footsteps echoed in the silent hall. Magnus walked quickly, trailed by Gyan and Dane. Magnus held his hands, fingers laced, behind his back as he walked. He thought to himself of his most recent accomplishment and smiled at the thought of another piece of his plan falling into place.

Gyan walked a few steps faster than his master, moving in front of Magnus, to open the door to the dungeon. Gyan found the brass key on the heavy keyring he carried and opened the door which creaked as if it had remained closed for centuries. *Perhaps it has been closed for centuries before,* Magnus thought to himself. *But now, now I finally have my enemies captured and occupying it.*

Magnus stepped into the dark chamber and immediately pulled a handkerchief from inside his cloak to cover his nose and mouth. The stench was almost unbearable. Magnus was not surprised when he heard Dane gag behind him. When Magnus's stomach had regained its composure, he stepped closer to the bars of the first cell. "Open it, Gyan." He said, his voice muffled by the handkerchief.

"Yes, master." Gyan responded dutifully, and he stepped forward with the keyring once more. The door was pulled open to reveal Magnus's three prisoners. His own keys to bringing Ansley back to him.

Magnus stepped into the cell. Gyan rushed forward with a nearby stool, but Magnus waved him off. "I will not linger."

Magnus stepped closer to the prisoner in the middle, with her hands chained to the floor. "Well, Bianca. It is nice to see you again." He said, disdain dripping from his lips.

The woman lifted her head to glare at him. "You may think yourself clever, but I know who you are and why you brought me here. You will never succeed, Magnus." Bianca spat at him, her voice almost a whisper.

Magnus chuckled as he lowered his handkerchief. He glanced in Rhys's direction. "I see you have enjoyed your company today? I suppose it has been some time since you have had another dreamwalker to speak with. Well, don't worry. We will correct that now." Magnus said as he snapped his fingers. Rhys's head shot up to look in the direction of the cell door as three guards entered.

"No!!!" Rhys screamed as he struggled to move out of the guards' reach. "Leave me. LEAVE ME!" Rhys roared, thrashing with renewed strength that he didn't have moments before. The guards cornered him before scooping him off the floor. They unlocked his chains and quickly bound his hands with rope before turning back to Magnus for direction.

"My study, please. Stay with him. I will join you soon." Magnus ordered.

The guards nodded and pulled Rhys out of the cell. Magnus laughed as he looked at the shock on Bianca's face. "This can be easy, you know. You can tell me where she is, or you can even summon her yourself." Magnus said, as he paced in front of Bianca. "Once she arrives, you are free to go. Free to live out the rest of your life in peace.

I have no quarrel with you."

"If you have a quarrel with Ansley, then you also have one with me." Bianca hissed. "You must have had a *horrible* mother if she taught you that family would betray one another so easily! I would never trade her life for mine, and I will never see her hurt!" Bianca finished, raising her chin to show her courage in spite of Magnus moving closer to her.

"Horrible mother? Yes, I did have one, but I was the one who taught *her* how family can betray you easily." Magnus turned away and walked to the door of the cell. Then, he paused for a moment to look back at Bianca. "Very well. I supposed you would be difficult, but it was worth a try. I will say, I do enjoy dramatic endings much more anyway." He finished as he left the cell and motioned for Gyan to lock the door.

Magnus began his walk back up the corridor towards his chambers to deal with Rhys. *What a weasel...*Magnus thought angrily. He had been angry that Rhys had denied him the opportunity to see Bianca's shock when she learned who Magnus really was. Magnus sighed deeply. "Dane, I suppose we should begin with the next stage. Please inform our followers of our success in capturing the grandmother and elder. They will be pleased."

"Yes, master." Dane replied as he turned and began walking down a different corridor, towards the gathered masses that had begun to support Magnus's cause.

Magnus continued with Gyan trailing him. "Gyan, how long do you estimate this stage will last?" He asked his advisor.

"I am not sure, my Lord." Gyan replied. "We will try to make our plans quickly, but without knowing where she is, we cannot be certain when we will find her. She is crucial to the next stage, as you know."

Magnus nodded and sighed again. "Well, let's try using the boy. Rhys may be able to help us locate her again."

"Yes, lord." Gyan answered as they stepped into Magnus's chambers where Rhys awaited his punishment.

CHAPTER TWENTY-EIGHT
Ansley

Ansley stood close to Kenna in the dream realm. Kenna stretched her fingers towards the ground and slowly lifted her hands. Small slivers of rock shot out of the ground and up into the air. Kenna held them easily and turned to Ansley, "Are you ready?" She asked.

Ansley nodded, moving away from Kenna. Once there was around six feet between them, Kenna let the rocks fly one by one towards Ansley, who practiced dodging them. Ansley moved as quickly as she could, but one rock caught her on her forearm, drawing blood. "Ouch!" Ansley yelled. "You aren't supposed to let them hit me!" She said to Kenna.

"How is this supposed to be realistic training if there is no danger, Ansley?" Kenna replied. "Damon wanted you to train today, and if you train with me, we do it my way." She added. Kenna knelt to the ground and placed her palms on the dirt. The ground began to shake and a light glowed under Kenna's hands. Worried, Ansley moved a few feet further from Kenna. "What are you...?" She started to ask, but then, Kenna had broken the ground into a deep chasm.

The ground near the chasm was tilting down, and rocks tumbled into the endless pit. Ansley's balance was off, and she fell scrambling onto her chest. She struggled to grab hold of anything nearby to avoid sliding down into the chasm, but there was nothing around her except dirt. Ansley dug her fingernails into the dusty earth as her feet went over the edge of the chasm. "Ahhh.... Kenna!" Ansley yelled, unsure of how to save herself.

"Ansley, I won't let you come to harm, but I will only rescue you if you absolutely need it. You must help yourself! Use your strength or your skills. Right now, I am no longer Kenna to you." Kenna responded, her voice moving as she walked in a circle around Ansley.

Ansley felt hot anger pulse through her fingertips as her grip began slipping. "But I am a seer! What do you expect me to do?" She yelled through clenched teeth. Suddenly, the earth began moving beneath her hands as another earthquake shook the ground. Ansley lost her grip and slid towards the chasm. Her body fell down, and she grasped desperately at the edge before finding herself in a freefall. Panic coursed through her, and her heart beat frantically inside her chest.

Ansley closed her eyes as her own screams echoed through her mind. All at once, Ansley felt a pulling sensation on her chest that lasted for just a moment before she collapsed onto a patch of soft grass. Ansley covered her eyes with her hands, trying to catch her breath. Then, she felt around her uncertainly. No injuries. No rocks. This was not right.

Ansley raised her head from the ground and saw herself in a field she did not recognize. She stood and turned in a circle and saw Kenna running towards her and yelling her name.

Kenna reached Ansley and spewed questions like a fountain, but Ansley was unable to hear them correctly. What had she just done? How had she gotten here? Had she transferred herself again?

*****

Kenna opened the door for Ansley as the pair entered

Damon's house. Ansley kept her gaze on the floor, trying to ignore the mounting headache she had. Rhyn met Kenna and her at the door to the kitchen and smiled at Ansley. Kenna shook her head briefly at him, and Rhyn moved to the side to allow Ansley to pass.

"What happened?" Ansley heard him ask Kenna. But she never heard her reply. She walked into the kitchen, mindlessly grabbed a cup of black coffee from Lya, and sat at the table. Her mind was drifting in and out of the present moment, and Ansley wondered if it was a side effect of what she had just experienced. She took a small sip of the brew she held and felt more grounded afterwards.

Ansley heard the door to the cabin open and quickly slam closed. She heard voices talking and recognized one as Mila's. Mila walked into the kitchen and spotted Ansley. "There you are! I've been looking for you." Mila said with a smile.

"Why?" Ansley asked, still weakened by her unusual experience.

"Someone is here to see you." Mila replied as she moved out of the doorway, allowing room for Josilyn to enter.

"*Ansley*! I am so glad I found you!" Josilyn said, as she sat down beside Ansley.

"What...what are you *doing* here, Jos?" Ansley asked in surprise.

Josilyn smiled and touched her friend's hand. "Your grandmother sent me of course! I arrived in Calvenia about two days ago, and I have been moving up the coast looking for you since then. I was lucky to meet Mila here in Dunbar this morning." Josilyn explained, glancing at Mila. Ansley could have sworn that Josilyn's cheeks reddened with her last comment, but in an instant,

Josilyn's attention was back on her friend.

"What happened to you? Ansley, you look horrible!" Josilyn exclaimed.

"Lots of things have happened since we left, Jos, but I suppose you mean *just* now. I'm not sure what happened exactly, but I think I transferred myself to a new dream location." Ansley said quietly, before taking another sip of coffee. It scalded her tongue, but the warmth felt good in her chest. "But never mind about that. Our biggest concern is that my grandmother has been captured, and we have to get her back before something worse happens to her." Ansley added. She paused before asking her friend, "Did you sense she was in danger before you left?"

Josilyn's eyebrows had risen in surprise, and her eyes were filled with fear. "No! She seemed safe enough. She was just worried about you. If I had known she was being watched, I wouldn't have left her, Ansley, I swear."

Ansley nodded sadly. Josilyn's fear faded from her face, and something stronger flashed across her countenance. This was the resolve Ansley had always loved about her friend.

"Tell me what you need me to do, Ansley. I am here to help you." Josilyn answered with a determination Ansley had never quite seen in her before, despite their years of friendship.

CHAPTER TWENTY-NINE
Damon

Damon laid down on his bed while Lya stood beside him. She had not left his side since the revelation they had shared at the table with Ansley and the others about the Calvenian government being involved in the attack. Damon kept glancing at her every few minutes, still worried for his family's safety. He was worried what the government being involved in this situation may mean politically for Calvenia, but he would die before he saw Lya or Mila harmed, even if it meant getting exiled from yet another country.

"Are you sure that dreamwalking is the best way to spend your time right now?" Lya asked softly. Damon noticed that she was keeping her voice low to keep the sound from traveling into the common room where the others prepared for dreamwalking together.

Damon nodded. "I think the best thing we can do now is prepare for any outcome, even the worst outcome possible. Continuing Ansley's training is important to prioritize before we begin digging for answers again. I fear that as soon as we go back to the hall of records, we will be in danger again."

"Yes, I worry you're right. Take your time then, dear. I'm not sure we can avoid that danger for long, but we will find the answers we need very soon. One way or another." Lya responded with a frown. She lifted her hand and placed it on Damon's cheek, and he leaned in to give her a soft kiss.

"I have work to do. Try not to fret while I am away, and *please*...keep an eye on our daughter." Damon said before kissing his wife's hand. Lya nodded with a smile, and she turned to walk out of the room. Damon let his head hit the pillow, and in an instant, he was in a dream.

*****

Damon stepped into the dream realm as fluidly as he would climb into a horse's saddle. He glanced around and was taking in the surroundings he had agreed upon: dense jungles with drooping vines, strange noises, and darkness that seemed to envelope him. Dreams could be so realistic, but the one thing that would make this setting real was missing. The animals. Animals were something that most dreams lacked, unless the dreamer had a specific attachment to one.

A heavy hand grasped Damon's shoulder, and he turned to see Rhyn standing behind him. He had lifted a finger to his lips to tell Damon to be quiet. Damon nodded silently, and Rhyn pointed out a clearing. Damon pushed aside the vines that obscured his view and glanced in the direction Rhyn had motioned. Damon saw Ansley sitting on a fallen log amidst the trees and hanging vines. She was waiting with a handkerchief tied over her eyes.

Damon moved closer to Rhyn and mouthed, "Where are the others?"

"Plotting somewhere on the other side," Rhyn whispered with a grin. He rubbed his hands together in anticipation and said, "Do you think this will help her?"

Damon looked up at Rhyn and saw fear in his green eyes. "We have to prepare her for the worst and most dangerous dreams. We cannot protect her every waking moment, and I fear that I did not prepare her enough with the training we started in Arvenia."

Rhyn glanced over Damon's shoulder at Ansley and frowned. "Shall we begin?" He asked.

Damon nodded and said, "You're up first." Rhyn grinned, and he stepped through the hanging vines, ducking his head to avoid the low hanging limbs of the surrounding trees. Rhyn walked several steps towards Ansley and held his hands up in front of him. Damon waited, unsure of what to expect of a wielder of air. It had been a long time since he had worked with one. Suddenly, a gust of wind blasted from Rhyn's hands in Ansley's direction. She fell off the log but rolled onto her hands and knees quickly. But Damon noticed something strange happening.

Ansley leaned her head down to the ground, murmuring to herself quietly. Quickly, she lifted her head to look in Rhyn's direction. She ripped the blindfold off her face and her eyes glowed eerily blue. Then, Rhyn was gone. Damon turned a quick circle, but he did not see the boy. He peered back at Ansley, and she was sitting up now, holding her head in her hands.

Damon ran through the vines and into the clearing. He knelt in front of Ansley and grasped her hands in his, pulling them off her face. "Where did you send him, Ansley?" he asked.

"I don't know." Ansley replied with a fearful look in her eyes. "I don't know what happened."

Damon let go of Ansley and yelled into the darkness, "Rhyn!"

Josilyn and Kenna ran to his voice and started when they saw Ansley was so upset. Kenna ran to her and brushed Ansley's hair from her face. "Settle down. It's okay. It's okay, Ans." Kenna whispered to Ansley. Then she pulled her into a hug as Ansley let out a sob.

"Rhyn!" Damon yelled again, cupping his hands

around his mouth. "Rhyn! Josilyn, help me find him!" Damon said to Josilyn who was standing dumbstruck in the clearing.

They searched for another ten minutes with no luck. Finally, an idea struck Damon. He walked back over to Ansley and Kenna. "Ansley," he said as he sat down beside her. "You have to bring him back now.*" Ansley sighed and covered her eyes with her hand.*

"I can try…" she said softly. Damon placed his hand on Ansley's shoulder to comfort her and waited to see if she would succeed.

The group was quiet as they watched Ansley try to summon this new skill. Then, Ansley's eyes glowed blue once more, and Rhyn appeared from thin air and fell onto the ground at her feet. He coughed violently and turned to his side to vomit water. He was drenched and shivered although the air was warm.

Damon, Josilyn, and Kenna helped Rhyn to his feet. Ansley glanced at him in guilt. "Where were you?" Damon asked. Rhyn shook his head.

"I dunno…" he sputtered, water dripping from his hair and off the end of his nose. "If I had to guess, I would say the Treacherous Seas. Thank the gods I can swim."

Damon and Kenna turned to Ansley. Ansley's face was stark white, and her eyes were bright. Damon did not have time to reach her before Ansley collapsed onto the ground. The others looked at Damon for direction. "Training is over. Everyone, get some rest tonight. I will take care of her." He said motioning towards Ansley's crumpled form.

"I won't leave her tonight until I know that she is okay." Rhyn said hoarsely. Damon nodded in agreement as Kenna and Josilyn disappeared from the dream. He let Rhyn go next and then walked over to Ansley. Damon had never done this before, but he had seen other

dreamwalkers reunite a spirit and body. He knew the dangers of leaving Ansley's spirit here unattended. If they did not help her find her way back, she may be lost in the dream realm. Dreamwalkers were considered "masters" of dreams, but they had a tendency to prefer dreams to reality. Gingerly, Damon picked up Ansley's motionless form and held her as he closed his eyes and left the dream.

*

When Damon sat up in the bed, he kept his eyes closed, trying to focus on holding Ansley's spirit in his arms. He moved with his eyes shut through his home to the common room, where he knew that her body lay. Thankful that he had avoided any bumps or obstacles, Damon released Ansley's spirit. Once he felt the weight leave his hands, he opened his eyes and was relieved to see Ansley sitting up in front of him.

"What happened?" She asked him. Her voice quivered, and Damon was reminded of her age and naivety, despite her extraordinary use of transference. Rhyn sat up from his makeshift pallet and waited for Damon's reply.

"I believe you used your transference again." Damon said, crossing his arms. "Kenna said you did it earlier today, so it seems you are learning how to control it."

Ansley shook her head. "I don't know where or how I sent him away. I could have *killed* him, Damon!" She turned back to face Rhyn and grasped his hand quickly. "I'm so sorry!" She whispered. A tear rolled down her cheek. Rhyn wiped it away gently, letting his hand linger on her face.

"Well, now that we know you can control it, we need more answers. Get some rest. Both of you. In the morning, we are going back to the hall of records." Damon turned away from the room and left Ansley and Rhyn, not wanting to intrude on their intimate moment. He walked into his bedchamber once more and unscrewed the top of the flask he had set aside with his cloak. He lifted the flask to his lips but knew whiskey would not drive away the memory of what he had just witnessed.

CHAPTER THIRTY
The following day...
Ansley

Ansley trudged into the hall of records, following Damon, Kenna, Rhyn, and Josilyn. Her head throbbed this morning, probably from her use of transference last night. She stifled a large yawn as she grouchily made her way through the hall. After her mishap in training, Damon had forgone all attempts at "playing it safe" by waiting to return to the hall of records. He hoped that they would find answers to at least one of the questions they now had regarding Magnus and Ansley, not to mention why the Calvenian government was targeting them as well. The sun had not risen yet, but Damon had insisted on starting early. It didn't matter to Ansley *when* they went anyway. She had not slept any after Damon left Rhyn and her alone.

The events of last night played over in her mind, and she shuddered. The air was turning colder still with the change of seasons, but Ansley knew it was not the cold that made her shiver. *How can something so alien and dangerous exist inside me? Something I cannot control and know nothing about?* She wondered sadly. Rhyn, who was walking in front of her, reached back and grabbed her hand. She smiled at him, and he returned her smile. At least he seemed to understand that she had not meant to send him away.

After Damon had left the common room, Rhyn and Ansley had sat up together talking. Their conversation played through her mind now as she held his hand tightly.

She had worried that he was furious with her, but he had been more worried about her than himself.

"Ansley, I am fine. I promise. Are *you* okay? You scared me, fainting like that." Rhyn had said to her.

"Yea, it was weird. I have never blacked out in a dream before." She had admitted. "Why do you think it happened?"

Rhyn had put his arm around her shoulders, and Ansley hugged her knees to her chest. "I think you just overexerted yourself. I am glad Damon knew what to do."

"What would have happened if he had not brought me back to myself?" She had inquired, almost afraid to hear the answer.

Rhyn had shrugged and said, "Let's not think about things that are of no concern right now. You need to rest."

Ansley had rolled her eyes at him then. "You know I can't after I sent you to the middle of the Treacherous Seas." Rhyn had chuckled and responded, "Me either. I still have salt water in my nose." He had coughed after that and beat on his chest humorously to lighten her mood.

Ansley dropped Rhyn's hand, as they walked in the hall of records, and thought of his brother, or Magnus, she supposed. So many things had happened since her inheritance ceremony, and it seemed that the list of things she didn't understand just continued to grow. She followed Rhyn past the table where Ceorl had sat with them before, and she dropped into a chair, happy to let the others do the searching this morning. A hand touched her back, in reassurance, and she smiled when she saw it was Kenna's.

Ansley waited at the table for the others to share anything interesting they found. It unsettled her to realize that today they were also searching for answers about her. Magnus was supposed to be the dangerous one. Not *her*. She sighed, folded her arms on the table, and laid her head down.

*****

"Ansley," A friendly voice whispered as a hand shook her shoulder, pulling her out of a deep, dreamless sleep.

"Mmm?" She answered, raising her head from the table and rubbing the sleep from her eyes. Rhyn sat beside her, and the others sat all around them with stacks of books partially obscuring their faces. Ansley knew hours must have passed since she first dozed. She had rested her eyes only intending to meditate peacefully to push away her troubling thoughts. She was surprised they had let her rest so long. Mila still stalked up and down the aisles in search of something. She must have joined the group at the hall of records while Ansley was asleep.

Rhyn placed his hand on her arm. "We think we found something." He said.

Ansley yawned and looked at the others. Damon spoke first, holding a heavy volume open before him. "This History of the Dreamwalkers, Book Four, outlines the events of a gruesome attack on Terra. It says, 'The king's guard left before dawn and positioned themselves among the Terrans. Each man, woman, and child were removed from their homes, questioned, under pressure if needed, and disposed of. King Deryn's search for what were called *skills* had drawn to a close. He had found these skills and the people who had hidden them from him all along."

"What does that have…" Ansley started.

"Wait, there's more. 'Deryn's necromancer, Dominic, was the first to discover the crystals," Ansley gasped in response to this statement and noted that the others' eyes were wide as well. They were taking in every word Damon spoke. "It says, 'Dominic was the one who discovered their use and assisted with *skill-removal* during this attack, later named the *Black Night*.' Well, that gives us answers about the crystals," Damon said, slamming the book shut.

"So, that's how the typicals got them. They had a necromancer helping them." Kenna added.

Damon nodded, "And Darby believed that Magnus is likely to have one too. Making him more dangerous."

Rhyn chewed on his lower lip in thought, and Josilyn met Ansley's gaze. "Did anyone find anything about Ansley's new skill?" She asked them.

Footsteps echoed in the hall, and Mila walked up to the table carrying one small volume. The book was small enough to fit inside a pocket, and Mila waved it in the air triumphantly before placing it in front of Josilyn. "This book may have some answers."

Josilyn looked up at Mila and smiled, blushing. "Thank you." Mila shrugged and took the seat on the other side of Kenna. Ansley noticed Josilyn's reaction to Mila but was too eager about the new volume to address it now. "What is it?" Ansley inquired.

"A book of myths." Mila replied with a grin.

"How can that *possibly* help us?" Rhyn asked, obviously annoyed with Mila's arrogance at finding the answer when the others had been searching fruitlessly for hours.

"It details how the dreamwalkers were made by the gods. If you read this translation-the first translation of the myth-it details the specific skills of the *first* seer." Mila stated. Rhyn looked dubious, so Mila gestured to the book and said, "Read it. You'll see what I mean."

Rhyn reached for the volume and turned to the chapter about humans and dreamwalkers. He read silently to himself for a few moments before handing the book to Ansley, his eyes wide with surprise. "She was right."

"Of course, I am right." Mila responded, crossing her

arms stubbornly. Damon looked in her direction and raised an eyebrow at his daughter, who simply glared back at him, challenging him to say something to her. Damon sighed and turned his attention back to Ansley.

"Go ahead, Ansley. Read it aloud for us, please." Ansley took the book from Rhyn, found the line he pointed to, and began reading. "Line 459 is titled, 'The Birth of the Dreamwalkers'," Rhyn shook his head and pointed further down the page. Ansley started again, "Okay, so it just went through how Stellos had betrayed the gods. Then, Matrisa appealed to Vito once more on behalf of her children. Here it is, Line 528 says:

'So, Kius and Vito decided that men were too easily swayed to have such an array of skills. To prevent a rebellion in the future, Vito chose to separate the powers forever, never to be connected inside a single dreamwalker again. He placed his hands over the world to spread them amongst the people.

"Wait!" Kius urged. He whispered into the god's ear to ask that a fifth skill be added to ensure the dreamwalkers had a secret weapon against Orco, and Vito nodded in agreement. Vito took a knife and drew a drop of blood from his hand. Then, he had Sophia, his daughter and goddess of wisdom, add a drop of her own blood. Vito poured the blood into a vial and then gave it to Kius, who took it with him into a dream. With Vito's help, he created a new dreamwalker. He made this dreamwalker female because he knew that women could sense the follies of men. Kius then knelt on the ground and poured the blood onto the dry earth. From that spot a tree grew with ripe apples hanging from it. Kius picked and gave an apple to the dreamwalker to eat, and when she consumed it, her eyes glowed blue. She glowed with the power of the gods. She had the power to move and destroy. But because she was mortal, Vito limited this new skill to only *one* dreamwalker. For Kius and Vito knew that mortals were too weak to be endowed with so much power.'"

Ansley finished reading, and when she looked up at the others, she saw them staring at her. She turned to Mila, and asked, "So, is *that* supposed to be *transference*? It never says that here."

"It doesn't, but I believe that's what you have been given, yes. I was bored earlier and started looking in the myths section. I started reading this one for fun and happened upon this different version of the familiar legend. I have a feeling that it's been censored from all other versions." She said calmly.

"But *why*?" Ansley asked.

This time, Damon answered. "Because you are given that power in case something goes wrong, and if others knew, they would surely kill you, possibly to take it for themselves."

Ansley swallowed, but her throat still felt dry. She turned back to Rhyn, whose gaze was steady and determined. "This changes everything, Ansley. Now we have a weapon."

"A weapon?" She heard herself ask him uncertainly.

"Yes." Rhyn responded. "We have *you*."

CHAPTER THIRTY-ONE
Kenna

When they arrived back at Damon's cabin, Lya was cooking for them. She had the kitchen table covered with so many delectable foods that Kenna's mouth began watering immediately. An aroma filled the room from a roasted turkey, and a soup made from carrots, potatoes, and a few other vegetables was still boiling over the cooking fire. Lya had also baked fresh bread and opened what looked like a new jar of jellied blackberries to use with the bread. Dessert was still resting on the stove-a pie filled with fresh apples. Kenna could hardly wait to dig into the feast.

Kenna's stomach growled angrily at her as she walked away from the kitchen to the room she was now sharing with Josilyn and Ansley. It was small, but the girls were all so thankful for Lya's hospitality that none of them minded the lack of privacy. Kenna glanced behind her to ensure that nobody had followed, and she closed the door quietly, securing the bolt. She could hear the others setting the table and readying themselves for that delicious meal. They would be too preoccupied to miss her.

Kenna walked to the bed, the only bed that occupied the room. She smoothed out the quilt and sat down. Kenna took a deep breath and reached inside her cloak to remove the volume she had hidden there. Kenna had chanced upon it while digging in the Calvenian history section of the hall of records. She ran her fingers over the cover, which was old, but still in good condition. The lettering was a shiny golden color, and a coat of arms took up almost the entire cover. This coat of arms was one that was familiar to Kenna, and it had caused her such confusion when she had noticed it earlier as she was searching shelf after dusty shelf of books for something significant. The coat of arms was made of two stallions. This was the same family crest that was displayed on one+ of the walls in Kenna and Edric's flat. The cover had baffled her, but Kenna had been even more alarmed when she had read the title. In bold letters across the cover, it read *The Calvenian Royal Family.*

Kenna still remembered how her breath had hitched after reading those words. In fact, she was not sure she had caught her breath since then. Her chest was tight, and she found it difficult to think clearly. But, she *needed* to know, so she opened the cover and began flipping through the pages.

Kenna was not sure what she was looking for, but within a few minutes, she discovered it. Almost at the end of the book, she found a large black and white portrait displaying a family, all with grim expressions. A father and mother stood side-by-side, and seated below them were four children. "The king and queen of Calvenia", Kenna read to herself. Two girls and two boys. The girls looked almost eight to ten years older than the two boys, but the father's hand rested on the shoulder of the oldest of the boys. No, the king's hand rested on the shoulder of his *heir*.

The child's face was round, still the face of a young boy, and his eyes were bright. He had an energy about him that filled her soul, even when just looking at his picture. The names of the children were listed below the photo, but Kenna did not read them. No, she would know that face anywhere. That was *Edric*, and she supposed this was his family. This was certainly why he refused to return here. Kenna tried to calm herself but could not quite stop the hot, angry tears from rolling down her cheeks. She wiped them away hastily. *He lied to me! He is no fisherman.*

Kenna read the heading above the picture and felt her heart stop for a moment. *Could this really get any worse?* It read, "The Last of the Royals-A Dynasty Falls". Kenna scanned the words briefly on the page until she found more details:

"Calvenia was initially a monarchy, established by conquerors who treasured the land for its fertility and the large expanses of fields that they used for raising horses. The ruling family passed control of the country to the eldest son for centuries.

It became clear in the last twenty years of King Sterling's rule that Arvenia was at odds with Calvenia. Arvenia had long sought full control of Orco's Pass to bring more trade into its capital, Avendale; however, Calvenia had increased tariffs on goods passing through the channel. Arvenia, primarily known for its trade in corn and vegetables, relied heavily on incoming trade for metals needed to make crucial farming equipment. At the same time, a small group of Calvenians despised the monarchy and sought to depose the royals and replace them with a ruling class filled with people who understood their struggles.

Arvenia infiltrated Calvenia with spies, hoping to take control of its resources, and these spies banded together with the Calvenian extremists. Together, they overthrew the monarchy by kidnapping the royal family and putting them all to death, including the youngest son, Edmund, who was only five years old at the time. Since that time, Calvenia has been governed by an elected leader. This leader has sought to throw off the influence of its neighbor and former ally, Arvenia, since they infiltrated Calvenia's borders. The fight continues to this day."

Kenna gasped and looked back at the picture of Edric and his family. He was probably only a few years older than Edmund when they were attacked. Kenna was unsure what to think about this new revelation. She was in shock. She touched her fingers to the young Edric's face thoughtfully, and said, "How could you survive such anguish, my love?"

"Kenna!" A voice called from the kitchen. Kenna slammed the volume closed and lifted the corner of the mattress to conceal it. She tucked the covers down around the book and stood to look in the mirror across from the wash basin. Kenna wiped the tears from her eyes and took a steadying breath. The others did not need to know about this. This was her burden. She unlocked the door and tried to walk into the kitchen as if her entire world had not just been shattered.

CHAPTER THIRTY-TWO
Ansley

To Ansley, the hours after she read about the gods' creation of transference in the hall of records seemed to pass without her. She was in a daze, reliving the words she had read aloud. Every few moments, someone would glance at her, trying to gauge her thoughts, but Ansley was pretty good at hiding them at this point.

After Lya served a glorious dinner that Ansley barely tasted, she quietly exited the common room and returned to the bedroom she was sharing with Josilyn and Kenna. Josilyn was in there already, changing into her nightclothes.

"Ansley, how are you doing?" Josilyn asked softly, her brow furrowed with concern for her friend.

Ansley shrugged. "About how you would expect. What are we supposed to do now? Now that we…know more about transference." She asked Josilyn.

Josilyn paused in folding the clothes she had worn that day. She looked up at Ansley, and just for an instant, Ansley saw fear there, but it was immediately buried beneath a blanket of hope. "Well, we regroup tomorrow and form a plan. Then, we go back to Arvenia together to retrieve your grandmother and Rhys."

"And what about Magnus?" Ansley asked, almost dreading the answer.

Josilyn raised one eyebrow and sighed. "We can't attack him until we are ready, and we aren't ready until we know a weakness of his."

Ansley nodded, ready to finish this conversation. She positioned herself in front of the mirror and used a comb she had packed in her traveling bags to detangle the knots in her long brown hair, just as she had done each night since she was a child. Josilyn did not say anything else, but she walked up behind Ansley and hugged her tightly. Ansley placed her hands on top of her friend's, and they remained that way for a moment. Then, Josilyn released her and moved towards the door, probably in search of Mila's company. Ansley had noticed the bond the two shared since Josilyn had arrived.

Ansley finished combing her hair, and then she pulled down the quilt cover that was on the bed. She scooted herself into the cool sheets and shivered for a moment until she grew warmer and more comfortable. Ansley looked out the small window to her right and was surprised to see a snowflake hit the glass. But she shouldn't have been surprised. The winter solstice was just a few days away. The weather had turned cold so quickly here in Calvenia compared to what she was used to in Terra. She reminisced for a moment about last year's winter solstice festivities and let her mind drift away from this place and her worries.

Ryker and Ansley had helped their mother cook a meat pie, filled with veal and potatoes. Leila, their mother, was a splendid cook and had been lucky to secure the meat from the butcher the day before. Ryker had begged to try the pie early, but Leila had insisted they wait. The meat pie was for dinner, and they would not eat without their father, Everett, and their grandmother, Bianca. After they had spent hours moping around the kitchen, Leila had finally allowed Ansley and Ryker to taste the fresh bread she had made. Their mother was very skilled when it came to jams, and Ansley's favorite had always been her mother's blueberry jam. Ryker had smeared the blueberries all over his hands and mouth, matching their younger brother Eli who sat nearby with a piece of bread clutched tightly in his fist. When Everett, their father, arrived after watering the animals for the night, his booming laughter had echoed off the walls of their home.

Ansley smiled to herself as she watched more snowflakes hit the window pane. How could her life have changed so much in just a year? A soft knock sounded at the door. "Uhh…come in." Ansley said, confused at who would be knocking on her door. Rhyn stuck his head in through a small crack.

"Do you mind if I come join you for a few minutes?" He asked hesitantly and continued, "If you are too tired, it's okay. We can always talk in the morning instead." He began to move quickly from the door, anticipating her dismissal.

Ansley sat up quickly in the bed, her long brown hair falling over her shoulders. "No, it's okay. I was just thinking about last year's winter solstice. Please, come in. You aren't disturbing me, Rhyn." She scooted over to the edge of the small bed to give Rhyn some room to sit with her. He sat down beside her and leaned his back against the wall. Rhyn smiled at her and asked, "Was it a good one? The memory?"

Ansley nodded. "Yes, but it hurts all the same." Rhyn did not answer. He simply waited for Ansley to fill the silence, knowing she needed to talk to someone. Her next question was probably not what he had expected though.

"Rhyn, why are we…. *connected*…the way we are? I have never met any other dreamwalkers who share that type of bond, and you said we have been connected for a long time, right?" Ansley inquired.

Rhyn turned to look at her. "I don't know, Ansley." He answered honestly. "I just assume the gods knew we needed each other." He added genuinely.

"Do you really believe they exist then?" Ansley asked Rhyn softly. He smiled at her question. "Yes, but it's difficult to explain why. I think I can *sense* their presence. I know they watch over me, and I know they try to help me when they are able."

"But how?" Ansley asked, turning herself so she was laying on her side, looking up at Rhyn.

"Well, do you ever plant something and doubt that it will ever grow, but then it surprises you and is ready to harvest just as your family is depending on it? That is where I feel Sali, the god of earth and the harvest. I know I am not skilled enough to grow crops, but when I plant them for my family, they do indeed grow." Rhyn looked at Ansley again and smiled.

"Is that all?" Ansley asked, a frown spreading across her face. She had hoped that Rhyn had experienced some divine intervention. She was starting to feel that they would need some type of supernatural guidance to defeat Magnus. The likelihood of succeeding against him felt next to impossible.

"No. Did you ever look at your mother and wonder how she could love you even when you were so naughty as a child? That love comes from Matrisa. If it was not for her influence, we would not be lucky enough to feel our mothers' love." He responded. "That is worth something, is it not?"

Ansley sighed. "And what of Poeno, god of justice? When will he strike down Magnus and save me the trouble?" Ansley retorted.

Rhyn grabbed her hand and squeezed it tightly. "I do not think the gods can do those things for us. It would mean we would spend all our time appealing to them when we need only to take the skills and gifts they have given us to do the hard work ourselves. Besides, if the gods took control of every difficult situation, others would not see their glory." Ansley looked into Rhyn's bright blue eyes and chewed on the side of her bottom lip. Then, she pulled her hand free of his and began rubbing her hands together. The room had grown chilly with the drop in the temperature outside.

Suddenly, Rhyn scooted closer to her, and he lifted her chin to his face with a delicate touch. "Ansley, in truth, I believe Amora bound us to each another. Only the goddess of love could have given my heart to you before I had ever met you." He said with a whisper that was warm against Ansley's lips. Then, he leaned in and delicately kissed her. His mouth was hot but sweet, full of eagerness but not indelicate. Ansley could feel his smile as he pulled away.

"I better let you go to sleep. I know you need it after the day you've had." Rhyn said as he stood from the bed and walked to the door.

"Rhyn?" Ansley called to him. He turned back to look at her with one hand on the door and his feet already outside of the room. "If you're right, then Amora made me the lucky one." She said with a small smile. Rhyn smiled shyly at her, and he closed the door softly behind him. Ansley sunk down onto her pillow and allowed herself a few moments to be a teenager again and enjoy a kiss from the man she cared about most.

*****

Ansley smiled at her friend, Josilyn, who was walking alongside a babbling stream. Josilyn knelt down and looked at the fish swimming with the current. Josilyn looked at Ansley mischievously and asked, "Do you want to see me turn into a fish?"

Ansley giggled before her smile melted away. "No, Jos.

Damon said we needed to train, and I don't know if he plans to come check on us unexpectedly. I cannot take one more scowl from him this week." Ansley tossed a pebble into the slow-flowing creek.

Josilyn stood and wiped her hands together. "Yes, Mila said he has been in a mood since the attack."

Ansley hmphed. "That makes sense, but I wish he wouldn't be such a grump. We have enough to worry about without worrying about dealing with his emotions."

Josilyn walked back to her friend and wrapped an arm around Ansley's shoulder for comfort. Josilyn's long, blonde hair fanned out behind them as the breeze picked up. Ansley glanced at the strip of white in her hair and touched it gingerly. Josilyn had been lucky that this was the only evidence of the attack she fell victim to about a month ago. Ansley sighed. "Well, let's do something worthy of telling him."

Josilyn smiled. "I have an idea. Do you mind if I use my skill to train you today?"

Ansley was not sure where her friend was headed with this idea, but she decided to trust her. Ansley nodded and waited. Josilyn closed her eyes, and after a few moments, her mark glowed. Ansley remembered first seeing the lion-headed creature when she had saved Josilyn from that attack. It was such a different mark from Ansley's simple oval-shaped eye.

Josilyn concentrated, and Ansley began to notice subtle changes in her appearance. Her hair shortened and turned black. Then, it fell into waves. She grew broader in the shoulders and grew several inches in height. Josilyn then slimmed down in the chest and muscles were visible beneath her clothes. But her clothes had changed too-to match her appearance. She now wore men's trousers and a white button-down work shirt. When Josilyn opened her eyes, they were blue.

Ansley took a step backwards and jumped when she felt her feet grow cold and wet. She stumbled through the stream and made her way to the other side. Josilyn, now a Magnus-look alike, followed her. Ansley lifted her hands, urging her friend to move away from her and thumped heavily to the ground. "Jos, please, I don't like this. Can you choose something else to try today?"

Josilyn smiled, and Ansley was surprised to see how much she did mirror even Magnus's movements. "Ansley, I thought I would never see you again, yet here you are." Josilyn stepped closer to her, and Ansley was surprised to hear Magnus's voice leave her friend's mouth. Ansley fell over a log that was lying behind her. She was starting to worry that Josilyn was actually Magnus after all, and he had tricked her once again.

But then her friend's face shifted back to her own, startling Ansley even more. "Ansley? Are you okay?" Josilyn asked, her concern audible. "I didn't mean to scare you! Come on. Let me help you up." Josilyn extended her hand out to Ansley as her mark glowed once more and her body changed back to her usual appearance. Ansley did not take the offered hand until Josilyn was Josilyn once more.

After a few minutes had passed, Ansley felt less apprehensive. She ventured to ask Josilyn the question that was on her mind. "Jos, what is your mark a representation of? It looks like a lion but isn't quite that..." Josilyn smiled broadly, "It's a chimera!"

Ansley frowned in confusion. Josilyn added, "A chimera is a mythological creature that has the head of a lion, body of a wolf, and usually the tail of a serpent. They also have wings!" Ansley frowned again, confused by this new revelation.

"But, why is it that?" Ansley asked in earnest.

"It represents what I am. As a shifter, I can be anything. A chimera is made of different creatures. It most accurately represents my skill, I suppose." Josilyn mumbled something under her breath, obviously hurt by Ansley's question. "I always thought it was a cool mark."

"Oh, Jos! I did not mean to....Jos?" Ansley started. Suddenly, the entire dream sequence changed, and she felt herself falling into a dreamvision. "Jos?"

Ansley felt a hand touch her arm, but she could not see it. "I'm here. What is happening to you, Ansley? Your mark is glowing." Josilyn responded. Ansley watched the dream shift into a dark chamber with chains dangling from the ceiling and more scattered across the dirt floor.

"I think I'm having a dreamvision. I have never been in a dream when I have had one. Stay close to me?" Ansley asked, blindly reaching for her friend. She felt Josilyn's hand grasp hers tightly. "I will not leave you."

Ansley watched as an older man approached and unlocked the chamber. The metal door creaked as he pulled it open for Magnus to step through. Magnus looked into the corner and began speaking to two huddled shapes there, but Ansley could not hear his voice. She guessed that this was not the important part of the dreamvision.

Ansley walked closer to the shapes in the corner and was shocked to see that one was Rhyn and the other was her. They were both dirty and had rips in their clothes, indicating that they had been here for some time. Magnus laughed suddenly, and then Ansley saw a shadow hit Magnus's servant in the head with a metal tool. When the shadow moved closer, Ansley realized it was Damon. The man had dropped to the ground instantly, and Damon ran towards Magnus with the fury of a tiger set loose on a hunt.

Magnus turned as soon as he had heard his servant fall. He unsheathed a small blade that he kept at his waist but hid it so that Damon did not see that he held it. Damon ran towards Magnus as fast as he could, trying to knock him to the dirt floor, but Magnus was ready. He stretched the blade out at the last moment, and Damon, not seeing it, ran right onto it. Damon stopped suddenly, his eyes opened wide in shock, and Magnus twisted the blade in his wound before viciously pulling it free.

Ansley heard herself scream but was unsure if it was her or her dreamself. Her eyes were glued to Damon's face, which turned white slowly as blood leaked through his clenched lips. Finally, his knees hit the floor, and just as she was about to run to catch him, Magnus leaned down towards Damon with the knife once more and plunged it into Damon's throat.

A guttural sound echoed off the walls, and Ansley turned away until she heard Damon finally fall to the floor after succumbing to his wounds. She felt hot tears run down her cheeks, and she tried to cover her mouth with her hand, but the hand was shaking too badly. Ansley fell to her own knees in shock, and then, the vision subsided. Josilyn sat face-to-face with her and began wiping the tears from Ansley's cheeks.

"Ansley, Ansley, it's okay. Ansley? What did you see?" Josilyn asked softly. Ansley let her friend pull her into a tight hug, the kind only sisters could share. Ansley spoke into Josilyn's shoulder as she felt herself sag with dread.

"It was Damon. I saw his death. I have seen it before, and it was not supposed to be this way. He...he...tried to save me from Magnus, and Magnus murdered him. He murdered him!" Ansley's pitch rose as she explained this to Josilyn, who was now stroking her hair.

"Well, what should we do?" Josilyn asked. "To keep

it from happening?"

Ansley shook her head. "I'm not sure." Despair filled Ansley as she lied to her friend, and the only plan she could see herself following began to unfold in her mind. She had to leave, and she had to leave without Damon being able to follow her.

CHAPTER THIRTY-ONE
Bianca

They had been here for at least three days. Bianca only knew this by counting the meals brought to them. They were in the dungeon and, she assumed, underground. No windows allowed light to shine upon them here. No, not here in this miserable place.

Bianca coughed to clear her throat which felt as dry as a piece of toast. Nothing helped though, and she knew that they had been given their last food and water for the day. Well, she *thought* of it as water. She was not actually sure what that liquid was. It was always a brownish color and smelled foul. Bianca had avoided it for two days until the thirst overwhelmed her. Alden, who had awoken from being drugged after the second day, had suggested Bianca hold her nose when drinking it. It helped, but Bianca knew that if she ever got out of this place, she would never look at a simple glass of water the same way.

Alden stirred, hearing Bianca cough. He lifted his head to look in her direction. Bianca took in his appearance. His clothes, once a dark brown set of trousers and a dark navy shirt with a brown cloak over it, were now mere rags. He was covered in dirt, and he smelled from not being allowed to wash. Bianca assumed she smelled just as bad as he did. There were dirt smears all over his face where he had tried to move his hair out of his eyes using his arms, which were still stretched above his head in chains. They had a bucket in the corner for…waste, but Bianca had moved it next to Alden, whose chains did not allow him free movement of the chamber.

Alden's eyes were bright with hunger and thirst. He mumbled, but Bianca could not distinguish his voice from the sounds of the guards laughing and playing cards nearby. Alden cleared his throat and tried again, "You okay?" He croaked.

Bianca nodded. "You?" Alden shrugged the best he could with his arms chained. Then he slumped against the wall and glanced down at his feet. "So, what chance do we have of getting free?" He asked her, all hope seemingly gone from his voice.

Bianca looked at Terra's chief elder and felt ashamed. She hated that he had gotten involved in this with her. Alden had been visiting when they were taken. "It doesn't look good. He doesn't even question us anymore. I worry that he will just dispose of us or use us to lure Ansley here, and both of those options are…not pleasant to consider." Bianca replied hoarsely, her voice cracking on several of the words.

Alden nodded in acknowledgement. "Yes. I am afraid of that too. Where did she go, Bianca? Why is she not in Terra?" Alden asked softly.

Bianca tried to muster some spit to swallow before talking again. Her throat ached. "She left with Damon for Calvenia. She said she was going there to train, but I did not believe her. I think she knew Magnus would be looking for her," Bianca said, gesturing to the locked door, "and she was determined to find a way to evade him. I sent Josilyn after her. I hope they found each other."

Alden nodded silently, and he closed his eyes to rest. Resting was important for prisoners, Bianca had learned. With the meager amounts of old bread and gruel served, their energy was easily spent on simple tasks. Bianca took his lead and laid down on the dirt floor of the chamber.

Her nose had adjusted to the smell now, so it no longer bothered her as it once had. She closed her eyes and pictured herself back in Terra, walking through the wildflower fields with her daughter-in-law, Leila. Bianca smiled with the memory and allowed herself to drift away to another, happier place.

*****

Bianca jumped as she heard the heavy door creak open. Magnus was quickly followed into the chamber by an older man and Dane. Bianca had not been surprised that Dane was alive. She just hoped his leg injury pained him horribly. He deserved that for handing her loved ones over to this monster. Dane had been the traveling companion of Kenna, and the pair had arrived in Terra a few months earlier looking for answers about the attacks taking place across the country. Bianca had helped Damon free Dane and Kenna from the pit they had fallen into in the Dream Hollow Mountains.

They had not discovered Dane's duplicity until Kenna, Damon, and Ansley had fought against him and the few members of Orco's cult working with him to steal skills from dreamwalkers. Bianca bristled when she saw him. Her anger burned within her like a roaring fire, so she held onto it to keep her strong.

Magnus walked over to Alden, and Bianca watched quietly, worried about what was about to take place. Magnus covered his mouth and nose with his white handkerchief, and he nudged Alden with his boot. Alden lifted his head, weak from the effort of the conversation Bianca and he had shared earlier. When he noticed who was looking at him, Bianca thought he straightened.

"Did you get what I needed?" Magnus asked through the handkerchief. Alden swallowed but nodded. Magnus turned to Dane and said, "He is ready. Unlock his chains please and bring the cot." Dane nodded, first moving towards where Alden sat. He unlocked Alden's arms, and the old man fell onto his face before rolling over onto his side. He reached out and touched Magnus's shoe, leaving a smudge on the top. Magnus moved his foot away from the prisoner and frowned at him.

Dane left for a moment, but when he returned, Bianca noticed two guards following with a medical cot between them. It had wooden handles on both sides for lifting the injured and transporting them to healers. They laid the cot on the floor, rolled Alden onto it, and lifted him from the ground. Bianca started.

"Alden?" She exclaimed with her gritty voice. "Wait! What are you *doing* with him?" She demanded.

Magnus turned to her and smiled, his eyes glinting. He walked towards her after nodding to the guards to leave the chamber. They took Alden out, and Bianca was even more confused when Alden did not put up a fight. Magnus knelt in front of her at eye level, and he said menacingly, "It seems that you are all alone *again*, Mrs. Black. You see, your friend was never actually your *friend*. In fact, he is most certainly your enemy. But I am glad that you trusted him enough to tell him the information I needed." Bianca's heart lurched into her throat, and she felt lightheaded.

Magnus stood and walked through the doors. She heard him yell at the guards to give her more water. "I want her alive! See to it!" He growled. The next few moments passed in a haze as she tried to comprehend what Magnus had told her. Alden…Alden *betrayed* her. No, Alden betrayed *Everett and Leila*. Alden made them lambs for slaughter. Alden…*Alden did this.*

CHAPTER THIRTY-FOUR
Magnus

Magnus followed his soldiers up the stairs into his castle as they carried the old man between them on the cot. He groaned when they turned it to the side to move through the twisting stairwells, but he kept his eyes open. The old man stared at Magnus silently, awaiting his attention. Magnus was content to let the man wait. He did not spare an extra thought for the man. Instead, his thoughts were on the information he had gathered. He needed it to find Ansley, and he needed to find her *quickly*.

Regin had been working his spell for some time, trying to perfect it. He had practiced on Rhys, but they had not been successful. Magnus assumed it was because the boy had no strength left for them to take. Regin disagreed. His most recent idea was that the spell was temperamental and needed to be used at a specific time to work properly. Regin suggested using it when the moon disappeared from the sky, in attempts to prevent Kius, God and guardian of the night, from interfering. Magnus had rolled his eyes at this statement, but he trusted Regin. And Regin had yet to disappoint him in that regard. Since they had been unsuccessful at securing Rhys's skill and allowing Magnus to take it from him, Ansley was essential to ensure that Magnus could not only use a skill but keep it. He tired of using crystals and wanted what had rightfully been his from his birth. He had been born to dreamwalkers and should have inherited like everyone else. Why should he suffer because of the events that unfolded before he was born? He deserved what he was owed, and he was going to get it, no matter the cost to everyone else.

So, Magnus impatiently followed the soldiers until they approached an opened room for guests. They entered slowly and lowered the man onto the bed. Magnus regretted putting his handkerchief away, for the man still reeked of the dungeons. The soldiers moved the cot and stood at attention in front of Magnus, awaiting orders. Magnus flicked his hand lazily in dismissal. Once the guards had exited the room, he approached the bed.

"Well?" Magnus asked, an edge to his voice even though he spoke softly into the darkened room.

The old man swallowed nervously, and said, "Sire, I am eager to speak with you, but I must ensure that our bargain…"

Magnus stepped closer to where the man lay, soiling the clean pillows with his filthy clothes and even filthier *commonness*. "Do not instruct *me*, old man. We had a bargain. I will honor it. Now, tell me what the woman said." Magnus hissed angrily. The man's face drained of color. He coughed once trying to dismiss the discomfort he now felt in Magnus's presence, but this did not unsettle Magnus. He merely waited for what he had been promised.

"*Calvenia*. She is in Calvenia with the others." The old man whispered, as if someone may actually hear his treachery this far from his homeland and from those he called his people. Magnus nodded stiffly and turned on his heel to exit the room. He had what he needed, and he would not waste another breath upon this worthless man in front of him. Before he turned, Magnus watched the old man spring quickly off the pillows.

"Wait! What of my granddaughter?" The man called in anguish. Magnus turned slowly, and he replied dryly. "She awaits you." Magnus took in the relief on the old man's face before he added, "In the afterlife." The old man sank back into the bed. Then he melted into the quilt and howled his grief into the soft, clean pillow. Magnus turned back to the door, eager to rid himself of the man's company. "Don't *worry*, elder. She died well." He said with a sneer as he slammed the door behind him, locking the man in his room. The man's angry shouts echoed down the hall behind Magnus. Magnus let the words slide off him, unaffected by their intended stings.

In truth, he had been lucky to find the elder's granddaughter. One of his followers had happened upon her in a dream and captured her in hopes of attaining the girl's skill. Her skill was one of extreme value and rarity. The girl was a wielder of air. Magnus had learned of the girl' capture just in time to use it to gain Alden's cooperation in helping him take Bianca from her home in Terra. The elder had been crucial to that stage of Magnus's plan, and without him, Magnus doubted that they would have gotten so close to Bianca without more violent measures. Magnus cared little for his followers to prize their safety over succeeding in his goals, but more bloodshed meant less followers for him to rely on when the time came for battle against the dreamwalkers. Magnus would not waste their lives on meaningless tasks.

Magnus stopped for a moment and listened to the elder's cries booming angrily against the heavy door of his chamber. Magnus shook his head at the man's ignorance. *Had he really believed that the girl would live? Surely not.* Perhaps, he had just been desperate enough to do anything in his power to save her. If that was so, desperation was the most powerful weapon Magnus could wield. He started walking away from the broken man again, considering these things and reminding himself to think on them more later.

CHAPTER THIRTY-THREE
Kenna

Kenna lifted a cup of lukewarm coffee to her lips. She had added too much sugar, but her thoughts were too preoccupied to worry with fixing it. So, she took another sip and tried to quiet her mind. Thankfully, Lya walked in with Damon. Kenna was happy for the distraction.

Lya moved to the fire to grab the coffee pot dangling over the fire. Damon sat in front of Kenna at the table. "Couldn't sleep?" He asked her as he scratched his beard and looked out one of the windows into the darkness. It was the middle of the night, and all was eerily calm and still. It made Kenna feel unsettled.

Kenna shook her head as she took another sip of her coffee, trying to wash away the unease. Damon ran his hand over his face and yawned loudly. Lya moved soundlessly around the kitchen as she filled two cups of coffee for her husband and herself. "Me either."

Damon shook his head slowly and looked at Kenna. "What should we do, Kenna?"

Kenna smirked behind her cup, her sassy nature getting the best of her. "Are you telling me that *you* don't have a plan?"

Damon frowned, and his eyes seemed to bore into Kenna with fire. "Of *all* times, Kenna. *Gods...*" He looked at Lya who gave him a stern look before seating herself at the table. She pulled a small basket of fabric towards herself, and Kenna noticed with surprise that it was something she was knitting. It struck her as such a mundane task to fill the moment when they were sitting around the table in the middle of the night discussing what could likely be their last battle. Lya sensed Kenna's attention and shrugged her shoulders. "Sometimes it is best to quiet the mind while the fingers work." Kenna watched Lya for a few more moments as she used her knitting needles to pull string together into the shape of a scarf. It was mesmerizing. Kenna's thoughts were pulled back from the work Lya was doing when she heard Damon clear his throat.

"What I *meant*, Kenna, was that I need your help with forming a plan. You and I are the only experienced dreamwalkers in this situation, and I am worried about relying on any of the ideas of the young ones. They have proven to be...*impulsive* in the past." Damon finished lamely and took a sip of his drink.

Kenna looked at her hands that lay folded on top of the table. "Yes, perhaps, but Ansley did help save us, Damon. You cannot deny her the credit she deserves." Ansley had helped to rescue them when Dane had lured them into a trap a few weeks ago, intent on taking their skills and using them to reach Jameson, Sophie, and Laurel, the other members of Kenna's tribe.

"That was...*luck.* Ansley is a child. Nothing more. And now she has been given such a hefty responsibility. Likely more than any of us will ever have to bear."

Kenna nodded. "Yes, you are right, but don't discredit her by assuming she will not be able to handle the burden. She has proven herself thus far, and I have faith that she will continue to surprise us with her strength." Lya smiled to herself and nodded in agreement, but Damon did not see his wife's response.

"She is....she is only a...."

"A *girl*?" Kenna added, raising her eyebrows at

Damon. "Please do not insult us," Kenna gestured to herself and Lya, "by insinuating that is some sort of...*weakness* to overcome. If anything, you have proven that men have less self-control than women in most aspects of their lives." Kenna pushed herself from the table and glared angrily at Damon. "You dishonor my mother's memory when you consider women so weak. You should know better. *You...*"

Damon raised his hands in defeat. "Alright, *alright*. Enough. You have said your peace, and I can't deny that you are right. But, she *is* a child and one that barely knows her own skills. We must come up with a plan to help protect her from Magnus as long as we possibly can. If he gets his hands on Ansley, he will destroy her completely and take his time with it. She has the skills he wants to fulfill some old hatred towards our people, and he will stop at nothing to either extract it from Ansley or use her to reach his own goals." Damon's face contorted in pain as he thought about this outcome. "I will not stand by and watch that happen. I will not *allow* it to happen. So, in the name of *all the gods*, Kenna, help me make a plan that ends differently. For *gods* sake, you *are* a woman, and I am sitting here asking for your help. Try not to always assume I am attacking you. Let's help each other."

Kenna chewed on her lip and nodded at Damon. "Very well, Damon. I am sure we can put together some sort of plan to rescue Bianca and Rhys. Where should we start?"

Damon opened his mouth, but he was interrupted by the sound of footsteps echoing through the small house. Josilyn ran into the kitchen, her blonde hair flying loosely around her shoulders and a piece of parchment in her hands. Her eyes were wide, and she was near tears. Kenna and Damon glanced at one another and hastily turned back towards Josilyn.

"Josilyn, what is it?" Damon asked softly, sensing her distress and feeling the same dread Kenna felt pooling in her stomach. Josilyn held the parchment with both hands and looked at it for a moment as a tear finally dislodged itself and fell down her face. Josilyn shook her head, closing her eyes in pain. "She's...she's *gone*, Damon. Ansley is *gone*."

CHAPTER THIRTY-SIX
Ansley

The wind whipped Ansley's hair furiously around her face as the ship raised its sails. The sun had not risen that morning. Instead, the clouds covered the sky, making everything dark and gray. Today, Ansley was thankful for that. She felt that it gave Rhyn and her extra cover as they fled Dunbar.

Ansley shivered from the chill in the air and wrapped her arms tightly around her chest to keep herself warm. She turned around and scanned the small deck of the ship for Rhyn but did not see him. She guessed he was below deck paying for their voyage home to Arvenia. Ansley still felt guilty about stealing from Damon, but it was the only way they could afford passage on a ship this size. She knew that if Rhyn and she were going to go back to Arvenia in hopes of arriving before the others, they needed to travel on a much larger vessel than the one they had taken to Calvenia.

Rhyn had scoured the docks in hopes of securing passage. Ansley knew they were lucky to find anything in such a short amount of time, but she was also amazed at the grandeur of the ship they had chosen. It was called the *Flying Maiden*, and a beautiful, hand-carved bust of a woman stood out boldly on the mast. Long hair fell down the sides of the woman's face, and her eyes were carved to show an eagerness for adventure. The ship was set to sail through Otto's Pass, but instead of traveling to Arvenia, they had planned a course around the southern-most tip of the country, into the Treacherous Seas. There was little good to be said of these waters. She felt uneasy even imagining what the crew may find there, but they had insisted that the *Flying Maiden* had traveled there safely once before. Rhyn had quipped that he too had traveled there safely before. Despite Rhyn's joke, Ansley and Rhyn had agreed this ship was their best hope in getting back to Terra, so they did not share their own opinions of the sailors' traveling plans. Still, the legends of sea serpents continued to torment Ansley's imagination as they continued on their journey. Thankfully, the captain had agreed to drop Rhyn and Ansley off at an island called Moreland before their ship continued on their journey south. Hopefully, she would be arriving in Terra by the time this ship reached the Treacherous Seas.

Ansley walked idly around the deck watching the crew attend to their duties. One sailor monitored the sails and adjusted the ropes attached to them when the winds turned. Another rolled barrels of supplies across the deck towards the lower decks for storage. It would be a long journey for them, so Ansley knew they likely had many, many crates full of food and other supplies they could barter with. Suddenly, the door to the lower decks was flung open, and the captain appeared in the opening. He smiled and took a deep breath of the sea air before striding towards Ansley.

Ansley tried to prepare herself. Rhyn had reminded her that their ship was solely manned by Calvenians. Tensions continued to grow between the two nations, as Calvenia tried to rid itself of Arvenia's influence over their lands. The sailors would not be pleased to know that Ansley was a native Arvenian, so she had to disguise herself the best she could. Thankfully, both countries had similar styles of dress, so it was mostly her accent that would give her away. Ansley smiled uneasily at the captain who removed his hat as he approached her.

"Morning, ma'am. Are the seas treating you well?" He asked with genuine interest at her reply. Ansley nodded and swallowed before responding.

"Yes, captain. Thank you. I was just getting some fresh air before I settle into my room." Ansley spoke with a faster rate of speech and tried not to use any Arvenian slang. It was surprising how difficult that was for her, and Ansley hoped that the captain did not notice anything amiss with her pronunciation of each sound. The captain nodded and scrutinized her for a moment. Ansley's pulse quickened, but she forced herself not to look away from him. She awaited his remarks with dread, expecting them to be orders to "drag the Arvenian scum to the brig". What he said surprised her, but not in that way.

"Are you ill, my dear?" The captain asked softly, his eyebrows raised. "You are much paler than when you came on board." Ansley felt relief flood through her, but she tried to maintain the pretense that the captain was misreading.

She nodded and fanned her face softly. "Please do not think poorly of me, captain. I have traveled by boat often, but the sea has been perilous today. I am afraid I may need to lie down." The captain nodded fervently and patted her on the shoulder.

"Yes, my dear. Please, rest, and let us know if we can ease your travel in any way. Eilene! *Eilene!*" The captain called. A young girl ran towards the captain, holding her skirts in her hand to keep them from tripping her. "Yes, captain?" she squeaked.

"The lady is ill. Please give her an early ration of dinner and a small pitcher of water. And see to it that she finds her rooms." The captain ordered. The young girl nodded and curtsied to the captain, which Ansley thought of as odd, before grabbing Ansley's hand and leading her in the direction of the lower decks. The girl walked quickly and almost dragged Ansley after her.

The captain smiled at Ansley as she left the deck and said in response to her confused look, "My niece. She will take care of you Miss…miss…what *was* your name again, dear?"

"Mila. Mila of the Svenians." Ansley said quickly, remembering her lessons on the history of Calvenia. The Svenians were a family that lived to the west of Dunbar and were experienced horse trainers. The lords and ladies of Dunbar often sent their horses to this family to ensure they were ready for competitions. Calvenians loved their horses, and that meant that any type of competition was considered sacred to them. The captain nodded approvingly and replaced his hat on his head before turning his attention to more important duties taking place on deck. Ansley turned her attention back to Eilene.

The girl led her into a narrow doorway, down a small set of stairs, and to the lower deck where her room was. When she opened the door, Ansley was pleased to see Rhyn inside, sleeping on a cot and snoring. Eilene's eyes had widened at Ansley, so Ansley said curtly, "My brother." Eilene then disappeared for several minutes before returning with a loaf of fresh bread, a lump of cheese, and a pitcher of cool water with a small teacup. Ansley marveled over the porcelain cup, so Eilene smiled and said, "My favorite. Being the only other lady on board, I thought you would appreciate it too." The teacup was pearly white with blue and pink designs around the outside. It had a small chip on the rim, which was lined with gold and shimmered when Ansley turned it. "This is *lovely*. Thank you, Eilene." Ansley said with a smile to the girl, who blushed. Eilene smiled again warmly at Ansley before letting herself out of the small room.

Ansley glanced at Rhyn again, who lay on his side with one arm tucked carefully under his head and the other hanging off the cot. His face was peaceful as he slept, and he continued to snore softly as the boat rolled across the wild waves of the sea. Ansley walked over to her own cot with her teacup of cool water, sipping it and thinking of the journey ahead. *I hope the others are not upset with me,* she thought as she sat down, trying not to spill her drink. She reached down and untied the laces of her shoes, removing them and placing them under the cot. Then, Ansley untied the bow on the back of the modest dress she wore and removed it as she kept a careful eye on Rhyn. She laid the dress across the bottom of the cot and pulled a nightgown from her travel bag.

She pulled this over her head and let it fall to her knees. Ansley pulled the coverlet back on the bed and slid into its warmth, laying her head on a feather-filled pillow. She sighed and let her fingers trace the lace design around the sleeve of her nightgown. Her mother's smile filled her thoughts, and she closed her eyes to picture her more clearly. In her mind's eye, her mother smiled warmly at Ansley, crossed the room with the nightgown she had just finished sewing, and held it up to her proudly. Then, she hugged Ansley tightly and kissed her on the head before sending her off to bed with her newly-sewn nightgown. When Ansley opened her eyes again, she eyed the white lace that was once so new. It was yellowed now and ripped in places from the wear it had withstood. Ansley's fingers traced the design once more as the hole inside her heart ached. It pained her to think that her mother's hands would never again sew such beauty, and just like this lace she had taken such care with, her memory of her mother would also fade with time.

Ansley sighed and flipped over onto her other side, facing the wooden wall of the ship. The creaking sounds and noise from the upper deck were loud enough to drown out the sound of her soft sobs. Ansley gave into her emotions and allowed herself to grieve in the quiet of the room that was so very far from her home.

*****

Ansley could not remember falling asleep, but she clearly was dreaming. She turned in a circle and tried to make out her surroundings. She was in a chamber that looked like a council room for a king. There were glass windows set high in the wall with windowsills taller than any man she had ever seen. The view outside the windows was breathtaking, and it was even more beautiful when the lightning lit up the sky.

Ansley turned away from the windows to explore a bit more. Her bare feet made no sound as she walked on the stone floors, and Ansley found that she felt like a spy who was sneaking around a castle. There was a large table in the middle of the room, and the chairs seated around it had red velvet cushions. Ansley ran her hand over the intricate carving on the wooden arms of the chairs. She had never seen something so ornate. She glanced up as lightning lit the room once more, and a shudder ran through her as she spotted a shadowy figure lingering in the doorway behind her.

The shadow stepped forward out of the darkness, and Ansley found herself holding her breath as she met the man's gaze. Magnus smirked at her from behind Rhys's face and trailed his hand along the chairs she had been admiring mere moments before she saw him. "Beautiful, aren't they?" He asked softly.

Ansley backed away from him, keeping the table

between them for protection as he edged closer to her. He looked up at Ansley and noticed her moving away from him. "Ansley, are you afraid of me?" He asked mockingly. Ansley was careful to keep her eyes on him as she continued to maintain a safe distance between them.

Magnus pulled a white handkerchief from inside his cloak and waved it towards her. "There. Now we can talk without you being worried for your safety." Magnus said with a laugh.

Ansley simply stared at him. "Why am I here? And why must you parade around as someone you are not? Do you enjoy torturing me by hiding behind the face you tried to steal my affections with? Why not wear your own face, and finally be honest about who you are?" Ansley snarled at Magnus. He chuckled.

"You are nothing if not entertaining, my dear." Magnus replied as he replaced his handkerchief back into his cloak. "Do you think I consider your feelings so much that I would go to such lengths to hurt you? Hardly. I have little time to consider my own plans let alone your silly thoughts and feelings."

Ansley swallowed the huge lump that had materialized in her throat. A tear escaped her eye, and she wiped it away angrily. "Then why am I here?" She growled in response.

Magnus smiled, and his eyes, no, Rhys's *eyes, twinkled with delight. "I have come to offer you a deal. A deal that I believe you will be unable to decline."*

"Well, let's hear it, then. I would rather not waste my night listening to you prattle nonsense." Ansley said through clenched teeth.

*"You clearly want an end to this…*disagreement *you and I seem to be having. You want your friends to be safe and your family…excuse me…your* remaining *family to be*

spared. Am I correct?" Magnus asked softly.

"You bastard!" Ansley replied angrily. The lightning flashed suddenly and echoed her fury towards Magnus.

Magnus inclined his head in her direction, acknowledging her accusation. "Yes, but remember that I am here and offering you what you so eagerly seek. Do not anger me, or I will rescind my offer."

Ansley seethed and wondered if Magnus could see the hate rolling off her in the darkness. "At what price?" She asked.

"The one you have always expected. I want your surrender. Completely, unequivocally, immediately." Magnus said as he turned away from her for a moment to glance out of the windows at the storm raging beyond the glass. "Or, I will come to Calvenia to collect you myself after I dispose of your remaining family and friends."

"And then what happens if I surrender? You kill my grandmother and all my friends anyway? How am I supposed to trust anything that slithers out of your mouth? You sound like a serpent promising me you will not eat me." Ansley responded. She could see Magnus's profile in the darkness and watched him smile and laugh.

"Ansley, my dear, you have a way with words. Have you ever been told that? I prefer to think of myself as a fox. Sly, sneaky, and unpredictable. Serpents are obvious in their...intentions." Magnus said as he stroked his beardless chin. He turned back to her. "I digress. Forgive me. You have my word that all of them will be safe when you turn yourself over to me. You are my target, so I have no interest in them. They are nothing to me, but do not misunderstand my meaning here, Ansley. That also means that I will not hesitate to dispose of them if I must." Magnus added matter-of-factly.

Ansley looked down at the table where her hands rested

before her. She turned them over and saw the lines running along her palms. A long time ago, her mother had traced those lines, looking for answers about Ansley's future. The line in the center of her palm was long and stretched the length of her hand. She remembered that her mother had said to her, "This is your life line. It is long and unbroken. You will live for many, many years." Ansley ran her index finger down this line and wondered if her mother had been wrong after all.

Magnus waited patiently for her response to his offer. Ansley looked up and asked softly, "Where will I find you?"

"Come to Avendale, and my agents will bring you to me. I eagerly await your arrival, but I have certain...responsibilities...that demand my attention at the moment." He said, as if discussing a dinner invitation.

Ansley ran her tongue over her teeth in thought. "And when I do arrive? What then?"

Magnus met her eye. "Will I kill you, you mean? No, my dear. That would be counterintuitive. I have many plans, but all of them involve you. You will be safe, but only if you are agreeable." Ansley expected as much. She nodded solemnly before adding. "I have someone traveling with me. He may be hard to evade. I will do as you ask in return for the promise of the safety of my grandmother and my friends. I want Rhyn spared like the others, and I want Rhys released as well."

Magnus raised his hands. "It will be done as you ask."

Ansley walked around the table and took slow strides toward Magnus until she stood in front of him, looking into the face that had grown so familiar and comforting to her. The face that was also Rhyn's face. She held her hand out in front of her, offering to shake Magnus's hand in agreement. "Then, we have an accord."

Magnus took her hand gently, but instead of shaking her hand, he lifted her fingers to his lips and kissed them gently. "We have an accord. I will see you soon, my dear."

Ansley cringed as Magnus released her hand, but just as she wiped her hand on her skirt, she woke with a start.

*

Rhyn knelt beside her cot. His hand was on the side of Ansley's face. Ansley felt the perspiration roll down her cheek. Rhyn frowned, his blue eyes full of concern.

"You were dreamwalking." He said, not questioning her but waiting for her to explain.

"Yes. He found me again." Ansley said as she sat up in the cot, pulling her hair over one shoulder and wiping her brow with her hand. Rhyn moved his hand away from her and awkwardly rested it on the edge of her cot, as if he was willing himself not to reach out to her. "He…was *taunting* me." Ansley added, trying to give Rhyn something that would keep him from guessing the true message Magnus had delivered to her.

"Ansley, are you alright?" Rhyn asked her softly. Ansley placed her hand silently over his as she thought about the journey ahead of them. She tried not to think about the amount of time they would have left together before she left him forever. Tears filled her eyes, and she looked up at Rhyn's handsome face. He had not shaved recently, and stubble covered his chin and neck. Ansley leaned forward and ran her fingers over his cheek. Rhyn closed his eyes and swallowed.

When he opened his eyes, fury and determination filled them. "I will not let him hurt you, Ansley. We will defeat him together, and we will free your grandmother and my brother. I *promise* you…I will *always* protect you." Rhyn said in a rush, and just as he finished his last word, Ansley pulled him by his shirt collar into her cot.

Rhyn climbed on top of her and held her face with both hands, kissing her tenderly at first before his kisses became more passionate. They kissed for what felt like hours before Rhyn finally moved away from her. He was breathing heavily, and his skin had grown hot under Ansley's hands. He paused, searching her face. Ansley only waited, wanting him to continue the work he had been doing with his tongue along her jawline moments before. Then, Rhyn's face slowly transformed with a smile that felt like sunshine to Ansley. His joy was contagious to her, and she soaked it up even as her heart broke with the knowledge that their time was now limited.

Ansley ran her hand along Rhyn's face and into his wavy black hair. Rhyn leaned forward once more and kissed Ansley's forehead before he stood and moved to the door of their room. Ansley glanced at Rhyn in surprise. Rhyn just shook his head. "Not here. Not like this, Ansley. We have time, and I would rather wait until we aren't in the bottom of an old ship, rolling around in the sea."

Ansley grinned and nodded. She rose from her cot and pulled her hair into a quick braid. "Very well. What shall we do now?" She asked Rhyn.

Rhyn smiled at her. "It's time for dinner, and I am starving. Let's go look for something to eat." Ansley smiled at him again and followed him out of their room. She could not help wishing that she was someone else, *anyone* else, who could live her life like a normal girl and even look forward to a future with someone like Rhyn. Unfortunately, she knew that she would never have that opportunity.

CHAPTER THIRTY-SEVEN
Damon

Damon tried to reel in his panic. He glanced around the dock for Mila, but he could not see where she had gone. The winds were high today, which would be good for traveling quickly. The dock was busy in the early morning hours, and sailors moved past Damon, oblivious of his presence. Damon moved quickly, narrowly avoiding being hit in the head with a large barrel that a sailor carried on his shoulder.

"Hey! Watch it!" The sailor yelled at Damon. Damon walked briskly down the dock in search of his daughter. He felt his cloak flap angrily in the wind behind him, only making him feel more irritable. Mila emerged ahead, and Damon noticed her handing a small bag of coin to a first mate. He nodded and pointed in the direction of a small vessel. Mila nodded in response and moved quickly to meet Damon and explain the plans for their travel.

"Well?" Damon asked impatiently.

"They will allow three to travel, but they only go as far as the next port." Mila said hurriedly. Damon shook his head in frustration.

"There is nothing else available?" He asked her.

"No. The other ships are traveling north or east. Nowhere near Arvenia." Mila answered him.

Damon nodded. "Then we will take it. One port closer to Arvenia puts us one port closer to Ansley. We will find something else once we get there." Mila nodded her agreement and hurried to inform the others. Damon glanced at the rolling sea and sighed. "Ansley, what have you done?"

*****

Mila returned to the docks within the hour with Josilyn following quickly behind her. Damon glanced at them both uncertainly. "You were supposed to bring Kenna. Why is *she* here?" He asked with confusion.

Mila glanced back at Josilyn and opened her mouth to respond to her father, but Josilyn responded first. "Kenna is still wounded. She is not fit for travel, so she will help us from Calvenia. You can summon her into a dream when we need her."

Damon nodded with surprise. They were right. Kenna was still injured, but now that left him with a young one and his own daughter for company on a dangerous mission. *How could things get any worse?* Damon wondered. Josilyn heaved her bag onto her shoulder and pushed past Damon as she sensed his frustration. Mila glared at her father and said quietly, "Josilyn is more helpful than you think she is. We are lucky to have her here." Then Mila stormed after Josilyn, and Damon quietly watched them board the ship that would take them south. Finally, he heaved his own travel bag over his shoulder and followed the young girls, hoping that his daughter was right about Josilyn. He certainly needed someone with some grit to help him chase down Ansley and convince her not to do something stupid. *Ansley will be the death of me.* He thought sadly, as he stepped onto the deck of the ship.

CHAPTER THIRTY-EIGHT
Two days later…
Ansley

Ansley stood at the railing of the upper deck and watched two sailors lower the anchor into the calm seas. It was a beautiful day, and the sky was empty of clouds. Birds flew overhead, and their calls echoed in Ansley's ears. She closed her eyes and breathed in the salty smell of the sea for the last time before she set foot onto land once more.

The sailors pulled a small rowboat to the edge of the ship and prepared to lower it into the waters below. Suddenly, Rhyn tapped Ansley on the elbow and nudged her forward. She stepped forward with her belongings bundled under her arm. A sailor offered her a hand into the rowboat that now dangled beside the large ship. Rhyn jumped into the rowboat after her, and three sailors followed him.

Once the five of them were settled, the rowboat was lowered very slowly. The three sailors in their boat attended to the ropes and ensured they would not come untied. Suddenly, the boat lurched, and Ansley felt the waves rolling beneath her. She sighed, happy to know that this part of her journey was almost over. Her soul was restless, and she glanced skyward hoping the gods would allow for fast travel.

The boat moved quickly in the calm seas, and Ansley watched the sailors pull the oars with considerable strength. The oars made ripples in the water around the boat each time they dipped into the sea. Ansley watched the ripples spread outward until they disappeared. She wondered how many ripples she herself had caused in the last months with her choices and actions to trust Magnus and his lies. How many ripples would her next choice cause in the lives of those closest to her? Ansley swallowed her emotions, and Rhyn, sensing her distress, placed his hand on hers reassuringly.

"Almost there." He said, gesturing to the shore.

Ansley nodded silently. "Moreland?" She asked him. He nodded.

"Yes. Do you know the history of the island?" He asked her, happy to provide a distraction.

Ansley shook her head. Rhyn smiled and said, "Ravyn of the Moreland people, from the lands to the northwest of Calvenia, was the first to reach our country to civilize our native peoples. She was an explorer and sought new lands for her country. This was where she first landed. The island was not truly named until many hundreds of years later when the kings agreed to name the island after her. They argued for years over whether it was acceptable to name a part of the country after a woman."

Ansley looked up at him angrily. "They would not name it after a woman when it was a woman who discovered their land? How have I not heard of this before? It was not something I was taught."

Rhyn nodded. "It was stricken from the history Arvenia provided to its commoners. The world is a strange place, isn't it?"

Ansley turned back towards the island ahead of her astonished by this piece of history she had never known. She felt betrayed and confused at how she could have been lied to about such an important detail. Then, a feeling of déjà vu hit her, and she found herself wondering if she was the one to blame for blindly accepting things told to her as truth without asking more questions.

*****

The island was more beautiful than anything Ansley had ever set foot on. The waters near the brown sandy shores were turquoise and lapped gently at her feet as she stepped onto land once more. Although it had only been a few days, Ansley felt that she had been on the *Flying Maiden* for months. The fresh air filled her lungs, and she felt calmer than she had since before her last dreamvision of Damon's death.

Ansley trudged through the wet sand, her feet sticking and making sucking noises when she tried to lift them up to take another step. Rhyn walked ahead of her and turned back frequently to check on her progress. She had opted for trousers today and was happy that she had done so. They were much lighter and cooler than any dress she carried in her travel bag. Ansley stopped for a moment and turned back to the seas, shielding her eyes with her hand to see the setting sun. The light threw beautiful shades of purple, pink, and orange across the horizon. Ansley gasped and took a moment to enjoy the beauty, one she may never experience again.

When she turned back towards the others, she saw that Rhyn had stopped walking to wait for her. He smiled at her warmly as she approached him. "Beautiful view, isn't it?" she asked him, speaking loudly over the sounds of the waves hitting the shore.

Rhyn's smile broadened as he said, "Yes. It is." He winked at her before turning around to follow the crew to the small village ahead. Ansley felt butterflies swarm in her stomach, but she pushed the thought aside. She had more important things to think about. She needed a plan, and she needed to make it quickly.

When they reached the village, the crew passed Rhyn and Ansley off to the parish leader. He informed them that there would be a small ship on the other side of the island leaving that night. The sailor lived on Arvenia's mainland, and he traveled between Moreland and Arvenia each day in search of fish to sell at the markets. Rhyn and Ansley crossed the island, which was only about a mile wide, found the dock they had been directed to, and refilled their packs with dried meats, cheese, and water. Once the sailor arrived at the dock prepared to return to his home for the night, Ansley and Rhyn were ready to board his small boat.

It was a modest fishing boat, but after an hour of rowing, it landed on the Arvenian coast, roughly to the northwest of Westfall. Ansley and Rhyn continued on foot along the well-worn dirt road towards the city for the night. The sky was cloudy, keeping the stars hidden. Ansley found that she was more anxious without their light. She had hoped to use them to navigate north to Avendale, but it seemed that would no longer be an option.

Rhyn was cheerful as always and guided Ansley slowly and patiently towards what they both hoped would be a warm meal and restful night's sleep. They talked some, but when silence fell between them, Ansley found it comforting instead of stifling, like it had been with many of her friends and other boys she had spent time with while growing up in Terra. This made her ache even more with the upcoming deception she had planned for leaving him on the road in pursuit of Magnus.

*****

Hours had passed since they had started on the road to Westfall, but finally, they arrived. They were sore, tired, and dirty, but they had finally reached one of the inns on the edge of the military parish. Ansley sat heavily on a chair in the tavern while she waited for Rhyn to secure them a room. She carefully removed her right boot and began rubbing and inspecting her foot. She shook her head as she found several large and painful blisters. *This is going to slow me down,* she worried, but Rhyn interrupted her thoughts by placing his hand on her shoulder.

She followed him up the steps to the rooms of the inn, and they entered a modest room at the end of the hall. When Ansley entered the room, she paused uncertainly. There was only one bed. She glanced nervously at Rhyn, who shook his head. "I will sleep on the floor with my bedroll. You take the bed." Guiltily, Ansley laid her traveling bag on the bed and began pulling out clean clothes to change into. She tried to push the thought of him lying on the hard, cold floor from her mind. She already felt guilty at the prospect of leaving him here alone tonight.

Rhyn sensed her unease and walked over to her. He placed his hand on top of hers and smiled sheepishly, misinterpreting her thoughts. "I have slept in much worse conditions. I promise, I will be fine." He patted her hand before turning away to unroll his blanket and bedroll. Ansley spent a few moments using the warm water from the pitcher that the innkeeper had placed on a side table to clean the dirt from her face and arms. The water was a refreshing reprieve from the heat of the day, so Ansley found it difficult to leave much for Rhyn to use.

Once they had settled, Rhyn on the floor and Ansley on the bed, they began talking about their journey this far. Ansley was surprised to hear that Rhyn had traveled this road before.

"Only once. My father, Rhys, and I came to Westfall to sell goods. It was a hard year, and we had made very little profit. Father was worried with winter approaching, so we made the journey in hopes of bringing home supplies before the first snow fell." He said, looking up at Ansley from his bedroll.

"*And*?" Ansley asked, wanting to know the result of their journey.

Rhyn chuckled. "Well, we did sell our wares, but we also lost half of our supplies on the journey home when our horse went lame. We couldn't pull the cart without her, so Father insisted we fill our packs with as much as we could carry." Rhyn laughed again. "I was determined to fill mine with more of the meats and canned vegetables than Rhys had filled his pack with, so I took out all my clothes and left them in the cart."

Ansley raised her eyebrows at Rhyn, waiting for him to continue. "Well, I learned my lesson within the day. A heavy snow started to fall as we journeyed the last few miles to our home. I had no cloak, heavy boots, or gloves. I caught a fever and was sick for a week. Father was furious!" Ansley smiled at his fond memories of his father.

"Did you get along with Rhys?" Ansley inquired.

Rhyn's smile died on his lips, as he realized that she had spoken of Rhys in the past tense, and he said softly, "Ansley, he is not dead. We will free him. You trust that, don't you?"

Ansley looked away from Rhyn, determined not to show emotion. Her attempts failed when she pictured her own grandmother, cold and huddled in some dark, unfriendly dungeon, awaiting who knew what. Tears flooded silently down her cheeks, and she covered her face with her hands, trying to hide from Rhyn. After a few moments, she heard him move and felt his strong, warm arms around her. She leaned into his shoulder and wept bitterly. He held her tightly and let her cry until her sobs turned to soft sniffles. When she had composed herself, she leaned away from his shoulder, and he held her chin in his hand. Then, Rhyn leaned in and kissed her gently.

Ansley soaked in his warmth and let all the grief and fear pour out of her. She focused solely on his hands, his lips, and his body. The two tangled together for some time until Ansley finally began reaching for the strings near the neck of Rhyn's tunic. His hand stopped hers, and they locked eyes for what felt like an eternity. Ansley was worried she had crossed a boundary, but then Rhyn let his hand fall away from hers.

Ansley moved closer to him on the bed and untied the strings of his tunic before pulling it over his head. Her gaze lingered on the muscles of his chest, and her hand trailed lightly down his back. His mouth met hers, and they fell backward onto the large bed. Rhyn's hands pulled up the edges of her nightgown, and Ansley let him remove it, shaking her dark hair loose over her shoulders. Rhyn's eyes glowed with a hunger that Ansley found she felt too. His hands explored her body until the two could resist each other no longer.

*****

When the candle had almost burned out and the silence of the room was filled with only Rhyn's soft snores, Ansley rose from the bed. She pulled on the set of traveling clothes that she had laid aside earlier and quietly laced her boots. She watched Rhyn carefully as she braided her hair back from her face. His face was slack, and his exhaustion from the days of travel was evident.

Ansley rose and pulled her traveling pack onto her shoulder. She wiped the tears from her eyes and turned away from where Rhyn lay resting, unsuspecting her deception. Her tears continued to fall as she walked down the stairs of the inn, paid the stableboy for a horse, and rode the mare quickly out of Westfall in search of what she assumed was her own doom. Secretly she hoped that in making this choice she would also ensure the safety of the man she had just abandoned in the night.

CHAPTER THIRTY-NINE
Kenna

Kenna and Lya sat at the dining room table and continued to drink coffee until Damon summoned Kenna in a dream with an update. Kenna responded to the summons but was disappointed with his news. At this rate, Damon, Josilyn, and Mila would not move quickly enough to catch up to Ansley and Rhyn before they docked at Arvenia.

Kenna pushed her chair back in frustration and excused herself from the table. Lya had just nodded silently after Kenna had shared the news, taking another sip of her hot brew. They had not slept since Josilyn had discovered Ansley's absence. Now Kenna was starting to feel the lack of sleep as she suppressed a yawn. She walked quickly to the room she had shared with the young ones, and she began changing into her traveling clothes.

She pulled on a pair of traveling pants, supple leather boots, and her heavy cloak that she fastened at her neck. Kenna knew where she had to go, and it would be a long ride. She walked back into the kitchen where Lya had not moved from her spot. Lya lifted her gaze to take in Kenna's change in appearance. She said nothing but lifted her eyebrows in question.

Kenna hesitated. She was in a hurry, but she was also troubled by the discovery she made several nights ago and hoped that Lya could share something to help her understand what had happened all those years ago to Edric's family. Kenna cleared her throat and sat back down in the chair across from Lya. "Lya, what can you tell me about the history here in Calvenia?" she asked softly.

Lya frowned in thought before smiling. "There are years and years to share, so unless you want a full history lesson, I'd suggest that you be more specific about the history you are interested in."

Kenna nodded, all business. "What about the last thirty years? Calvenia was not always led by elected rulers. What happened to the monarchy? Why did the power shift?"

Lya nodded as she sipped more of her coffee. "Well, it is not a happy tale, as I am sure you would expect. Changes like that rarely happen in a way that is beneficial for the rulers who are cast out." Lya looked at Kenna's face, gauging her reaction. Then she continued, "We had a ruling family since Calvenia was established as a separate nation from Arvenia. The family was respectable enough. I was just a young woman when the rebellion happened."

Kenna waited, twiddling her fingers under the table as she tried to contain her anxiety at hearing the story from a local. She wondered if Lya could sense her unease. Lya gave her a look that suggested she could, but then she began speaking again. "The country had changed. People were not happy, and the king was not changing fast enough with the times. A group of people decided they were ready to make that change happen, so they took it upon themselves to see that it did. They infiltrated the castle in Dunbar, and they captured the Royal family. We were never told exactly what happened to them, but the Calvenian people understood that they had been removed from the picture. We never saw them after that day, and nobody knows where or *if* they were even buried. The children too…" Lya finished shaking her head sadly and sipped on her coffee once more.

Kenna sat back in her chair, absorbing the information. She had to admit that she was disappointed that Lya had not shared more. Kenna tried to accept that the best source of information was the one she did not want to ask. She stood from the table and said, "Thank you. Lya, please don't tell anyone that I asked about it. Also, I need to leave for the day. Would you mind if I take one of your horses?"

Lya nodded and stood as she began leading Kenna to the stable behind the house. Before she walked out the front door, Lya asked softly, "Did I not give you what you needed?"

Kenna cleared her throat uneasily. "Do not trouble yourself, Lya. I will find out what I need to know one way or another." Then she followed Lya out to the stables, trying not to shiver from the bite in the air.

*****

Kenna dismounted her mare, happy to be on the ground again. She led the horse to the nearest tree trunk and tied the reins around it tightly. Then, Kenna stretched her left arm, trying to relieve the strain from her recent wound. It had not fully healed, and the ride had caused her pain. She patted the horse on its neck in thanks before walking towards the small cabin ahead. Kenna was not sure what had brought her here, but she knew this was where she was supposed to be.

Kenna raised her hand to knock on the door, but the door opened, saving her the effort. Kenna let her hand drop back to her side. Darby smiled at Kenna as if she had been expecting her since they had left her home over a week ago. She moved aside and held the door open for Kenna. Kenna stepped over the threshold, hopeful that Darby may be able to help her save Ansley before she did something foolish, but Kenna also hoped this meeting would shed light on the troubling truth of Edric's past.

CHAPTER FORTY
Ansley

Ansley yawned and covered her mouth with her hand as her horse neared the capital of Avendale. The lights of the town pulled her towards Avendale like a beacon, and even though Ansley saw the sun rising to the east, over her right shoulder, she felt that ahead of her was only darkness.

Ansley took a deep breath trying to quiet her racing thoughts. She wondered if Rhyn was still sleeping or if he was awake and looking for her. Her guilt grew into a sob, surprising her, and she quickly covered her mouth with her hand again to quiet her sorrow. Ansley wiped her eyes on the back of her sleeve and took deep breaths until she knew that she could face what was coming.

The sun rose in the sky, lighting up the landscape ahead of her. Ansley saw the stables outside the city. She led her horse in that direction, trying to focus only on what was in front of her. The city was still sleeping, but there were a few signs of it coming back to life. The stable boys were filling the horses' troughs with fresh water from wells, and the owners of the stables were opening the large doors to let in fresh air for the horses.

Ansley stopped her borrowed horse near the water trough and let her drink. Ansley slid off her back and removed a small sack of coins that she had placed in the saddlebag. A man with greying hair and spectacles approached her. "Good morning, miss! How can I help you?" He asked as he grabbed her horse's reins, ready to direct the mare into the stables behind them.

"I am going into Avendale for a few days. Maybe a week. Can I leave my horse here until I return?" Ansley inquired, thinking silently to herself that she would likely never see the poor beast again.

The man nodded. "Of course. We usually charge a set fee upon drop-off, and we will charge you the rest when you pick up."

"That works." Ansley said, opening her sack of coins. She gave the man three pieces of silver, even though he only asked for two. She knew she would not be returning, but he did not. The least she could do is offer him something in return for accepting her lies.

After the man led her weary horse to the stables and fresh hay, Ansley began walking towards the city. It was hard for her to believe that she had been here maybe only two months ago with Magnus. Her life had changed so much since then, but the city was just the same as she remembered.

Owners were opening their shops and stands. There were clothing stores, grain and supply stores, market stands, and small inns serving breakfast. The owners of the inns had the servers standing in their doorways yelling at passerby to try to bring in customers. Some were successful, but most were just annoying.

Ansley avoided the noise as much as she could. She found that the noises increased her nervous energy. Ansley walked to a small market stand selling fruits and bought two apples and an orange. Then, she meandered down the street until she found a stand selling dried meats. She bought a small package and found a shady step outside a temple to eat her breakfast.

Ansley ate the meat slowly, savoring her last meal free from captivity. *What am I doing here?* She asked herself anxiously, before hastily standing and tossing her remaining fruit into her pack. Then, she stopped as an older woman walked past her on the street. She was walking hand-in-hand with what appeared to be her granddaughter. The girl was giggling, and her grandmother was smiling, probably at something the girl had said to her. Ansley deflated and sat back on the step, unable to leave knowing that somewhere, her own grandmother was probably in chains. Ansley took another bite of her apple and resigned herself to her fate. So, she waited.

*****

Ansley wasn't sure what she was supposed to be looking for. She had sat in the same spot for a few hours, and no one had approached her. Only about an hour ago did she feel the strong pull to dreamwalk, and guiltily, she pushed it away. She knew Rhyn was trying to summon her, but she could not let herself see him. If she did, Ansley worried that she would leave before meeting Magnus.

She stood and decided to walk around a bit. Maybe she needed to make herself more visible to Magnus's lackeys. Ansley had taken only a few steps before a hand closed around her wrist in a vise-like grip. Ansley instinctively tried to pull away, but the hand did not let go. Ansley looked into the face of a woman and was shocked to realize this must be the one who was coming for her.

"Keep walking. Do not stop like a *fool*. Do you want the guard to stop us?" The woman hissed into Ansley's ear. Ansley kept walking, but the woman's grip on her never loosened. Ansley took small glances to try to get a picture of what the woman looked like. She wore baggy brown pants that were tucked into black leather boots, common for most women these days. The woman also had a hunter's green cloak on with the hood covering most of her face in shadow.

The woman hissed at Ansley again, pulling her around by her arm to face forward as they walked on. "You are making it *more* obvious!" Ansley stopped trying to look at the woman and instead continued walking. They walked down the streets of Avendale, but as they approached the castle gates, the woman steered Ansley quickly to her right into an alleyway. She pushed Ansley against the stone walls of a building and held a knife to her throat. Then, the woman pulled her hood off, revealing a striking face and an ever more striking head full of dark auburn hair that fell long past her waist.

"What is your name?" The woman asked softly, pressing the knife into Ansley's neck.

Ansley tried to swallow, but the knife edge was pressed so hard against her skin that she felt the sharp bite of the blade. Ansley closed her eyes and said, "It's Ansley. Of the Blacks."

"I thought so. Very well. We must be off. We have a long ride from here." The woman said as she put her knife back into her belt. She grabbed Ansley's wrist once more and spun Ansley to face away from her, towards the end of the alley, that eventually turned into a small dirt trail. Ansley marveled at how such a trail could exist without the guard finding it. Then, Ansley jumped in surprise as the woman bound her hands tightly together with rope. Ansley gasped in shock, but the woman simply finished tying her hands and then pushed her forward.

Ansley stumbled, and the woman laughed. "Come *girl*. You did not expect to be treated like *royalty*, did you?" Ansley's voice caught in her throat as her fears were realized. The woman tied a rope around Ansley's waist. Ansley caught sight of the woman's face once more and was surprised to notice how young she was. She must only be a few years older than Ansley. The woman's green eyes sparkled with what seemed like hate. When the rope was secured and the knots were tight, the woman tugged on Ansley and led her down the small path.

They walked for a short time before reaching a pair of saddled horses that were grazing near a grove of trees. The woman helped Ansley onto her horse, keeping Ansley's hands bound and the rope around her waist. With the end of the rope, she tied the horses reins together before mounting the second horse. She did not even glance back at Ansley before spurring her horse onward. Ansley's heart shattered into millions of pieces as she watched her freedom slip away. Then, she wondered how someone who did not know her could hate her so much already.

CHAPTER FORTY-ONE
Kenna

"I knew you would return." Darby said as she closed the door behind Kenna. Kenna looked at her quizzically before replying.

"Do you know why I am here?"

Darby smiled, her gray eyes appearing sad. "Yes, unfortunately. My dreamvisions come to me as pieces of a puzzle. Once the events unfold, I can piece them back together, but I have never been very good at preventing things from happening." Darby motioned to her kitchen table. "Please, sit. Can I get you anything?"

Kenna shook her head. "Just water. Please, I understand that you don't know our whole problem, but it has become rather urgent. Can you tell me where Ansley is?"

Kenna sat in a chair as Darby fetched a pitcher of water from her ice box. "No. I do not know where she is, but I know she will be with Magnus soon."

Kenna felt the blood drain from her face. She swallowed hard and asked, "What else do you know of him?"

Darby frowned. She sat with Kenna and folded her hands together in front of her. "Other than what I told you before, not much. He is *ancient*. Older than any dreamwalkers I know, but he is no walker."

"How can that be?" Kenna replied. "Typicals live only for a short time, whereas we endure."

Darby sighed. "The last time you were here, I mentioned necromancy. Do you know much of it? I am old, child, but even when I was born, the necromancers were being exterminated. There were very few left at that time, but there are even fewer now. Yet they still exist. Here and there."

"What does that have to do with Magnus?" Kenna asked, still confused by the direction the conversation had taken.

"Everything!" Darby exclaimed angrily. "*Don't* you see? Necromancers have the powers in the waking realm that we have in the dream realm. They have greater power and can extend life as well as take it. That is why they were feared. Their magic is...*unnatural*." Fear was clear in Darby's eyes, and Kenna could not help but wonder how someone so old could fear anything.

"And you think he has one? Helping him?" Kenna added.

Darby said, "Of course he does. He could have many for all I know, but there are other things about him you need to know. He is an advisor to the Arvenian king."

Kenna's eyes widened in surprise and fear. "The king? Our king? Why did you not tell us these things before we left your home? If you had told us then, we may actually have had a good plan that would keep Ansley from getting hurt!" Kenna accused Darby.

Darby closed her eyes, and for once, she looked her age. She sighed again. "Yes, you are right, Kenna. But I could not keep her from him. She had to go for certain events to take place, and whether you admit it or not will change nothing. Wheels have been set in motion, and those wheels were always meant to move this way. Seers can see what will happen, but we are not always meant to prevent. Sometimes we are simply meant to guide."

Kenna felt herself fuming. "So...how did you *guide* Ansley? It seems like you guided her straight to her death."

Darby remained calm, despite Kenna's accusation. "I guided her to begin asking questions. She needed to know what she was."

"Well, we all know now, with or without your help. *Listen*, I have come a long way, and I am tired, dirty, and worried. I do not have time to sit here with you and discuss your failings. Why don't you tell me how you *can* help, so I can get on my way?" Kenna asked, irritation flooding through her words.

Darby's lips curved into a small smile. "I can tell you about your husband. That's really why you are here, is it not?"

Kenna stared at Darby until Darby said, "Edric's history is a sad one, but you cannot blame him for hiding it. He is a *refugee*, Kenna. He would be put to death, simply for his name."

Kenna looked away from Darby. "He should have told me."

"Perhaps. But maybe he wanted to start a new life, and maybe you were the crowning jewel of that life." Darby said softly.

Now Kenna sighed. "There is *more* to it than that. I know he is hiding something else. Can you see what it is?" She asked Darby hopefully.

Darby shook her head. "No, child. I can only see his heart."

"And what is in it?" Kenna asked quietly.

"You." Darby replied. "Only you."

CHAPTER FORTY-TWO
Ansley

Ansley had lost track of the hour and where they were exactly. All she knew was that her legs and back ached. Her arms, though, hurt the most. With her hands tied, she had to lean forward to stay on the horse. She was just miserable.

The woman had not spoken to her since they had started riding. From what she could determine, Ansley thought they were moving northwest, but she could not be certain. Every hour or so, Ansley would once again feel that pull to dreamwalk. She did not know if it was Damon, Josilyn, or Rhyn, but she assumed Rhyn would have alerted the others to Ansley's disappearance by now. They were probably searching through Avendale for her if the others had made it back to Arvenia. She could not help but hope they came across her. She had known all along that sacrificing herself for her friends and family would not be pleasant or easy, but so far, it had been *horrible*. Ansley had expected Magnus to treat her better than this, and she worried what may happen to her next.

Suddenly, Ansley noticed the woman was picking up speed. She raced their horses down a very large hill and through a small stream. They raced faster and faster, until Ansley could barely keep her seat. She shouted, but the woman did not turn to look at her. The woman led the horses into a forest, and Ansley closed her eyes to keep from screaming again. They were moving so fast, it looked as if her horse would run right into a tree trunk.

Then, all at once, the horses stopped. Ansley felt her stomach lurch to keep up with the movement. She opened her eyes and vomited into the grass on her left. The woman turned then, looked at Ansley's face, which had grown pale, and chuckled again.

When Ansley finally looked up, she saw a small castle ahead of them. It was made of stone, and there was a gate with a bridge leading to it.

The horses continued on towards the castle, and Ansley prepared herself for an unhappy reunion with her grandmother and Magnus.

*****

The guards untied Ansley's hands after pulling her down from her horse. Her knees had buckled, and she had almost fallen face first onto the polished floor. The guards had caught her, but they were not gentle about it. Once the ropes were removed from her wrists, they began searching her for weapons.

They found only the small knife tucked into her waistband. One of the guards tucked it into his own waistband before lifting a set of chains. Ansley's heart began hammering. "What *harm* can I do? I'm just a *girl*..." she said pathetically.

The guards looked at one another, questioning their orders, but they soon decided that it was in their best interests to follow them. They chained Ansley's hands together. Ansley was surprised to realize she preferred the chains to the ropes. At least her shoulders did not ache from the constant strain.

The guards led her through the halls of what Ansley assumed were servant's quarters. They finally approached a set of stairs and descended until they no longer saw windows shining with the sun. One guard lit a torch while the other pulled Ansley forward down even more stairs. Finally, the stairs ended. The floor was dirt here, and Ansley grimaced at the smell. They must be in the dungeons. The guards led her on, finally stopping outside a large cell. She saw no one inside, but then her attention was directed to the figure standing in the shadows ahead of her.

He leaned against the bars casually, as if he were meeting Ansley in a tavern instead of a dungeon cell. When he stepped out of the shadows, Ansley was surprised to see that he looked different.

Magnus had grown his beard out, and his hair was longer with curls drifting down towards his ears. He wore what looked like a cream satin shirt, riding pants, and boots that shone like gold. He had a red cape streaming down from his shoulders, and Ansley noted with disgust, there was a small crown of thin gold perched upon his brow. When the guards saw him, they stopped immediately and went down on one knee.

"Your grace." They both said quietly. Magnus waved his hand, and the guards stood again. Magnus took a step towards Ansley, who moved away from him. The guards grabbed her arms and kept her in place until Magnus was nearly nose-to-nose with her.

"Welcome. You look like you could use a warm meal and a bath." Ansley stared at him in contempt, and Magnus grabbed her chin tightly, turning her head to the side. "We made a bargain, and I am very pleased that you have held up your end. Now it is my turn."

Magnus released her face and stepped back. He motioned to the guards to follow him, and he walked past a few more cells before he finally stopped. He gestured inside. The guards released her, so Ansley stepped forward to look through the bars. Her heart lurched when she saw two figures inside, leaning against the stone wall. It looked like they were sleeping.

"Open it." Magnus said. The guards stepped forward and unlocked the cell. The figures inside shifted but did not look up. Once the doors were pulled open, they finally looked to see who had arrived.

"Nana!" Ansley screamed, running forward to see her grandmother. Magnus reached Ansley first and grabbed her around her waist, holding her back.

Ansley struggled against his grasp, but as her eyes settled on her grandmother's face, she stilled. Her grandmother's eyes were bright, and dirt was smeared on her face. Her clothes were in tatters and covered in dirt too, probably from sleeping on the filthy floor. But she was unharmed. Bianca stood and moved as close as she could manage with the chains around her wrists. "*Ansley*? Is that you?"

"Yes, Nana. It is alright. I am here to help." Ansley said quietly. Bianca shook her head.

"You should not be here. You are *foolish*, child. Why have you done this?" Bianca said in a rush, emotion fueling her words. Ansley was hurt by these words, but she knew why her grandmother said them. Unwilling to be chastised for her choices in this moment, she turned to Magnus who had released her and now stood behind her.

"Let her go. You have me, so free her. *Now*." Ansley said through gritted teeth.

Magnus inclined his head and turned to his guards. "You heard her. Do as she asks." The guards looked between Ansley and Magnus, hesitating. Finally, they moved to Bianca and removed her chains. Bianca tried to rush toward Magnus, but the guards stopped her by tripping her. Ansley gasped as Bianca hit the dirt floor. The sound echoed throughout the cell.

The two guards scooped Bianca off the floor and began to drag her out of the cell. Bianca lifted her head and reached towards Ansley to grab her hand, but the guards pulled her away before Ansley could move close enough. "Wait!" Ansley yelled in protest, but the guards had already moved out of sight. Ansley turned on Magnus. "How *could* you!"

Magnus shrugged his shoulders. "I said I would release her. I did not say that I would allow lengthy family reunions." The guards returned without glancing at Ansley. They waited for Magnus to direct them further. Magnus merely pointed to the other slumped form in the cell and said, "Him too. Have the physician look him over before he is released." The guards nodded and moved towards the figure.

Ansley was not surprised to see Rhys raise his head, but she *was* surprised to see the shape he was in. His face was covered in scars and bruises, and it looked like he was unable to walk on his own. Rhys was extremely skinny, just a shadow of the handsome figure she had seen in her dreams. Ansley ran forward this time out of Magnus's reach and touched Rhys's face. Rhys opened his eyes, and his face lit up with fear at the sight of her.

"Ansley! What are you *doing* here?" He groaned, his voice barely audible.

"I am so sorry, Rhys. Please, forgive me for all of this." Ansley said, as the guards pushed her out of their way.

Rhys turned his head back as they passed her and said in a louder voice, "It was never your fault. This is not your crime to account for!" But then, he too was gone. Ansley tried to hold back her tears as she heard Rhys's protests as the guards carried him up the stairs to freedom. Her attention was drawn back to Magnus who smiled at her and raised his hands in the air with his palms facing upward.

"There. We have both held up our bargains. Now, *shall we?*" Magnus asked. It was obvious he was quite pleased with himself. Ansley wiped her tears away angrily and followed him out of the cell. What else could she do at this point? This had been her choice, and she had made it. She had gotten all that she had asked for, so now it was her turn to cooperate.

Ansley followed Magnus back up every step into the castle once more. The halls were full of the afternoon light, and the setting sun turned the walls to red, as if warning Ansley of the dangers ahead. *If only the sun could burn this place down.* She thought dejectedly. Ansley followed Magnus down hall after hall, until finally he approached a wooden door. He removed a key from his pocket, and Magnus unlocked the door. He motioned for Ansley to enter. When she did, her breath caught in her throat.

"You are a guest here. For your services, I will provide you with comfort. You need not live in the dungeons like a prisoner." Ansley looked around at the room. It was painted cream, and there was a large four-poster bed in the center of it. A giant patterned rug covered the polished floors beneath the bed, and there were four large windows looking out towards the west. Ansley noted the bars on the windows before looking back at Magnus in question.

"I said you are a guest here. I did not say you were free to go as you please." Magnus responded. He motioned to the windows. "Recent addition. The windows were too lovely to nail boards over. I hope you enjoy the view. I always do this time of day. Make yourself comfortable here. It is now your home." Magnus turned away from her and exited the room, closing the door loudly behind him. Then, Ansley heard him turn the key in the lock, sealing his prize inside her new cage. Finally, alone, Ansley sank to her knees and sobbed.

CHAPTER FORTY-THREE
Damon

Damon shouldered his traveling pack as he followed Josilyn and Mila down the ladder to the rowboat. They had finally reached the shores of Arvenia and had docked near Westfall. Damon had heard no word from Kenna or Ansley since he left Dunbar. The silence worried him.

Mila and Josilyn chose seats in the small row boat and smiled at one another. Damon sat across from his daughter and watched her closely to distract his thoughts from Ansley and their predicament. Mila's cheeks were flushed as she spoke to Josilyn, and Josilyn was grinning from ear to ear, chiding Mila about something. Probably some joke between the pair of them. Since they had left the harbor in Dunbar, Damon had felt oddly like the third wheel. He was not sure how it made him feel, considering it was his daughter that was starting a new relationship.

Mila laughed, a rare sound, and a smile erupted on Damon's face. *If she's this happy, it cannot be too bad. Besides, Josilyn seems nice enough.* Damon thought to himself as he turned away from the pair to stop eavesdropping on their conversation. Damon glanced ahead to the harbor of Westfall. He saw soldiers marching and patrolling along the dock. This was the part of Arvenia reserved for training of troops. Damon had heard many things about this parish over the years, but he had never visited it.

Suddenly, Damon felt a tug inside his chest upon what seemed an invisible string. It had been many, many years since he had felt this pull from another dreamwalker's summons. He gave in and allowed himself to drift into a dream, hopeful that he would be meeting with Ansley. He needed to talk some sense into that girl...

*

Damon appeared in a dark room as soon as his eyes closed. A large wooden table was in front of him, so he sat and waited. Then, a hand closed on his shoulder, causing him to jump. He turned to see Kenna behind him.

"Sorry! I didn't mean to sneak up on you. I was just trying to find a spot to stop riding for a moment, and I couldn't be here when you fell asleep. I have news." She said as she walked around the table and sat down. The room was empty and plain. Damon was always amused with how dreamwalkers could create the most beautiful spaces sometimes and on other occasions, be so unimaginative.

"What is it? Is she alive?" Damon asked. His heart felt like it was being squeezed by an invisible hand as he waited for her response.

"Yes." Kenna responded. Damon breathed out in relief. "But, he has her, Damon. I went to see Darby, that old seer near Dunbar. She told me that it was Ansley's fate to go to Magnus. She had every chance to warn us, but she didn't. She could have cost Ansley her life." Kenna added with frustration.

Damon frowned. "Fate? Fate has nothing to do with it. Ansley made a choice, and it could cost her everything and us everything too. Darby chose not to act out of superstition, and now we have to deal with the consequences!" Damon said, his voice growing louder with each word. He slammed a fist on the table in frustration. "Did she tell you anything *helpful?"*

Kenna nodded and said, "Magnus has a necromancer. Maybe a few, and apparently, he is an advisor to the king. King Orlan." She looked at Damon meaningfully. Damon didn't miss her meaning.

"Gods. We may never find her, Kenna." Damon replied. Kenna just nodded. They sat staring at one another for several minutes until Kenna's eyes widened. "Damon, I think I have a plan."

"I hope it's better than mine." Damon said sullenly.

"You have one too?" Kenna asked uncertainly.

"Yes, but mine involves mostly whiskey and weapons." Damon said as he scratched his beard.

"We have to find Bianca. She may be able to lead us to Ansley. If Ansley turned herself over to Magnus, there is a small chance that he released Bianca and Rhys, Rhyn's brother. If we can locate her, we may be able to get to Ansley before she is in any real danger." Kenna said, her words rushing out of her.

"Hmm." Damon said thoughtfully. "I like it. What should I do?"

Kenna responded, "Try to summon her. Try to summon Bianca. Seers are not as talented when it comes to summoning, but I need all the help you can offer."

Damon nodded. "I will do everything I can, and Josilyn and Mila will be happy to help too." Kenna smiled. "Send word to me if you reach her."

*****

Bianca and Rhys had been given one horse and a very old wagon when they had been thrown outside of the castle. Bianca may have been disgusted, but she was too hurt to feel anything else. Poor Rhys was still very weak, so she positioned him in the back of the cart and took the horse's reins herself to steer them towards Terra. As they rode in silence, Bianca could swear that she heard her heart breaking into more and more pieces. *Why did Ansley come? He will destroy her!* Tears fell silently from her eyes, blurring her vision and making it difficult for her to stay on the path. The cart lurched wildly as one of the wheels rolled over a large stone on the path. She heard a loud snapping sound, so she promptly stopped the old horse to investigate.

Rhys sat up in the cart, disoriented. "What was that? Are you okay?"

Bianca climbed down to inspect the horse's legs and the cart wheels. "Yes, I am fine," she cursed under her breath as she noticed the broken axle on the front left wheel of the cart. "Unfortunately, our cart is not." Bianca kicked the cart wheel in anger until she could no longer feel her toes. Then she sat down in the dirt and let her anger roll over her in waves.

Rhys simply looked at her from where he sat. She knew he understood, and frankly, there was nothing either of them could do to fix the situation. The wheel was just another frustrating element to their dilemma. Bianca sat for what seemed like hours beside the broken cart. When she finally felt her anger burn out, Bianca noticed that the sun had begun to drop in the sky. She stood. She knew they needed to find water and shelter before night fell. They may have a cart, but that monster had not given them anything else.

Bianca felt it just as she started to climb into the cart once more. She felt that familiar pull, and her heart exploded with hope. She allowed herself to be pulled into a dream, hoping to see her granddaughter's face.

*

When Bianca closed her eyes, she was surprised to see Damon instead of Ansley. Fury overtook her, and she marched right up to that solemn man and slapped him as hard as she could. Damon's face snapped in the opposite direction, and when he looked back at her, blood trickled from the corner of his mouth. He wiped it gingerly but said nothing. He knew why she had hit him and knew better than to scold her, even if he was her elder.

Damon stretched his jaw and said, "Well, since that is out of the way, Bianca, we need your help. Have you been freed? Can you help us reach Ansley?" He said quickly, maintaining his distance from her.

"Of course, I am free, and why am I free, Damon? Because Ansley traded her freedom for mine. This is all your fault! You lied to my face and then turned around and allowed my granddaughter to go to that monster! You should be ashamed of yourself, you worthless, son-of-a-" Bianca said angrily but Damon raised his hands in the air to stop her.

"Yes, yes. I know, and you're right. I had no right to betray your trust like that, but I did. Now I am trying to fix it, and I need your help, Bianca. So would you rather waste your time chastising me, or would you prefer to tell me where in the gods' names you are so I can save your granddaughter's life?" Damon's face was alight with anxious energy that Bianca had never seen in him before. She deflated.

"Do not fail me this time, Damon." She breathed. Her sorrow echoed through her words with the pain she felt at being ripped away from Ansley.

"You have my word, Bianca. I will not." Damon said, placing his hand on her shoulder.

CHAPTER FORTY-FOUR
Ansley

Ansley cried for hours in her lovely room. She threw pillows off the bed. Pulled the curtains from the windows, and she threw the one glass vase into the empty fireplace. Glass shards erupted and flew in various directions across the floor. Ansley looked at them for a moment and wondered how she could avoid cutting her feet. Then, she was struck by an idea. She rushed forward and began sweeping the shards of glass below the grate of unburned wood in the fireplace. She scooped soot and scattered it over the shards to keep the light from reflecting on them. Ansley found the biggest piece of glass and tucked it into her waistband to hide until the time was right.

She had just stood and was wiping her hands off when she heard the key turning in the door. Quickly, Ansley threw herself onto the bed, laying as if asleep. When the door was flung open, she sat up as if waking because of the noise. Four armored guards marched into the room, while two more stood at the door, keeping watch in the hallway. Ansley sat up on the bed in alarm as the guards approached her.

The men did not speak to her. They barely even glanced at her as they grabbed her arms and forced her to her feet. One guard stepped forward with two sets of chains. He grabbed Ansley's wrists one at a time and closed the rusted metal bands over them. The chain connecting her wrists was much smaller this time, and Ansley could barely separate her hands. Then, the guard knelt to the floor and snapped another set onto Ansley's legs. Ansley looked at him in surprise, unsure what exactly was happening now. The guard stood and grabbed her by the arm, pulling her out the door. Ansley stumbled as the chains around her ankles pulled taught. She tripped and fell. The guards let her hit the floor without making any effort to catch her, and her head smashed into the polished stone.

Ansley's vision went dark, but she still tried to push herself up from the floor. Her head swam, so she let herself sink back to the cool stone. She distantly heard a guard mutter, "*Dreamwalker* trash…" and then felt a sharp pain in her stomach where his boot made contact. Ansley gasped for air, but then she was dragged from the floor by two of the guards. The one that had put chains on her stepped in front of her face, nearly touching his nose to hers.

"You *knew*, didn't you? Didn't you!!" He screamed in her face. Ansley winced and tried to back away from him, surprised by his anger.

"What? I-I don't know what you mean. I did as he *asked*." Ansley gasped in response, trying to catch her breath in between words. The guard raised his hand to hit her, and Ansley closed her eyes in anticipation. The blow never landed though. When Ansley felt brave enough to open her eyes, she saw that the guards had parted. Magnus now stood in front of her. Rage was radiating from him in silent waves. His blue eyes erupted with fury.

"Ansley, my dear. I am sorry to *disturb* you at this hour, but I am afraid I have need of your presence in the dungeon." Magnus said softly, his voice barely audible. Before she could respond, Magnus turned and left the room. Ansley was carried forward by the guards. One pair flanked Magnus, and the other flanked her.

They reached the dungeon much quicker than they had

left it. Magnus led them to the first cell, a small one in comparison with the one that had held her grandmother and Rhys. Magnus turned and motioned for the door to be unlocked. His face had turned white with the rage simmering beneath his calm manner. Finally, he erupted.

Magnus grabbed Ansley by her shoulder and dragged her into the dungeon. He threw her upon the dirt floor and shouted at his guards, "Secure her!". They responded quickly, happy to meet his needs and avoid his wrath themselves.

Ansley's chains were locked to a set of chains along the wall. Then Magnus moved towards her once more, standing over her where she sat on the hard ground. His voice started low and gained volume as he continued. "We had a deal, Ansley. You told me you had upheld your part, and now I find *him* trespassing in my castle! How *dare* you betray me! I promised safety for all of your *worthless* friends and family, and this is how you respond? You will *regret* this." Magnus's eyes narrowed as he said those last two words.

Ansley's heart began hammering in her chest. She had no idea what Magnus was insinuating, but it was not too difficult for her to guess who *he* was. Magnus moved towards the wall to allow two of his guards to enter. They carried a man between them. His head lolled, but it was just as Ansley had feared. It was Rhyn.

"This *boy* was discovered after he attacked two of our guards and seized the keys to the dungeon. I assume he was attempting to *free* you?" Magnus growled at Ansley.

A cry escaped her lips, and she stood and tried to move to where the guards held Rhyn. Her chains stretched taut as she pulled helplessly against them, trying to yank them free from the wall. Then she turned to Magnus again, ready to beg. "Please! He had nothing to do with this. This is between *us*. He has nothing of value to you!" She screamed.

Magnus looked at Rhyn for a moment. "Perhaps you are right. Guards!" Magnus called loudly. Ansley turned back to where the guards were, in hopes they would release Rhyn's arms, but one guard unsheathed his sword and laid the bare blade over the back of Rhyn's neck. "If he cannot help, why should I keep him?" Magnus snarled at her.

Ansley's eyes widened in fear. She had trusted him. She just realized how foolish she had been. She had trusted Magnus, and he was a lying monster. This was all *her* fault. Rhys, Bianca, and now Rhyn. Ansley stood tall and calmed herself. Magnus waited for her response.

"You will let him live." She said quietly.

Magnus smiled, his eyes widening. "Oh?" He chuckled and looked back at Rhyn. "Why is that?"

"Because if you don't, I will never give you what you want." Ansley replied.

"And what do you think I want?" Magnus asked.

"Revenge." Ansley said simply. Magnus's smile faded, replaced by a cold look of hatred.

"So, it is true. You are Rosalie's legacy. I was right after all." Magnus breathed.

"No, I may or may not be her legacy, but I am most certainly *your* doom." Ansley replied, looking into those black eyes as she spoke. Magnus smiled and laughed suddenly at what Ansley said. The guards looked nervously at one another, awaiting orders. Finally, Magnus turned to his guard holding the sword, the one that had shouted at Ansley in her room earlier. The guard lowered his sword and sheathed it.

"Very well, Ansley. I will play your *game*. I will allow him to live, but it will be on my terms. I will be back shortly. You may regret this decision you have made. Trading your life…for his." Magnus turned to exit the door, his red cape flowing elegantly after him.

Tears filled her eyes as she watched the guards drop Rhyn to the floor and exit behind Magnus. "Never." Ansley said to herself softly. "*Never*."

*****

Ansley waited in the dark, staring at Rhyn's motionless shape crumpled on the floor. Finally, after what she guessed were several hours, Rhyn stirred. She heard him groan as he lifted his head. His eyes were unfocused as he pushed himself to his hands and knees in front of where she sat, just out of his reach. When Rhyn finally saw her, he froze. "Ansley?" he asked tentatively.

"It's me, Rhyn." Ansley responded, her voice breaking on his name. Rhyn hurriedly made his way over to her and grabbed her in his arms. He held her tightly, and the room melted away just for a moment. Ansley closed her eyes, trying to imagine they were somewhere else. Rhyn finally let go and held her at arm's length, examining her.

"Are you alright? I am sorry it took me so long. I lost your trail in Avendale. I was so close, and…" Rhyn started. He stopped talking when Ansley started crying. His dirt-covered fingers wiped away the tears on her cheeks, but Ansley continued to sob. Rhyn pulled her into his arms once more and held her until she quieted.

"Rhyn, I…" she started, but Rhyn shook his head.

"Don't, Ansley. I know why you left me. I forgive you." Rhyn said as he brushed away a strand of hair that had fallen from her braid into her face. Rhyn's hand stopped as he glanced at her temple, where her head had hit the floor. He inspected her head closely and hatred filled his eyes. "They did this?"

Ansley did not answer. Instead, she offered Rhyn what hope she could. "He is *free*, Rhyn. They let your brother go. He is alive, and he is free." Rhyn stared at her as if she was crazy before saying, "Ansley, you know I love Rhys, but I will not let you do this. I will not let you sacrifice yourself for everyone."

Ansley's eyes filled with tears once more. But before she could answer, Magnus's voice echoed through the cell. "I am so sorry to disappoint you, Rhyn. Ansley has already bargained away her freedom. If *you* are lucky, maybe I will allow you to keep yours." Magnus stepped up to the door and unlocked the cell. He held the door open for a man wearing a green hooded cloak that entered behind him. His hood obscured his face, but when he drew closer, Ansley noticed what he was carrying. A glass jar filled with a boiling orange concoction.

Rhyn moved in front of her, but Magnus laughed softly. "Do not *try* me, boy. I dealt with who I assume was your brother. I can deal with you also." Rhyn's face turned bright red, but he clenched his jaw shut. He looked nervously at Ansley who grabbed his hand and squeezed it tightly. The man wearing the hood stepped closer and waited for Magnus to lock the door behind him.

When Magnus had turned back away from the locked prison door, the other man removed his hood. The man was shorter than both Rhyn and Magnus, but his confidence radiated in the way he carried himself. His hair was short, and his nose was sharp. He turned to Magnus, "Are you ready?" He asked him.

Magnus nodded. The man handed him the glass of orange liquid. "Remember. Slowly…" the man said. Magnus glanced nervously at this new man. Then, he lifted the glass to his lips and drank. He drank until half of the glass of liquid remained. Then, he returned the glass to the man's open hand.

Magnus looked warily at him before clutching his stomach. "Regin...it *burns*." Magnus said, as he bent over in pain.

Regin nodded and circled his master. "Yes, your grace. It is working." Magnus moaned, and Regin gently touched him on the shoulder. "She has to drink now." Magnus looked up at Regin's face and nodded, still in obvious pain.

"Do it." He said to Regin. Regin did not hesitate. He drew a short dagger from his sleeve and held it to Rhyn's bare throat. Rhyn tried to fight him off, but then Regin sliced lightly until blood trickled down into Rhyn's shirt collar. Regin's green eyes met Ansley's. Her heart beat frantically.

Regin said simply, "Make your choice. Your skill," he said, looking at Rhyn who was trying to push the dagger from his neck. "Or his life." Ansley nodded without hesitation and reached for the glass. Regin handed it to her, dragging Rhyn along with him.

"No, Ansley!" Rhyn shouted at her, but she had already tipped the glass back and downed the hot, orange potion. As soon as she finished drinking, Ansley dropped the glass. It shattered as she fell to the floor, writhing in pain. She heard shouts and voices in the cell, but she could not focus on anything but the pain she felt as the liquid seared her throat and exploded in her stomach. The fire burned and grew until Ansley thought she may be sick from it. She rolled over onto her hands and knees, but a rough hand grabbed her wrist, pulling her across the floor.

Ansley felt a sharp pain slice across her palm, and then her hand was pressed hard into someone else's. The fire she felt filling her entire body found an exit and quickly began pouring from the cut Regin had made to her hand. Ansley opened her eyes to see that her entire body was glowing and light poured from her palm into Magnus's.

Rhyn lay on the floor staring at her in fear. Then, he grabbed the abandoned dagger Regin had thrown aside and ran forward, eager to save Ansley.

Regin looked up from where he knelt, holding Ansley's and Magnus's hands together tightly. "If you break the connection, she dies!" He growled at Rhyn. Rhyn stopped suddenly and dropped the dagger. He rushed to Ansley's side and fell to his knees unsure of how to help. Ansley looked at him in horror, her body still burning with the fire from the potion. But then, she felt it ebbing. The fire seemed to be burning out at last.

Ansley looked at her feet and other hand and saw that she was no longer glowing. Her skin was pale, and she felt lightheaded. Light continued to pour from her palm into Magnus's. He sat on his knees with his face to the ground, howling in pain himself as Ansley's skill poured into him. Ansley watched it leave her body and suddenly felt herself shiver. Her arms felt heavy, and she fell heavily to the ground.

Rhyn pulled her onto his lap and touched her face. His eyes were full of tears as he called her name. She could not hear him. She could not hear anything. Her ears were filled with a loud humming noise, and her vision grew more and more cloudy. The only thing she felt was a distant burning in her hand and Regin's strong grip on her wrist.

Then, Rhyn stood, carefully lowering Ansley to the floor. She was too weak to move, so she turned her head to see that Regin had been battered over the head and now lay unconscious on the floor. Ansley's hand was no longer held against Magnus's. Magnus lay face-down on the ground and did not move. Ansley turned to look for Rhyn but a sudden movement drew her eye. A familiar face swam over hers.

His lips moved, but no sound met her ears. Damon's eyes were full of fear as he touched Ansley's brow hesitantly. Then, she finally heard him. "...not let go, Ansley. I will *not* let you. I made Bianca a promise, dammit, and I intend to see it through. *Ansley*! Come back to us!! Do not give in this easy! You are stronger than this!" Damon shouted at her and gently squeezed her shoulders. Ansley blinked the tears from her eyes, and they ran down her face into the dirt.

She saw more movement to her left, but before she could look, someone moved into view above Damon as he knelt over her. Damon turned his head a moment too late, and Magnus thrust Regin's dagger into Damon's chest. Damon's face contorted in shock, and he looked down where the hilt protruded from his wound. Blood fell from him onto Ansley where she lay below him on the dirt.

Horror filled Ansley, and she tried to reach for Damon, but her arms would not move. They were too weak. Damon grabbed Magnus's wrist that held the hilt still, but Magnus twisted viciously, causing Damon's hand to drop once more. He leaned forward, his eyes burning at Magnus, and finally Magnus pulled out the dagger. Blood poured from the wound in Damon's chest as he fell onto his side. Magnus stood over Damon and wiped the dagger on a corner of his cape. He sneered and glanced momentarily at Ansley. Then, he fell screaming to his knees once more.

Suddenly, light poured from his outstretched hand back into Ansley's. Ansley pulled herself to a sitting position, as her skill returned to her. Her back arched in response to the power that poured back into her body. Finally, the transfer ended, and Ansley's mark burned as it once had when she had first been marked in her trials.

She saw several figures move around her as she

suddenly felt a surge of power. Rhyn crawled to her and grabbed her arms. "Ansley!" He shouted. "Are you alright?" Ansley turned to see Regin pulling himself to his feet near where they sat. He had retrieved his dagger and snarled as he lurched in their direction.

Ansley wrapped her hands around Rhyn's wrists, and he looked down for just an instant before he realized what she was trying to do. "Ansley, don't you *dare*!" He screamed at her. She was not sure she could use it at will when she was not in the dream realm, but she had to try. Ansley closed her eyes and thought of the furthest place she had ever read about. She reached out and placed her hands on Rhyn's chest, and then, he disappeared.

Moments later, Regin reached her. Rhyn was long gone, and Regin could not harm him now. Regin growled and slapped her across the face with a force strong enough to send her to the ground. Ansley fell and when she opened her eyes, she stared into Damon's. He lay in front of her, struggling to breathe and holding his hands over his chest, trying to stop the blood from flowing out of him. Blood bubbled at his lips, but his eyes stayed on hers. Then he closed his eyes for an instant, and Ansley understood. She closed hers too and immediately fell into his dream.

*

Damon grabbed her roughly with both hands. "I don't have much time, Ansley."

Ansley nodded at him. "I know. Damon, I am so sorry!" She said helplessly, ashamed that she had led him to such a horrible end. All for what?

Damon shook her shoulders roughly. "Listen to me!" Ansley eyes focused on his. "It is up to you now. The others can help you, but they will not be able to reach you here. Do you understand?"

Ansley nodded. "Yes, Damon."

"You have to fight him, Ansley, and you are strong enough. Look what you just did to Rhyn in the waking realm. Magnus will destroy us all if you cannot find a way to defeat him. Do you understand me?" Damon asked her desperately. Ansley placed her hands over Damon's and noted that they had grown cold. *"I will fight him, Damon. I won't allow him to win this battle. I swear this to you."* Damon's eyes started to haze over, then he closed his eyes as if he was searching for something in his mind. Ansley squeezed his hands tightly, and Damon frowned as if trying to see her through a heavy fog.

"Damon, I swear to you. I will end this." Damon nodded once, and then, he disappeared into thin air. Ansley turned in a circle looking for him, but it was too late. Her fellow Seer, her master, her friend...was gone.

*****

Kenna felt an uneasy sensation as she fell into a dream. Looking around, she noticed the haste of the dream. The shadows edged closer and closer to her, barely maintaining their distance. She tried to push them away, but they would not listen to her commands. This dream was fading already.

A pair of hands grasped Kenna's arm urgently. She turned, afraid of what she may find, to see a pale face with black eyes that had an unnatural shine to them. Kenna gasped as she took in Damon's blood-soaked shirt, and the blood spurting from a wound in his chest. Unable to stand any longer, Damon fell to his knees. Kenna made to catch him, but instead, they fell to the ground together. She grasped the dying man in her arms trying to help him any way she could. It was no use. They both knew it.

Damon coughed and tried to find his voice. "The truth. You need to know, Kenna...," he sputtered, wincing in pain. Kenna used her sleeve to wipe the blood from his face. Damon coughed again and added, "Your mother. She was elite too. She died from the sickness. Not by her own hand. She knew...she knew..." Damon's eyes began to lose their glow, and Kenna held her breath as she soaked in the words he had whispered into the darkness surrounding them. The words he had used his last moments to share. "She knew the truth." He said, closing his eyes to rest or to give in to death at last.

"She knew what, Damon?" Kenna asked urgently, knowing his time was almost spent.

"Her father. Her father...she got the sickness from him. He passed it on to her." Damon whispered; his voice barely audible. "Your father didn't know. She couldn't tell him."

Kenna shook Damon lightly until he opened his eyes again. "Damon, I don't understand." Damon's lips had started to lose their color. He looked at Kenna, sorrow lining his face. "She was elite, Kenna. Just like you, and it drove her mad. Her skill...killed her." Damon added weakly before his chest stopped moving. Kenna placed her hands on Damon's bloodied chest.

"Damon. Damon! No, it can't be. It doesn't make any sense! Damon, gods damn you!" She yelled as tears started to roll down her face. Damon heaved one more breath and whispered his last words while keeping his eyes closed. "Don't make her mistakes. Don't let it take over." Kenna held Damon's body until it disappeared in her arms, a mist of the man she had known. She covered her face, anguishing the death of a friend and the horrors of the secret he had imparted to her. As she stirred back to reality, Kenna lost sight of who she was. She fell into a pit of despair and stayed there, unwilling to be found. Unwilling to be rescued.

*

Ansley opened her eyes to see Damon's staring blankly back at her. She lay in shock at the events that had unfolded. Her mind separated itself from her body as she was dragged to her feet by guards and led back to her bright, cheerful room. Magnus snarled at her before closing the door and promising her he would be back to "try again" as soon as more of the potion was ready. Ansley said nothing in response to his threats.

She sat heavily on the large bed and stared out the windows. The sun had started to rise, and sunlight filtered over the treetops. Ansley watched it until its power filled the sky, and her eyes hurt from looking at it too long. She swore to herself at that moment, as her palm smeared bloody streaks on the beautiful quilt on her new bed, that she would not fail Damon. She would not fail her grandmother or her parents. She would not fail Kenna, Rhys, Josilyn, Mila, or Rhyn. She would not fail herself. She would defeat Magnus, and she would watch that monster burn before her time was done.

CHAPTER FORTY-THREE
Magnus

Magnus sat at his desk in his chambers as a crowd of servants flitted around him. His head thrummed still from the power of her skill. It had been his, his alone, for just moments, but he had felt it. Magnus knew what she could do, and he had it just for a few moments. The blood rushed loudly in his ears as he thought of all that had unfolded in that cell.

He glanced down at his hands where Damon's blood still coated them. The servants were too busy attending to Magnus's face and the cuts on his legs where the broken glass had cut deeply into him when the skill was flowing into his body. Magnus did not even remember when he had cut himself, but it was obvious now how badly he was injured. There was a gash across his left calf and three long cuts below his right knee. Blood was also smeared over his shirt, cape, and pants. The servants were relieved to find that this was not the blood of their master.

Magnus glared at Regin in the mirror ahead of him. He stood behind him, waiting silently for orders. Blood dripped slowly from the side of his head near his right ear, but Regin paid no mind to it. He waited. Expecting his punishment.

Magnus snarled, "Regin, you said this would work." Regin's eyes met Magnus's in the mirror, and Magnus swatted at the servant attending to the cut on his palm where the skill had poured into him. The servant hastily moved away and settled on removing the blood from

Magnus's face where he had smeared it when he had rubbed his face in frustration over their failure. *Flitting around like a knat*...Magnus thought angrily but allowed the servant to continue working.

Magnus's gaze settled back on Regin. He waited, fuming as the silence drew on. Finally, Regin spoke. "It was working, your grace. It was complete. It just did not *seal*. When that...boy *attacked* me, I was unable to seal the wound properly." Magnus glared at Regin, waiting for him to finish explaining. He didn't.

"Then what happened? How did she get it back?" Magnus asked angrily. Regin did not flinch at his master's tone. He simply said, "She called it back."

"*Called* it? It is a skill, Regin! Not an animal!" Magnus snapped. The servant who had been sewing the gash in his leg dropped his needle, and it swung from Magnus's leg. The servant made eye contact with Magnus who glared angrily at him until he retrieved the needle and continued working.

Regin cleared his throat. "It *is* hers, sire. If she calls to it and the exit wound has not been sealed, it will obey."

"So, we try again?" Magnus asked Regin. Regin nodded. "We try again."

"When do you think..." Magnus started, but suddenly his head fell forward. His servants caught him as his eyes closed.

*

Magnus opened his eyes and saw a ghost standing before him. His breath caught in his throat as he stepped away from it. It could not be...this could not be happening...

"Hello, Magnus." The ghost said. Magnus stared wildly at the wraith as it moved toward him, closing the distance Magnus had put between them. Magnus took two

steps away from it and held his hand up in front of him.

"Stay away from me!" He shouted. The ghost of his brother laughed.

"Still superstitious I see!" Rhael said mockingly. Magnus stopped moving and glanced at the man standing in front of him. He was solid, and he did not look like a ghost. But he had to be...He could not be here. He was dead.

Rhael circled him slowly. "You took the girl. You should not have done that."

Magnus swallowed. His brother's blue eyes stared into his own. He did not have the same face Magnus had last seen last before his mother, Rosalie, had transferred him to safety away from Magnus.

"You cannot take her skill. It will rip you apart." Rhael added. Magnus narrowed his eyes at his brother.

"Why are you here? Come to gloat from the grave, brother?" Magnus jeered. "That is all you can do now. Your bones rot while I live on. Even a dreamwalker such as yourself could not outlive me...a typical."

Rhael's smile faltered. "Not a typical anymore, brother. You have played with magic, but you have forgotten that magic has consequences. You cannot run from them forever."

Magnus watched Rhael move around him in another circle. "I am here to tell you that fate is looking for you. Even now, the god of death, Orco, has written your name in his book. He searches for you and will not stop until he has collected you. You will burn, and you cannot escape him."

Magnus sighed. "Threaten me if you want, but do not bring the gods into this, Rhael. This is between us. Not them."

Rhael stopped walking and turned towards Magnus.

"Mark my words, Magnus. Your time draws near. And when it arrives, I will be waiting." Rhael leaned forward and pushed Magnus out of the dream.

*

Magnus sat up from his bed where the servants had laid him. He held his hand out towards where Regin sat to his right. Regin stood nervously and moved toward him. "Your grace?" Regin looked at Magnus's hand. It was shaking.

Magnus said softly, "Regin, get to work on that potion. Make it fast. Our deadline approaches."

*****

Mila sat up from where she lay on the grass. The stars glittered above her as she looked around at the others.

"Did it work?" Rhys asked. His voice echoed around them in the still night air.

"I distracted him, but I don't know how much time it will give us." Mila said. Josilyn put her arm around Mila's shoulders and gave her a hug. Mila lifted the very worn book from the ground and handed it to Bianca. "We are lucky that I found this. Without it, we would never have known anything about Magnus having a brother."

Bianca frowned and nodded. "Sometimes the gods smile upon us."

"You did great." Josilyn whispered into Mila's ear, following it with a soft kiss on her cheek.

"We must hurry if we hope to find your brother," Bianca said to Rhys.

"We should focus on Magnus instead of finding Rhyn." Mila said defiantly. "He is the one who killed my father."

Bianca looked at her sadly. "He is, and we will not let him get away with that. But we cannot face him by ourselves. Between the four of us, we are simply two shifters, one injured seer, and an old lady. We have no hope in defeating Magnus without help." Mila nodded in agreement, but she pursed her lips in frustration.

The group gathered their things and began moving toward Westfall to find a boat willing to return them to Calvenia. Mila and Josilyn each supported Rhys by putting his arms around their shoulders. Bianca led the way in the dark, fueled by what Mila guessed was anger.

"Bianca?" Rhys called. Bianca stopped, and Mila and Josilyn helped Rhys cover the distance between the group and her. Rhys stopped and searched for the words he wanted. Finally, he spoke.

"Do not worry. Ansley is a fighter. Magnus has no chance against her." Rhys said, confidently.

Bianca sighed. "You don't know how right you are, Rhys. But she will rip our worlds apart trying to destroy him, and it is our job to make sure she does not have to."

Mila nodded in agreement. Bianca turned and continued walking south. Mila moved slowly with Rhys's weight on her shoulder. She hoped silently that Ansley gave that bastard the very thing he deserved. A knife right through his heart. She trudged along with the others throughout the night, eager to avenge her father's memory.

EPILOGUE

King Orlan huddled in a corner of one of his advisor's chambers. His personal servants and staff were inside the room with him and had just moved the large wooden table against the door to keep the intruders from entering the room.

It was in the middle of the night, and the guards had raised the intruder alarm and requested that the king lock himself in his quarters. Orlan argued that he felt that would be where the rebels would look first, so instead, he marched himself to one of his advisor's chambers. The poor man had been dead asleep and snoring, but when he saw the king at his door in the middle of the night, he had quickly dressed and ushered him inside.

King Orlan was afraid. It was true that there were many things that scared King Orlan, but this was by far the worst experience he had ever been put through. He was unsure how things had ever escalated to this point. Arvenia had enemies, yes, but to have an attack on the capital with intentions of kidnapping the king? Orlan tried to remain calm, but his hands trembled with the prospects of being captured.

Suddenly, a loud banging on the door rang out in the room. All of the servants and the advisor turned as one to glance at their king. Orlan stared dumbfounded at his people, and wondered how loyal they would be when the time came for them to prove it. Then, the staff seemed to snap out of the momentary stillness and desperately began trying to keep the doors closed. A small gap appeared in the doors, and a sword chopped from the other side at the hands attempting to hold the doors closed. Men yelled and fell back with wounds gushing blood. Others tried to rip the swords from the hands of their foes, but they were not successful.

In a matter of moments, the servants were overwhelmed, and the doors were thrust open. A small number of soldiers pushed their way into the room and rounded up Orlan's staff and servants. They bound them all, and Orlan was relieved to see that aside from those who had manned the door, no harm was intended towards his people.

A man entered as the guards gained control over the room. Servants were led out of the room in iron manacles or with rope-bound hands. The man that had entered was tall with broad shoulders. He had dark hair, and his skin was a rich brown. His eyes fell over the servants being led away before they finally landed on Orlan. Then, the man's eyes narrowed.

"Nate!" The man called. A soldier stepped forward to his leader's side.

"Sir?" The soldier inquired. The leader said nothing, but he pointed silently at Orlan where he huddled unnoticed in the corner of the darkened room. "Is that…?" the soldier started.

"Yes. Please bring him to me." The man requested calmly before turning to his other soldiers. "Out!" He shouted in a booming voice. The soldiers stood to attention, saluted him, and dragged the last few prisoners they had captured from the room. Guards rushed forward towards Orlan and dragged him across the floor in a most undignified manner until he sat on his knees in front of this rebel leader, the same one, he presumed, that had haunted his nightmares for the last several months along with the thoughts of war.

The man focused his attention on Orlan. Orlan felt heat spread under his shirt collar and swallowed with difficulty. Hate seemed to roll off this rebel, so that did not bode well for Orlan. The man's light green eyes seemed to bore a hole into Orlan's face. Orlan bent his bald head to avoid looking at this rebel. Prisoner he may be, but he did not have to cooperate with these...*traitors*.

Orlan felt a strong hand grab his chin and force his face upwards. The leader now sat nose-to-nose with him. Orlan held his breath and waited for this man to share his intentions with him.

"You *filth*. You have sat on this throne, rotting away while I took control of your country. You let others rule for you and did nothing to help your people. But you did try to help Calvenia, *didn't* you?" The man whispered, every word dripping with disdain.

Orlan swallowed again and felt his face grow even hotter. It couldn't be...besides, that was not Orlan's intention...how could this man know anything about that deal he had made so many years ago? Orlan's thoughts raced, but he held his tongue. The man finally released him and stood.

"You don't even know who I am, do you?" The man asked him quietly. Orlan shook his head quickly and finally spoke to his captor. "Please, I have gold, silver, jewels. Take what you wish. Please, mercy!"

This last word set the man's face on fire. He turned to his closest guard, drew the sword at his side, and turned back to King Orlan, placing the sword tip in his double chin. Orlan tried to pull his head away from the weapon, but the guards holding his arms did not let him budge. The sword felt cold against his throat and made Orlan's heart race with fear.

"Mercy? *Mercy*? How dare you ask for mercy when you needlessly saw to the slaughter of my *entire* family!" The man growled at Orlan through gritted teeth. Orlan felt the shock wash over him like a bucket of cold water. Orlan's eyes widened in surprise and fear, unlike any he had felt before.

"*Lord Edric?*" Orlan asked tentatively. The sword tip then pierced his neck, and Orlan felt panic rise in his chest as the sword split the skin it touched. Blood rushed from his wound, and the guards released Orlan's arms. Orlan quickly grabbed for the wound on his neck and tried to staunch the blood. But the wound was too deep, and Orlan sunk slowly to the floor onto Edric's shiny black boots. He looked helplessly at Edric as he felt his life leave him, and finally felt regret for the crimes he had committed against the royals of Calvenia so many years ago. His thoughts centered on Edric as his face was the last thing Orlan saw before he finally collapsed on the floor, dead.

*****

Edric handed the sword back to Nate, and Nate sheathed it. Edric used his foot to roll the king onto his back. *What a waste…*Edric thought as he looked at the useless lump that had assisted in his family's regicide. Nate waited patiently for orders from his king. Edric turned to his friend and shook his head in shame.

"What have I *done*, Nate?" Edric asked him quietly. He looked at the floor once more where the king's blood stained the carpet. "I have killed him, and now I am just as guilty as he was."

Nate relaxed from attention and placed his hand on his king's shoulder to comfort him. "Your grace, King Edric, you have avenged those that you loved and the life you lost. You are *not* him, but now that you have removed their king, you can ensure that his country does not suffer as ours has at the hands of Magnus. One less obstacle to stopping him has been eliminated."

Edric nodded and placed his own hand on Nate's shoulder. "Thank you, friend. Now, go. We have much work to do." Nate smiled at King Edric and turned to leave the room. Edric looked back at King Orlan where he lay on the floor at his feet. Now it was time for the real work to begin.

The Gods of the Dreamwalkers

Vito- Creator of the world and "father" of the people
Matrisa- Wife of Vito and "mother" of the people
Cassis- God of war
Amora- God of love
Sophia- God of wisdom
Sali- God of the earth and all things that grow
Caeli- God of the air
Ondo- God of the waters
Kius- God of dreams and sleep, pulls the moon across the sky each night
Poeno- God of justice
Orco- God of death and destruction who delights in struggles of the people and seeks to destroy all that his brother Vito holds dear

Dreamwalker Family Lines of Arvenia
(by constellations)

The Bear: Blacks
The Fish: Fischers
The Serpent: Asps
The Hunter: Mannes
The River: Brooks
The Eagle: Scouts
The Stallion: Galloways

Characters

Alden Black-lead council member for the elders that has led the elders for over ten years. Brother of Daro.

Ansley-a seer who has the gift of transference.

Aryn-young man who was Darius's son (captain of the guard). His father forced him to help the soldiers attack and kill dreamwalkers on the Black Night.

Bianca-Ansley's grandmother. Everett's mother and a strong builder before she passed on her skill to Ansley in the inheritance ceremony following the death of her son, daughter-in-law, and grandsons.

Braddock-local dreamwalker of Bolivar who is helping direct the search of Ansley, Rhyn, and Kenna. Well known in Bolivar and has connections.

Ceorl (Kay-orl)- old records keeper of Dunbar, Calvenia. Passed his skill on and is "retired". Grouchy and disapproves of Arvenians.

Damon- Exiled Arvenian seer who comes to train Ansley. Former lover of Kenna's mother and unintentional murderer of Kenna's father.

Dane-Builder that can control water that joined Kenna's tribe one year ago. Betrayed Kenna, Ansley, and Damon by helping to turn them over to Orco's Cult in hopes of aiding Magnus.

Darby-wise old seer northwest of Bolivar. She has had dreamvisions of Ansley and Kenna's group. She offers to give information to help aid their task. She appears young even though she is over one hundred years old.

Darius-captain of the guard when Dominic led the

Black Night raid on the dreamwalkers in Terra.

Daro Black-newest council member for the elders of Terra, younger brother of Alden. Wise, like his brother, but has only served for the elders in the last year.

Dominic- A necromancer who stole crystals from the dreamwalkers and experimented upon dreamwalkers until he found a way to use the crystals to extract their skills. Initiated the Black Night.

Edric-Kenna's non-dreamwalker husband, from Calvenia. He works as a fisherman, and Kenna knows little of his family.

Edwin-deceased husband of Bianca, who died at forty-six along with two of their children of fever during a disease outbreak.

Eli- Ansley's three-year-old rambunctious younger brother that was murdered by members of Orco's Cult.

Everett-Ansley's father. A dark haired, burly and joyful man. The strongest builder in his family since his great-great-grandfather Callan. He was a farmer in Terra whose specialty was corn. Used to serve as a parish leader.

Finley-previous king of Arvenia. He died when Orlan was seventeen. Strong, well-liked by Magnus. Died in an assassination attempt by Calvenia from a wound to the gut that had festered.

Grady-neighbor of Ansley's that lives with his wife and young child. Takes over the family's farm work after Ansley's parents are killed. Almost murdered by her parents' killer.

Gyan-Magnus's most trusted advisor who has been with him for years. Knows all of Magnus's plans and secrets and desperately wants Magnus to rule Arvenia.

Jameson-elder of Kenna's tribe, persuader, bachelor. Approached Kenna to ask her to join his tribe ten years ago. Always stands on the moral high ground, doesn't believe that people are bad, and prefers to see the good in others.

Ciaran (See-air-an)-Damon's friend from when he was a child that offered to help him kill his brother to steal his skill.

Joseph, Jackson- Sons of Bianca who lived in Westfall by the sea as soldiers, or at least began training.

Josilyn-Ansley's friend from childhood. Shifter, recently inherited. Long golden hair, green eyes. Tall and thin. Rarity of blond hair in Terra. Envied by the other girls her age for it, but she had a kind heart. Josilyn's family moved to another cottage when the girls were little, making it hard for them to stay close to each other. Attacked by Orco's Cult recently when they tried to extract her skill with a crystal. Ansley saved her, but Josilyn still has a strip of white hair from the attack.

Jyskar- captain of Deryn's army.

Kenna-a builder who lives in Willow, with her husband. Elite, orphaned due to Damon's love affair with her mother. Taken in by an old man when she was young. Manages a general store on the dock at Willow and teaches in the winter seasons.

King Deryn-King of Arvenia when Rosalie was living. Granted Terra to the wild mountain people and anyone else who wanted to pay the low fee for the acres of land. Worked with Dominic to orchestrate the Black Night to steal skills of the dreamwalkers using the crystals Dominic had given him.

Laurel- A member of Kenna's tribe for four years. She was attacked by Dane to force the tribe to respond to the dreamwalker attacks by going to Terra to speak with the elders.

Leila-Ansley's mother. A slim, woman with black hair to her waist. A talented builder as well. Loved lilies of the valley. Of the family of Brooks, but not related to Rhyn and Rhys.

Lya (L-ai-uh)-Damon's typical wife who lives with him in Calvenia. The mother of Milavida.

Magnus-son of Rosalie's and twin of Rhael who tried to murder his mother and kill his brother so he could steal his skill. He was unsuccessful, but he spent years tracking Rhael unsuccessfully. He has also learned of his mother's skill of transference and made plots to use it to break open the dream realm. He is also the leader of Orco's Cult.

Margaret and Stephen-dead siblings of Everett and children of Bianca. Died at seven and three, respectively.

Milavida-Damon's daughter, named for Kenna's mother. Recently inherited her skill and is a shifter.

Mirena- Deryn's queen.

Mrs. Seicar- Josilyn's landlord in Arvenia. She works at the Seven Stag's Tavern.

Orlan- current king of Arvenia who does business with Magnus. Took over Arvenia at seventeen after his father died. Is nervous in his dealings with Magnus. Married to Queen Aileen and has heirs. Orchestrated the overthrow of Calvenia's royal family.

Queen Aileen-Orlan's wife, formerly a princess of Tortia. Her children take after her looks.

Quinn Brooks-council member for the elders. Very wrinkled, and much older than Bianca. Elected to the elders ten years ago and works to preserve their history into books.

Regin- Magnus's necromancer.

Rhael-Rosalie's son, twin of Magnus. Inherited his skill and was transferred by Rosalie to save him from Magnus.

Rhyn (R-ee-n)-Rhys's twin. Identical looks, but he is the one who is actually tied to Ansley. He seems to anticipate Ansley's feelings and respects them. Rhyn is a wielder of air, and he inherited at the age of eleven.

Rhys (R-ee-s)-seer in Ansley's dream. Four to five years older than Ansley. Grew up outside of Avendale near the Spruce Mountains with his parents and twin brother. Inherited a few years ago. Held hostage by Magnus who is using necromancy to allow him to possess Rhys's body and mind. Of the Brooks.

Rory-Damon's older brother. Jovial, smiles often.

Rosalie-a dreamwalker living in Terra when the mountain people were first invited to the land. Mother of Rhael and Magnus. Trapped in the dream realm and is now an old woman. Was a seer and had transference. Was of the family the Galloways.

Ryker-Ansley's nine-year-old brother, who she suspected would begin to emerge in the coming year. He was to turn ten a week after his murder. He was soft spoken and had a love for animals. He especially worked well with horses.

Ryker-eldest son of Bianca, who crossed the sea to start a new life. Closest brother to Everett.

Sadie- Ansley's aunt in Avendale, who moved to escape farm life.

Sophie-shifter in Kenna's tribe that enjoys tricking others with her disguise, a little too carefree for Kenna. In person, she is short but curvy with beautiful light brown skin and amber eyes.

Stephen-Rosalie's husband. Asked her to marry him before he moved to Terra to start a new life as a farmer. Died protecting her in the Black Night. Had blonde hair and dark brown eyes like his son Rhael.

Vida-Kenna's mother. Had an affair with Damon and died after her husband was accidentally killed by Damon.

Milton Keynes UK
Ingram Content Group UK Ltd.
UKHW020234250424
441687UK00004B/170